D1428340

SEPTEMBER IN THE RAIN

BY THE SAME AUTHOR

Peter Robinson

SEPTEMBER IN THE RAIN

A Novel

Holland House

This is a work of fiction. Although portions of *September in
the Rain* are derived from real events, each character in it is a
composite drawing upon several individuals and the author's
imagination. Place and time have been adapted to suit the shape
of the book, and with the exception of a few public figures,
any resemblance to persons living or dead is coincidental. The
opinions expressed are those of the characters and should not
be taken for ones held by the writer.

Hardback ISBN 978-1-910688-08-3
Paperback ISBN 978-1-910688-10-6
Kindle 978-1-910688-09-0

Cover : Vincent Van Gogh.
Detail of *Enclosed Wheat Field in the Rain,* November 1889,
Philadelphia Museum of Art, Philadelphia

September in the Rain"
By Harry Warren And Al Dubin
All Rights Administered
By Warner/Chappell North America Ltd

Cover design by Ken Dawson

Typeset by handebooks.co.uk

Printed and bound by TJ International Ltd, Padstow, Cornwall

Published in the USA and UK

Holland House Books
Holland House
47 Greenham Road
Newbury, Berkshire RG14 7HY
United Kingdom

www.hhousebooks.com

NOTE

Though based upon a series of events that took place over forty years ago, *September in the Rain*, as its subtitle says, is a work of fiction. When not invented, its characters resemble only in outline their originals, and are composed for fictional purposes. This novel has been the recipient of a great deal of advice from many loved ones, friends, family, and acquaintances. I warmly and gratefully thank them all. For their particular care and attention to this book, I would especially like to acknowledge the help of Kate Behrens, James Peake, my editor at Holland House, Robert Peett, and Marcus Perryman. Surviving faults and weaknesses are, of course, my own.

'Cette vie est un hôpital où chaque malade est possédé du désir de changer de lit.'
Charles Baudelaire

20 SEPTEMBER 1975

The yellow breakdown truck pulls off and halts outside an Agip petrol station bar. Pushing the stiffly sprung door, the driver throws back his blue anorak hood and shakes off the worst of the rain. Behind him come the two of us, bedraggled from the storm, wet through, with limp hair and blank faces, eyes blinking in the neon as if startled out of a troubled night's sleep.

Head down, with your long dark hair dripping from the rain, you've retreated to a corner as far as possible from the counter and customers. And there you'll stay, your face still wet with tears or the rain, shivering beside the chrome stands where dolls in plastic bags and soft toys for souvenirs are dangling on display.

The breakdown truck driver walks across the marble floor. It's muddied with the feet of transients through the small hours of this Saturday morning. Reaching the polished counter, he orders and falls into conversation with the few men standing there. Not much to tell: he hadn't understood what the two young people were trying to say. Someone had pressed a button on the red emergency box beside a crash barrier down the hard shoulder. He'd stepped out of his truck, into the pouring rain. But there wasn't a car in sight, and the breakdown man was only a mechanic getting through his long night shift.

'*Polizia!*' you had cried. '*Polizia!*'

So the mechanic had slung our wet rucksacks onto the back of his truck, bundled us into its cab, and driven directly to the Agip service station where, yes, he would

3

phone the police. Now he's asking the barman for use of the phone to make a quick call to the *polizia stradale*. That's right, he had found two foreigners alone on the autostrada towards Como at about half past four in the morning. They were soaked to the skin, and there was definitely something wrong because they were saying '*polizia*' over and over. Then he puts the receiver back into its cradle. The police would drive over to see for themselves.

By the bar, the workmen are starting to stare towards the souvenir stands. You're still silently shivering in amongst the bric-a-brac, not responding to anything I might try to say, standing stiffly and slightly stooped. Puddles are starting to form about your feet, further muddying the barman's floor. Here he comes out from among his shelves of bottles and glasses with a mop, wiping clean arcs around him from the counter to the door and back again. Seeing our disarray, he's left that part of his floor to look after itself.

His phone call finished, the breakdown truck driver has turned to the other men standing at the bar. Now one of those nightshift workers is venturing across the floor towards the reddish smears from the wet clay earth. It's streaked up the legs of your jeans, and even on the elbows and front of your clothes. The mechanic, it seems, has encouraged this other man to come and find out what the matter could be.

'*Bist du Deutsch? Sprechen sie Deutsch?*'

You don't so much as look up.

'*Inglese,*' I reply.

He shrugs incomprehension.

'*Mia donna …*'

'*Sì,*' says the workman, nodding.

But I don't know how to say it, and stumble over noises in pretended Italian.

'*Cosa?*' says the workman, with a kindly but puzzled expression. Now he's looking sideways towards you, your head still lowered among the toys. The workman shrugs his shoulders.

Look, this is my hand pointing out into pitch darkness, pointing towards the clatter of September rain on roofs and leaves. Then this is the shape of a gun being pointed, index and middle finger, the barrel, the thumb raised like a cocked trigger.

'*Ah, si, pistola,*' he says. '*E poi?*'

It's a ghastly game of charades. The nightshift workman gasps, seeming to understand. He looks askance at you again, hunched there amongst the teddy bears with their flexible arms outstretched, your eyes fixed firmly on the barman's floor.

'*Venite, venite ragazzi,*' he says, gesturing towards the service station counter. The rain is still pouring in the blackness outside. Rivulets are coursing across the plate-glass windows, fusing and dividing as they run. The interested workman crosses towards the glistening chrome surfaces. Looking around as he walks, he waves an arm in a way that clearly means follow—which is what I do, alone. Up at the counter, the barman is busy with his coffee machine and at first takes no notice of these new arrivals. Now he's pouring drinks into short glasses and talking with his regulars. Finally, one of the workmen directs his attention towards me standing there, a bedraggled boy with dripping wet hair drawn back from his face. The mirrored wall behind the barman's back is lined with brightly labeled bottles; bits of a suntanned English face are reflected between their curves and variously coloured contents.

'*Due caffè, per favore.*'

'*Corretti?*' asks the barman.

Correct?

'*Sì, sì.*'

'Sissy,' the barman says, parodying my impure vowels. Then, after producing the two espressos, he adds a measure of brandy into each of the small white cups lined up on his freshly wiped bar.

There are a few loose coins in my damp trouser pockets. I slide them onto the counter, gulp the coffee down, and take yours over to the souvenir stands. You're shivering still with your arms clasped about you, long straight dark hair parted in the middle but falling forward and closing around the head to hide your features. A few traces of the red mud cling in the lank brown strands. You're wearing my shapeless, crumpled summer jacket, its shoulders and back darkened from the soaking. Other night workers and travellers are swiveling round and glancing towards you. They're talking about those *ragazzi inglesi*, making guesses about what must have happened outside in the rain. You sip at the coffee, holding the small white cup near your face with both hands.

The *polizia stradale* pull up outside and two uniformed men step in. One is carrying a short carbine with a wooden butt. Now they too are trying, with the aid of the German-speaking workman, to discover what the matter can be. Only they aren't able to hear anything they might understand, just the loud noise of a raised voice speaking a language that none of them knows. But the two traffic policemen can gather from the breakdown truck driver and assorted bystanders that this is none of their business. Nothing about what's occurred sounds like a motoring offence. Quite simply it will have to be reported to the *Questura* in Como.

How can this policeman not be concerned about what has happened out there in the rain? What are the police for here, if not to investigate crime? Yet it's not the policeman's job to explain for our benefit, and explain in English, that Italy has half a dozen, entirely independent categories of police. Now here in front of your face comes a waggling thumb.

'*Autostop*?'

No, it is none of their business. The senior of the two will have to spell it out.

'*La polizia*,' he begins saying slowly and loudly, '*più vicina … è … a Como … dovete … andar*e … *a Como … ragazz*i.'

Then he turns his attention to you. Your arms remain held across your breasts, hands clutching your sides as if doing the best you can literally to pull yourself together.

'*Coraggio*! *Coraggio*!' he says, resting a large hand for an instant on your shoulder. At which you visibly stiffen. The two policemen turn, step out into the watery early morning light, and are gone towards their blue squad car parked by the door. In they climb, and drive away.

'Courage?' I gasp. 'And would somebody like to tell me how we're supposed to get to Como? Hitch-hike?'

Momentarily, you look up. You're standing a slight

distance from me, your state made worse by the policemen's visit. But that considerate workman has foreseen this difficulty too. He's leading somebody across from the small crowd gathered by the bar. This man in a light blue overall is a pump attendant at the petrol station and will be driving into town at the end of his shift. So the thing is to wait until the attendant clocks off, pointing at his watch, then he'll drive into Como, turning an invisible steering wheel with his hands, and make a detour by way of the *Questura*. The what?

'*Polizia?*'

'*Sì ... polizia.*'

At regular intervals other workmen and drivers come in from the road. They glance around and catch a glimpse of you huddled among the dolls and bears, me standing helplessly beside you. These newcomers appear to think nothing of it. Buying their refreshments, now they're being filled in by the barman or a customer about whatever our story is supposed to be.

They don't seem surprised, turning around to take another look at us standing over here. It's as if this sort of thing happens all the time. This nonchalant attention, added to the policeman's consoling gesture, is piling on your agony. It almost begins to seem worse, even worse than what had taken place out in the dark. The safety of some neon light and the company of those others from the small hours has been so quickly transformed into a purgatory of curiosity—as if we're already dead, come back to haunt the scenes of our last moments like a pair of unappeasable revenants. It feels like being the blurred black-and-white photos of car accident victims in the Sunday morning editions.

Back turned to them now, standing between you and the bar, I'm making an attempt to shield you from those customers' eyes. Underneath your thin summer clothes, my damp red-smeared jacket, and the flowery smock you made yourself, your body quivers and quivers. The nightshift might come off around six-thirty. And it's just after five-fifteen by the bar's electric clock. The best part of an hour has passed already. Like a compulsive hand-washer, whenever there's a lull the barman comes out with the mop and attacks his muddy floor. Outside, the rain has begun to ease. A row of Lombardy poplars is forming itself from the blackness, swaying slightly in the middle ground, with an outline of mountains starting vaguely to sketch itself onto the far distance. What promises to be a warm early autumn day begins to lighten through the bar's glass panels, a landscape's routine emergence from the dark …

Now the Agip employee is walking out to his Fiat parked beyond the petrol pumps. The air felt chill and fresh across the drying asphalt as we followed him. Car windows down to get the pleasure of this refreshingly cooled atmosphere, he set off without a word. Dawn was lightening on the road. That storm of the early hours had rinsed the sky. Distances stood out pellucid and near. A town came into sight around the wide curve of the lake's edge. Lines of cable cars led up sheer inclines to the levels of houses and villas high above its glistening water. The streets were almost empty, silent but for the occasional roar of a car, or the clatter of a shutter being raised.

Finally, the mechanic pulled up at a curb. Was this Como? So which one of those nondescript buildings would be the police station?

'*È quella là, la Questura,*' he said.

The mechanic was pointing towards a dusty-grey frontage with barred and meshed windows, on the opposite side of the street. Treated with a generous indifference by the man in the light blue overalls, still I felt a relief in having climbed out of his car, to have removed our rucksacks from its boot and stood away.

'*Auguri ... e buon viaggio,*' the man said.

At the street's edge, undulating tarmac flaked into recently coagulated dirt. The doors of the Questura di Como were firmly locked and with no sign of life inside. A film of grime covered the grilled windows. It was nowhere near eight o'clock—which was the time a notice announced the building would be open.

'Let's try and find something to eat,' I suggested.

You looked up at me a second time. A few yards ahead the road began to widen. Not much further, a side street appeared to lead off to the left. Some distance down, on the right, a pile of chairs was stacked against the wall.

'That looks like it might be a café. Why don't we try down there?'

'If you like.'

The place looked dingy, but quiet and anonymous—like a good place to hide. Its door wasn't locked, though there seemed to be no one inside. A sharp tang of floor disinfectant suffused the air. Then came the usual hesitation between the vulnerable feeling of staying outside, and the fear of being caught in some impossible situation. But, as if in response to my anxious peering, a middle-aged woman appeared from a passage behind the bar. The skin around her eyes was tightly wrinkled and discoloured. She was emptying impacted coffee grounds from the café's red and silver *Gaggia* machine.

The woman hadn't said a word, which probably meant it was all right to stay. You didn't wait to find out. Making your way between the chairs and tables to a place in the far corner, you dropped the grey pack on the floor and sat down. Smears of the same reddish clay mud were visible all over the rucksack, and on the frayed ends of your jeans; similar encrusted traces of the night were mottling my trouser legs, and the tan desert boots I'd bought in Florence.

'What shall I get you?'

'A hot chocolate,' you replied.

'That's a good idea. How about a brioche? They've got some by the look of it.'

'No, I don't think so,' you murmured. 'My stomach's not feeling that well.'

Rehearsing the phrase in my head, I crossed the café to where the woman was putting things into a case on the bar.

'*Due cioccolate, e un brioche, per favore.*'

The proprietress had her hair in curlers under a floral headscarf. She pointed to the transparent container that opened on the customer's side. It displayed a few doughnuts, croissants, and biscuits.

After what seemed like forever the two hot chocolates were placed on her wooden bar top. At the table with its red gingham cloth, barely raising the cup from its saucer, you drank in slow, loud sips—the rain-despoiled hair in fronds like cypress trees about your face, a face in shadow.

Giving all my money to you had been such a stupid mistake. As if putting myself at your mercy could have possibly been a token of trust. That way I had seemed to make the promise, but you would have to keep it. If only we'd gone into any of the restaurants whose menus we studied that day. It was just a few minutes after not going in that last one when everything went horribly wrong, and then worse and worse in a helpless slide. Why didn't I just insist on staying at a hotel in Rome till the trains were running again? If only I hadn't got into the back.

Those loud sipping noises at an end, you put the drained cup down. Drinking like that was a thing that always managed to get under my skin, and despite what had happened in the last four hours it was painfully upsetting to feel it once again. Now your speechlessness sank in to me like a mute rebuke. What was there to say that might ease or appease you? What was there to say at all? Brought together in adversity, or driven apart by it, now the worst thing that would ever happen to me—it had happened to you.

After quite some while lost in tangles of thoughts like those, with both our chocolates finished on the gingham, I finally managed to say something.

'We needn't wait for the police station to open, need we? We could just try and get to Switzerland somehow, and there'll be trains.'

But you looked up at me in blank astonishment.

'No,' you said. 'It has to be reported.'

'But why put yourself through even more? What good would it do?'

'What is it with you? Don't you understand? If he gets away with it this time … don't you see?'

So that was how you would do the right thing in the circumstances, whatever came of it. Since you could never guarantee the results of your actions, and people always blamed the social worker, the only course was to do what you believed to be right. Not that I thought anything like this at the time, feeling even more crushed by what seemed my cowardice in the suggestion that we go straight home. Leaving the table, going up to settle the bill, I felt myself retreating towards the woman at the bar. Now the proprietress was announcing a price. Then there was the usual fumbling to match what the woman had said with a tiny bundle of dirty coloured paper. Muttering the word '*moneta*', she handed back five caramels and a piece of chewing gum for change.

At a distance, on the far side of the road from the Questura, we stood waiting. Then, finally, someone appeared. He was wearing what looked like a fireman's uniform, but without the helmet. Approaching the heavy wooden doors of the Questura, the custodian unlocked them and stepped inside. We remained still a moment, then, picking up our rucksacks, crossed the road and paused at the entrance while I tried once more to decipher its public notice.

'Go on, just open the door.'

The building's central entrance let onto a waiting room with a grilled reception cubicle immediately opposite. There were doors on either side of it. All round the room were dark-varnished wooden benches. Its walls had been painted a deep matt green, but, nevertheless, there were scuff marks of soles clearly visible at the floor angle, the signs of recalcitrant suspects perhaps.

You sat down on one of the benches. The officer had taken up his place inside the cubicle. He must have cut himself shaving that morning: a minute piece of tissue paper remained attached to his chin by the tiny circular bloodstain on his jaw.

'*Buon giorno. Dica.*'

'*Polizia? Parlare ... con la polizia ... per favore?*'

After looking into the foreign face, the man spoke and must have been asking why we needed the police. But receiving by way of reply no more than an embarrassed shake of the head, he must have been trying to explain that we needed to wait, in response to which there came neither reply nor movement. So the uniformed man was obliged to jab a finger firmly towards the benches where you were already sitting against those dark green walls.

A clock above the grilled aperture moved slowly round with stubborn shudders. At some distance down a corridor, behind one of the two doors opposite, came the sound of another door banging. Then through the entrance, somebody arrived for work. He greeted and spoke briefly with the custodian in his cubicle. Now it was happening at shorter and shorter intervals. Before disappearing through one of the doors, each new arrival would glance momentarily over towards us sitting there. The clacking of their leather soles resounded along the marble passages that extended beyond those doors.

Did the uniformed man understand what we needed? When he spoke with the other men arriving for work, was the custodian even mentioning our existence? We would just have to wait and see.

'*Seguitemi, ragazzi,*' said a stocky man in his mid thirties, a plain-clothes detective whose gesture beckoned towards the left-hand door. We followed him along a narrow passageway with offices off to the left and a faded red carpet. Then the detective invited us into a small room crammed with wooden desks, heavy black phones, big grey typewriters, and filing cabinets. On the desks were dark sunglasses; overflowing ashtrays; pink newspapers filled with sports reports … Half a dozen large policemen, mostly in shirtsleeves, were lolling against the walls, slumped in swivel chairs, or casually perched on the edges of desks. An acrid smell of stubbed-out cigarettes assailed my nostrils.

'Avete carte d'identità o passaporti, per favore?'

From an inside pocket came the blue booklet with its gold lettering. The detective began to leaf over the pages, stopping first at the one that said it remained the property of Her Majesty's Government of the United Kingdom and might be withdrawn at any time. Then he opened the page that asked those to whom it may concern to allow the bearer to pass freely without let or hindrance, and to afford the bearer such assistance and protection as may be necessary. Finally, he found the page with the personal details. There was the photograph of a seventeen-year-old boy in a black school blazer. His unwashed strands were tucked back behind the ears to avoid compulsory haircuts. There were traces of acne above the bridge of the nose. He had a peculiarly pouting mouth caused by the need to suppress an urge to giggle at the photographer's fuss and palaver. The detective glanced into the face of the bedraggled twenty-two-year-old standing in front of him just to confirm that they were one and the same person. They were.

Rummaging in your rucksack's front pocket, there you found the official piece of paper, issued by the British

Consulate in Rome not twenty-four hours before, valid for one journey only: a return to the British Isles. The detective who asked for the documents opened a drawer in the heavy wooden desk, took out a form and inserted it into the Olivetti typewriter. He would mispronounce a detail from the papers, turn, receive a nod, and type the details onto the form with just one fleshy finger. He was making mistakes. Neither of us corrected him. As the letters of your family address were being stamped into the thin white sheet of paper by the typewriter keys, your face appeared a mask of homesickness and longing. There you stood, the personification of a desire to be removed at once from that place and returned, against the dictates of distance and time, into somewhere warm and secure, somewhere like your own bed in the family home beside the Solent. But you would not die, not for now anyway, nor, for that matter, be changed into a nightingale. Yes, you would undergo the physical examination. It could be no worse than what you'd already endured.

When the detective finished his typing and handed back the documents, another older-looking man took over. Then he must have asked you to tell him what happened. You were trying your best, first in a smattering of high school French —

'Nous sommes venus ici par la pousse ... et à l'heure du quatre du matin ... quelqu'un ...'

Perhaps the detective didn't know the language or couldn't fathom your accent, because he shook his head and turned to one of his colleagues.

'Cosa dice?'

'Non lo so.'

'Qui c'è qualcuno che parla Inglese?'

'*Penso di no.*'

'*Beh, devo trovare un interprete.*'

The detective picked up the phone and spoke quickly into its dark shell. As he returned the receiver to its cradle, he began again chatting with those around him. He was half-sitting, half-leaning on the edge of the desk, one leg swinging nonchalantly. After some minutes the phone rang and the same detective listened, the receiver balanced between his ear and hunched shoulder.

'*Squadra volante, Como,*' he said. '*Si, si.*'

Then he pointed towards a second handset on the desk nearby. One of the other detectives picked it up and offered it to you.

This was how the exchanges went. First the detective standing beside you would ask a question:

'*C'era un atto sessuale completo, con penetrazione ed eiculazione?*'

Then you would hear an adaptation of the phrase:

'Would you tell him if the sex act was complete; if the man achieved complete intercourse and an orgasm?'

And I heard you answer: 'Yes.'

'*Il consenso per quest'atto era estorto con minaccia o violenza?*'

'Did the man use threats or force to be permitted to do this act?'

'Yes, he threatened us with a gun.'

'*Si, l'uomo lì ha minacciati con una pistola … e in quale luogo si sono verificati questi fatti?*'

'And where did these events take place?'

'In his car.'

'*Nella sua macchina.*'

Then you remembered we had tried to memorize the

car's number plate.

'The number plate …'

'*La targa della macchina …*'

The detective leant towards a note-pad lying on the table.

'Do you remember what it was?' You turned and asked me.

'MI653420 … or possibly 4320.'

So you repeated it to the voice in the receiver.

The translator said the numbers in Italian. Then the detective spoke again.

'*Tipo della macchina?*'

'A dirty beige Ford Escort,' I said, and remembered one more detail. 'There was a World Cup football in the boot.'

'*Cosa?*' said the detective, and you repeated that fact.

'*Un pallone dei mondiale di calcio nel bagagliaio.*'

'*E l'uomo?*'

'Could you describe the man?'

You glanced around once more, inviting further help from my memory.

'Yes: he was short, dark-haired, fairly thin, with a small moustache, and he was wearing a dark red tie …'

You repeated the details into the mouthpiece then added:

'… and he'd been drinking.'

When the detective had all the information he needed, he thanked the interpreter at the other end of the line and replaced the receiver. Now he was speaking to a colleague at his elbow. The other man immediately telephoned to what must have been the offices in Milan where vehicles were registered. His sentences contained the possible numbers and make of car. More details were jotted down on the desk pad. The detective nearby suddenly pulled open a drawer, took out a large black automatic pistol, a magazine and handful of bullets, assembled the clip, pushed it into the handle, and inserted the gun into a shoulder holster under his light-weight shiny grey jacket. He closed the desk, announced something to the others, and immediately two of them left the office. They appeared to be almost in a hurry.

You were preparing yourself for the physical examination you supposed would be required to substantiate your story, but none of the policemen had even so much as mentioned the possibility. And now the uniformed man from reception was showing us out of their office.

'I can't believe this,' you said. 'What's happening now?'

The uniformed man led the way back down the green corridor past those other doors and over the threadbare carpet weave on which the detectives walked each day with their suspects and criminals, victims and informants. Then the more senior plain-clothes officer appeared. He was explaining rapidly but with expressive gestures that we were free to go. Now you really were astonished. But it did seem as if the police would escort us to the border, still a distance to the northwest somewhere.

'*Fino a Svizzera?*'

In response, the uniformed man stepped into the bright morning air and pointed to the right, along an avenue.

'*La corriera per Chiasso si ferma lì,*' he said.

'So now we have to take a bus!' you exclaimed, seeing where his finger had pointed.

Alone together once again, we set off in the direction of

a post in the crumbling road—the sign for where the bus should stop. Family greengrocers, butchers, tobacconists and cafés were beginning to open; displays of produce, tables and chairs were arranged on the pavement edge. These businesses seemed precariously close to the flow of traffic, cars and lorries mostly travelling north. Housewives wearing headscarves were setting about their chores, dropping in and out of tiny shops, the places so modest it seemed impossible they could ever keep going. Older men sat with drained cups and newspapers, or absently scanned the familiar street. I could hear the hiss of a coffee machine. It scented the drowsy air. This one was called a Jolly Bar.

There at the far end of summer, evidently on our way home to Germany, we must have looked to anyone who cared to examine us as if we'd had quite enough of Italy and would be glad to return to school or work or college. The sun was dispersing the last of the morning's early mist that shimmered across the expanse of Como's lake. Some attenuated cloud was drifting above the steep mountain slopes. Along fenced-in wharves jutting into the water, powerboats and yachts were moored. The outboard motor of a fishing craft could be heard spluttering into life. A first steamer was approaching the shore.

Finally, a yellow bus appeared amidst the traffic. At the last minute, it halted by the post where we were standing. The bus was crowded round the entrance and the automatic doors closed so quickly they caught your rucksack, leaving half of it protruding from the bus. Some passengers had noticed this disaster and were smiling by way of consolation, trying to attract the driver's attention. Doubtless there was the usual sign that expressly forbade doing this while the bus was in motion. Anyway the driver took no notice, and only when he pulled up at the next stop could your damp sack be retrieved from the door.

You were gazing intently at the footprint-grimy floor of the bus, whose motion impinged in the form of legs and shoes on the pavement, passed at speed as the vehicle accelerated. The bus was taking a road that led northwards beside Lake Como and up towards the border. Early risers had loaded surfboards on to roof racks and were motoring out for a day by the shore. Now the bus was travelling along a winding road, mist plumes rising from the woodlands, slowing through almost deserted ports, past advertising signs, furniture warehouses, pizzerias, bars, telegraph and power lines. At furthest distance, through the thinly layered cloud, white tops reached above, their crevices etched with last night's snow. Then the Alps were emerging, and, with them, Switzerland: thick pines and outcrops of rock interspersed with tiny mountain villages, their small inns by the roadside, fairy-tale castles perched on precipices, a fogginess hanging in the highest branches of fir trees.

Across the frontier there'd be no rail strike. Trans-European expresses would be starting out for Paris. We would probably arrive at the Gare du Lyon and have to go by Metro to the Gare du Nord. Once there, boat trains would be leaving for one of the channel ports and then Dover, then London and home at last.

The bus was slowing to a halt within sight of the border. Everyone was picking up bags and descending. We made to follow them, shouldering rucksacks and walking with the other passengers across the frontier into Chiasso. As we went through, a customs official, or perhaps a policeman, smiled and pointed out the way to the station. Coaches of a train were rushing above as we entered its booking hall. The indicator board announced that an express for Paris would be leaving within the next half an hour. I tried to buy some tickets with the Italian money kept back for just this purpose, but the booking clerk behind her grille would not accept the currency.

Still, there wasn't the least problem finding a *Wechsel-Cambio-Change* place near the station: Chiasso was a town full of banks. The exchange rate and commission charges were better not thought about. But we didn't have a choice. So I queued at a till and asked to get the minimum required converted into Swiss Francs. The narrow slot under its sheet of armoured glass was like nothing so much as a *bocca della verità*, but with yet more misunderstandings to bore the official for whom it was just another ordinary day.

We passed the barrier and descended the underground walk that led towards the platform. Climbing the dusty steps together, your eyes were fixed it seemed on some distant, different memory. With the holiday in ruins all about us, I was feeling sorry, blankly staring at your squashed, misshapen pack, borrowed for those weeks in Italy, thickly encrusted with that same red mud.

We had both kept looking back through the rain-speckled window of the breakdown truck's cab to make sure our belongings, thrown against a crane outside, amongst its forest of orange cones, weren't about to fall off and be lost on the rain-soaked road.

Platform Three was to the right at the steps' head, and it was deserted. There in the silence a white cloud floated above the empty railway lines. You let your sack fall to the dusty ground. Then, collapsing with relief at having reached this place of safety, you began to shake once more—but now with silent sobs as well. Standing beside you, with my shoulders pinned back by the narrow canvas straps, arms hanging uselessly, I could do no more than slightly raise my hands, palms inward. Only you were too overwhelmed by your own wretchedness to notice that gesture which might have been of care, intercession, exhaustion, or even something resembling remorse.

Coaches that would make up the Paris train were being shunted towards the platform. Immediately they halted we climbed aboard and found an empty compartment. The first thing you did was step over to the window, lowering the blinds and then sitting down with your back to the engine. Then you turned and opened the flap of your rucksack, placed on the seats as a deterrent against other passengers who might think to come in. The buckles undone and strings untied, you fished among the carefully folded wad of your possessions. Searching around in there, you drew out a toiletries bag and change of clothes.

'Watch our things,' you said, 'while I go and have a wash.'

You slid the stiff compartment door open, stepped into the corridor, glanced around to find the nearest lavatory, and then set off to the right.

I could imagine you sensing the faint draughts of cold air below, washing yourself all over in that confined space, rinsing the dried red mud from between your toes, and taking the morning's pill from its silver card, baffled by the fact that the flying squad hadn't felt they needed to examine you. While you may have been doing these things, I sat gazing absently from the express train window. Petals of marigolds in pots were fluttering by the ochre-washed wall of a station building. A railway employee went past spearing litter and placing it in a black plastic bag. Then the silences and quarrels of those two weeks in Italy began to tumble out once more.

On our very first Sunday morning in the country, dropped off by the main road from Brunik heading south, we had all but given up thumbing and simply stood bickering beside the curb.

'Just leave me alone!' you had shouted. 'God, I'm going home. The first town we get to I'm taking the train.'

'But you can't do that: the travellers' cheques are all in your name.'

'Well, that was your brilliant idea,' you came straight back. 'I'm going to cross this road and get a lift into town and change them all at the first bank I find. You can have yours and then, I mean it, I'll get a train out of here.'

'But do we really have to, now that we've come this far?'

Which was when an open-topped saloon veered over and offered a ride. The Austrian couple in the back squashed up and all six of us made the last part of their drive from Stockholm along the swerving autostradas as far as Florence. They were from Carinzia and heading for Amalfi, where the Swedish currency earned in a Saab factory would keep them in comfortable hotels till the end of September.

'So tell me, now, do you have any idea if this is the road to Rome?'

That was as we climbed towards Fiesole two days later.

'Well, for God's sake, just ask someone, will you?'

And Piazza Navona, the sun at its zenith, would forever be associated with a fight about whether we could afford one more ice cream. The very next day, somewhere down near the Tiber, tired and hungry, we were fussing about a suitable restaurant. I was feeling too timid to ask did they do a tourist menu. Had it started because we'd stopped talking to each other?

'Oh please just do something,' you complained. 'Tell me why does it always have to be me?'

Exasperated, I had walked on ahead, leaving you to catch up in the heat. It was only a few minutes later, not exactly sure where we were, wandering along a narrow street with high blank walls on either side, you walking on the outside, that the terrible sequence began. I should have been on the street side of you, I realized now. Why didn't I guess why the Vespa with the two boys on it was revving up behind? We were terribly tired and hungry—too wrapped up in what was not going right between us. Being robbed like that was a daily occurrence. It could have happened to anyone. It happened to you.

Now, in a green dress with tiny red flowers printed on it, like poppies in an early summer cornfield, you stepped back into the compartment. Your legs below the knee were both bruised. You held out towards me a bundle of clothes.

'Do something with these for me, will you?'

Outside the compartment, the door closed, wondering what to do with them, I was carrying your jeans with the frayed ends, stringy and damp; a small pair of pants; your pale blue blouse with a button hole badly ripped at the front; and a crumpled white bra.

Stepping down from the carriage, I looked to the left and right. At the far end of the platform, knots of points and sidings snaked away beyond the station, its signal boxes and trackside huts. The trees' scorched leaves hardly stirred in the glittering air. Then taking a few quick paces,

I thrust the bundle deep into a half-full rubbish bin at the platform's head.

Back in the compartment, a nun was picking fluff from her habit, a spindly old man in a trilby had settled himself by the door, and an overweight matron with two noisy toddlers was unpacking some plastic bags of refreshments and finding a handful of comics to keep the blond, mop-headed infants entertained. These would be our nightlong companions. Undeterred by the blinds or the scattered baggage, they had asked if there were places free and taken up their positions.

Put out that we wouldn't be able to lie across the seats and get some rest alone, I lifted the rucksacks onto the racks provided, first taking out a book to read. The fat mother leaned across and raised one of the blinds. The narrow space with those people had made it impossible to speak.

Now with a jolt the train was in motion. Opposite me, your eyes were shut and your head had slid over to be cushioned by the compartment wall. Your dress lay crumpled from long folding against the skin of your body, shaken slightly as all were by the movement of the wheels. You opened your eyes, aware that we were moving. Far too late, I attempted to give you a warm and tender look. But you immediately curled back into the seat to rest once more.

Asleep, all tension seemed to flow from your body, to be painted across the landscape which unfolded and rolled up beyond the carriage window—for the rest of that day through the St Gothard Pass. Tiny hamlets were constructed in patches of steep but cultivated land, the surrounding forest so thick no sunlight could penetrate it, great crags obtruding from the slopes. Narrow pathways twined around and up above. They would catch my eye a moment and be gone, replaced by columns of smoke rising from hidden chimneys or farmer's fires.

The train trundled on through precipitous pasture with rugged cows cropping where they could, inaudible tinkling bells on leather straps around their necks. There were herds of goats. A wiry deep-tanned farmer waved to the coaches from his byre. Moment by moment, your head would slip forward on the green-padded carriage wall. You would be woken by the jolting over points, or discomfort of your position, would look blankly at me reading, draw your head back to the upright of the seat, and shut your eyes to sleep.

Your oval full face, its small mouth drawn tight and hair limp from the crown, rocked gently from side to side on the column of your neck as if it were saying 'No' over and over. I tried to sleep too, but, my eyes closed, the sounds and glimpses would come out of the dark—and with them the series of *what ifs* and *if onlys*, the *should we haves*, and *might have beens* that I couldn't then begin to unravel. The only way to keep them at a distance was to stare and stare at the page below. When you awoke, you would have been able to make out, upside down, it was *Florentine Painters of the Renaissance* that appeared so absorbing, my eyes enlarged behind the thick lenses, reading page after page, retaining nothing at all, yet seeming entirely lost to you in art.

You had eased yourself backwards in the seat and stretched out your legs. It was night outside and somewhere in central France. The shadowy reflections of the compartment's inhabitants, people attempting to get some sleep, were only just more visible than the phantom countryside beyond. From time to time a gathering of lights would promise the outskirts of Paris. Looking up from a discussion of tactile values, I would find the lamps dispersing in countryside and darkness yet once more.

Framed in the panel above your head was a black and white photograph of a French chateau. It had thick, crenellated towers with pointed tiled roofs and dominated its valley from the summit of a small, steep hill. Around its walls were the roofs of a village grown up in the castle's shadow. The foreground contained a lake, glistening, still and silent under glass. Looking into that picture, I could feel the tiredness and ache of more than thirty-six hours without sleep taking hold. Over and over on that journey through the night, you would seem to blink awake. As I looked across to try and offer a smile of sympathy, you would close your eyes and leave me to the blurred, swimming pages of my book.

PART ONE

CHAPTER 1

Every now and then an opening or private view will bring me up to London. Whenever it happens, as like as not the mood will seize me to get off the Tube at Holborn and walk round by way of Boswell Street to take another look at those places once more. I can see myself emerging yet again into that leafy square, standing for a moment in front of the Italian Hospital, its ornate black cupola surmounted by a crucifix, *Ospedale Italiano* and *Supported by Voluntary Contributions* picked out in faded red lettering. The Italian has two flagpoles at splayed angles, and a shield above its entrance. Although its flaky pillar moldings have now been carefully restored, the sight of the place will still start a fugitive nostalgia for those months spent working as a porter at the National Hospital for Nervous Diseases. Founded in 1859 as the Hospital for the Paralysed, it has again recently changed its name to something more patient friendly, a name that doesn't mention nerves or diseases.

Being a porter at the National was my first real job of any kind. No longer a teenager, hardly an adult, I would collect my pay packet in the hospital's basement every Thursday from mid-March through to the end of August, then slip away down Powis Place and round the corner to deposit a portion in a savings account at the Lloyds Bank there. We were going to Italy in September.

In the extra year of your social sciences degree, you found a training placement at the Hospital for Sick Children, just round the corner in Great Ormond Street, the place that still owns the copyright to *Peter Pan*. By now we had been together for the whole of university; and so, in a year off before taking my place at the Courtauld, I decided I would follow you down to London for my gap year, as it's known now. And what a gap it would end up making, more like a great gulf fixed. The first few weeks were spent sleeping on the floor of a borrowed flat in White City, just beyond the BBC Television Centre and Westway flyover. While I was crashing on the floor there, a Manpower Agency offered me a bit of temporary work at a warehouse in nearby Park Royal. But then the students came back from vacation and wanted their living room all to themselves.

An early edition of *The Standard* produced that first real job of mine at the National. The head-porter knew of some accommodation near the Arsenal football ground, which is how I came to be renting a tiny bed-sit in Alexandra Grove, off the Seven Sisters Road, opposite the grassy, tree-lined hillocks and paths of Finsbury Park.

Back in the Seventies, remember, when you started at The Children's Hospital, you were staying in a Christian hostel near the Earl's Court Tube. Sharing the room was a vicar's daughter training to be an occupational therapist. She was intent on living down her upbringing and would come back late in the evening, put her head round the door, and ask if she could possibly have the room to herself for an hour or so. *Of course, of course*: and so off you would go wandering along the rows of shop fronts in search of a coffee bar open that late.

'It's so completely shameless,' you said with an apologetic smile. 'I could never do a thing like that to anyone.'

Which meant that on the two or three times we met, down in the place's communal lounge, I would have to keep my emotions parked.

'So how is it going on the Barrie Wing?' I asked.

'Alright: it's dispiriting, though, you know, the way you go into this, yes, vocation, because you want to do some good, make a tiny difference, repair a bit of damage … but then you see the birth defect cases they have up there on the wards. It's heartbreaking. They should be giving out medals to the nurses. And the tragedies you have to listen to each and every day.'

I could only try and sympathize.

'Still, it's better than those social work placements up North,' you add, shaken by the depths of despair involved in getting through the practical part of your degree.

'I don't know,' you were saying, 'maybe there's something more for me in hospitals.'

'Maybe there is—and, anyway, a change is as good as a rest,' I tried.

'And everyone always blames the social worker. If you intervene you're meddling bureaucracy, if you don't you're culpably neglectful. Not that I wasn't warned. When I first went up for my interview, Jean Minton finished off by taking me over to the window, pointing down at the rows of slate roofs and saying: "All this can be yours …" I should have known she was quoting the Bible.'

Leaving the North had meant we were no longer living together. Reluctantly, I agreed it would be a waste of my year off to hang around the town where we'd graduated, and you were never entirely at ease in those northern tearooms we used to frequent. After two years of being together in the place you had decorated and furnished with the choice items from junk shops and house clearance sales, we left behind our tiny flat across the footbridge over the railway lines; you complained as much as everyone else about the grit and smut blown about by the wind. Most of the textbooks, papers and things were heaved up into my mothers' attic till there was somewhere more permanent to send them. Only now we were working in London I couldn't stop myself wondering why you didn't seem to regret the fact we were no longer living together.

No one could accuse us of not trying; but the places were always too expensive or too far from Queen Square. In the end, we answered a few ads for flat shares in the personal columns of *Time Out*. One evening, the door to the flat in question was opened by a swinging-London-survivor who promptly offered glasses of wine and ushered us into a party of strangers who'd all answered the advert, or else had jointly composed it. Their spare room would be allotted to the lucky partygoer on the basis of superior charm and sociability. Definitely not our bag: we gulped down the wine and made our apologies.

Nor did my bed-sit off the Seven Sisters Road offer much of an alternative.

'So why don't you come over to Alexandra Grove?' I asked.

'Oh I couldn't, I couldn't,' you whispered. 'It's just so cramped and sordid.'

No, there wasn't much space in that single bed of mine, nor around it; the thing took up more than a third of the entire place, not that you ever agreed to try it, and anyway even the thought was against Mr. Power's pinned-up regulations. The rent was £5 per week for an oblong six foot wide. It was reduced in size, though, by the rudiments of furniture packed into it: a rickety bedside table, a utility chest of drawers, a metal-topped table with a gas ring, and a wardrobe with an inventory of fixtures pinned to the back of its door. Above the gas ring were sun-bleached duck egg curtains, behind them a window that showed a brown brick wall cut into with a mirror-like aperture. The tenant from the window opposite had to be a man, judging from the off-white nylon shirts hung drying in the breeze, and from the thirst for beer evidenced by the row of empty cans that formed a bright stockade along its sill. After dodging the furniture, with less than a hop, skip and jump, you'd be perched on the top landing of a precipitous flight of stairs, to the left, the sink with its white tubular heater, to the right a locked door. One day after work, happening to glance that way, I discovered the landlord, Mr. Power himself, rummaging among the dead wine bottles and faded heaps of pornographic magazines he kept hoarded there.

Nor when you found something more suited to easing my frustration did it actually amount to an improvement. Now you had an attic bedroom rent-free in exchange for being on duty most evenings with a group of reforming drug addicts at a halfway house in Stanhope Square. The lads who spent their time playing snooker in the basement were usually very jumpy. One or two had quickly taken a fancy to you, managing with their over-intimate approaches to start some piercing pangs of an unsuspected jealousy in me.

After clocking off and hanging about for a few hours in Earl's Court, I would take the Tube back to Finsbury Park, moodily remembering our student life in St Luke's Square. Light from a street lamp through the flat's white curtains faded before reaching the table, leaving the rumpled bed in shadow. You would be there with just a white sheet pulled up to keep off the chill, gazing absently at the room's cracked grate while I got up to make some tea. One time, back turned, as I wiped my face with a towel, you were suddenly stage-whispering some tender words of love. Throwing back the sheet as I turned around, you kicked one small foot over the side of the bed and affected a mildly erotic smile. Only there was a red flush at your neck, and goose pimples along your forearms, like emblems of a precarious innocence, or of my inexperience, hardly disguised by that momentary mock-brazen look.

But while I yearned and fretted on the Tube home about our not sharing a bed any more, you had evidently accepted we couldn't live the student life forever. These constraining circumstances, you seemed to say, would have to be put up with for as long as it took to move on.

Despite the difficulties, it was really something to be working deep in the heart of London, in Bloomsbury, where the Darling Family lived, or where the Vorticists instigated their Rebel Art Centre around the corner in Lamb's Conduit Street. And around that corner too was Harold Monro's Poetry Bookshop, the place the Georgian poets would meet and recite their latest works. Going by those spots every day was like being an extra in the film when you'd already read the book. Sometimes, after working, I would wander off towards Tottenham Court Road. From one square to another, I read the various publishers' names and the blue plaques where those great writers had achieved their immortal works ... or pressed my nose up to that antiquarian bookshop window with its unaffordable Tavistock edition of *Reflections on the Nude*. Lunch hours were often spent in Russell Square with sandwiches and Klee, Kandinsky, Berenson, Gombrich or Wollheim, as I began to work my way through the preliminary reading list supplied by the Courtauld Institute. To keep up, I would hurry over to Dillons bookshop for a snack in their basement café, or the British Museum— where a T'ang Buddhist Painting exhibition was on all that summer, right down to the end of September.

The leaves turned brown early that year. There'd been no rain for weeks; by August the grass was scorched. A seemingly endless sequence of bright days followed upon one another. Sometimes, if we were lucky, a faint breeze would ruffle the robes of patients being wheeled from the Italian to the National under Queen Square's shady chestnut trees. We would go past the public benches where outpatients whiled away the time before their appointments. It was my job to manoeuvre them around the children playing, then push on by the black water fountain marked UNFIT FOR DRINKING and the rows of red telephone boxes where people would be calling relatives to let them hear the latest news from the consultants. We would continue into Outpatients so my passengers could receive their various treatments. Then I would wheel them back again.

The New Wing at the National, with its private ward on an upper floor, has a choice of entrances. The left displays the word HEALING above the door. The right has the word RESEARCH. Both are ornamented with bas-reliefs in the style of 1930s neo-classicism. It was as if I could decide to enter the building by means of the one idea or the other. But these days, on my occasional returns to Queen Square, its grass damp and littered with the leaves of brown from the previous autumn, I find myself wondering how I might even try and attempt the impossible—and go in through both doors at once.

The journey by wheelchair from the Italian to the National took practically no time at all. Just two curbs had to be managed by the porter and endured by the patient. The others were provided with handy ramps for easing the transit of hunched figures in pyjamas and dressing gowns or nightdresses and bed-jackets that formed a daily feature of life in Queen Square. Steps led up to the stained-wood entrance doors of the Italian, also avoided by means of a ramp. Pale cream net curtains hung in its ground-floor windows. Back then you could distinguish its porters from those at the National: they had blue coats, whereas I wore a short white jacket. Porters would negotiate the clattering grilles of the old-style lift to the wards. They would help the nurses manhandle the patients out of bed, or give the poor creatures an arm if they were among its walking wounded. Then we renegotiated the iron lift doors, and headed out down the polished corridor back towards its main entrance into Queen Square.

The nurses who worked inside the Ospedale wore yellow uniforms with white aprons, and starched white cones pinned to the tops of their heads. Many were Italian, or of Italian extraction, with jet-black hair, olive skins and intriguingly mobile features. They too made me long for the Italy I had never seen, only read about in books, whose paintings studied in illustrations had so much inspired me. All through that scorching hot summer in the mid-

Seventies everyone appeared in holiday mood. Within the railed precincts of the square's garden, off-duty ancillary workers, porters, nurses, doctors, secretaries, hotel staff and recuperating patients would be sunbathing on the bone-dry ground. People were getting to know each other, choosing out new friends and confidantes from chance acquaintances and work-mates. It would help them through the routines of those long and sultry days.

The private patients being wheeled from the *Ospedale Italiano* could be seen wrapped in bandages, or swathed in veils and headdresses. Shrunken within loose clothes and veils, which fluttered against their sickly skin outside, they seemed entirely withdrawn from Queen Square's party mood, where, as wheeled patients approached them, great flights of pigeons would rise into the leafy air.

CHAPTER 2

My sister Christine always wanted to go into advertising. Sometime back in the mid-Eighties, she took me along to a dinner in St John's Wood with that friend of hers, the trainee therapist and, her work associate, an account manager with one of the bigger and better firms. Perhaps to impress his new girlfriend, the account manager spent the entire evening dominating the conversation with a sales-pitch about what a fantastic operation he worked for, how everyone was treated equally, right down to the receptionists and doorman. The chief executives were such nice guys—hard headed, but reasonable. Everyone really looked up to them. He even reported, perhaps for my benefit, that these philanthropists went in for sponsoring opera and avant-garde art, buying into the higher emotions, as it were.

'But,' I asked, as he paused to fork some buttered parsnips into his mouth, 'don't you have any sense of metaphysical worthlessness?'

The momentary silence was only underlined by the sounds of plates and cutlery.

'What on earth do you think?' was all he said, returning to his slogans and the tale of his tribe.

'I can just imagine what he thought of you, you spirit broker!' my sister laughed as she drove us back to her flat. Putting the Peugeot into fourth, she was accelerating out across an almost empty Waterloo Bridge in the early hours of a Sunday morning. Having managed to go easy with the spirits after dinner, my head was already clearing as the

Festival Hall and the Hungerford Bridge went by. Along the river, beside the Savoy, the pleasure-boats' lights still glinted on the murky Thames below.

'By the way,' she said, after a few minutes' quiet as she threaded her car through that maze of roundabouts and exits heading south, 'I happened to meet an old friend of yours last Saturday.'

We were held up at yet more traffic lights; the road in the other direction was deserted, tempting her to inch forward out across the junction.

'It was at Belle's wedding … Isabel, come on, she was at university with you. I was her lodger, remember, till she and her bloke decided to take the plunge.'

'So who was this friend of mine?'

'Alice something-or-other … at least that was the maiden name, if I could only remember it, the name she said you'd know her by.'

'How come she knew we were related?'

'She recognized a family resemblance!' my little sister said—a tall slim blonde, still in her twenties, eleven years my junior, with a broad white smile, a tiny turned up nose and hazel eyes.

There was a grinding noise as she crunched the gears.

'If I were you, I'd get someone to look at that.'

'And this is the man who wouldn't know the difference between a clutch and an embrace!'

'You should use that on someone more deserving,' I said.

Tower blocks and red brick terraces, miles of deserted pavements went by. The earliest morning traffic was just an occasional car moving smoothly past shadowy segments of grass, dimly sketched out by a neon streetlamp among the leaves of Clapham Common.

'So what was she like then?'

'Isabel?'

'Alice.'

'Homely Scottish mother,' my sister said, 'with three or four kids. Still managing to keep her looks. Husband a schools inspector. Living somewhere up in Shropshire. Converted farmhouse type of thing. Thinking of going back to teaching when the kids are a little older. Not quite your type, I'd have thought.'

'Funny, that's exactly what *sh*e said.'

My sister made a tricky right-hand turn across the carriageway.

'Curious coincidence, you answering that flat-share ad,' I found myself saying to half-change the subject.

Alice and Isabel were inseparable at university. When she graduated, Isabel, practically a Sloane Ranger from birth, managed to wangle herself a stopgap job in a theatrical costumier's near Drury Lane. But within a few years she'd presumably started her training as a child psychotherapist. Come to think of it, wasn't it Isabel's encouragement that decided Alice on giving up and moving down here? Following a frankly admitted homing instinct in your choice of final-year placements, you too had made the journey south.

'She did ask after you,' my sister conceded.

'Isabel?'

'Alice! And she spoke rather warmly of you too, I'd say … Did you have some kind of a thing going on back then, or what?'

'Sort of.'

'What sort of "sort of"?'

'The usual sort —' and I crooned the hook to *Just One*

of Those Things.

'And what did your wife think about that then?' she asked. 'Can't imagine Mary didn't find out. You being such a hopeless liar, and all.'

'Well, yes; but we weren't exactly living together at the time.'

'Interesting,' she mused, 'and I always thought of you two as the ideal couple, the great inseparables, two peas in a pod, all your eggs in one basket.'

'The ideal couple: as if we were yoked together …'

'She wanted to know if you got married in the end,' my sister continued. 'She asked if you had any children.'

'Naturally, you filled her in on the details.'

'How could I?' She laughed. 'You never tell me anything!'

'Come on,' I said, niggled by her harping yet again on that bit of family myth, 'you know we got married.'

'You must admit, though, you do tend to keep things to yourself … things like this Alice whatever-her-name-was.'

'And what if there's nothing to tell?'

'Now I don't believe that for a moment. Everyone's got skeletons to rattle, but if anyone so much as touches your cupboard door, up come the defences, on goes the mask, and there you are, standing on one leg with a distant look in your eyes, gazing off somewhere and saying precisely nothing!'

'Have it your own way,' I shrugged.

'So how is Mary?' my sister asked.

'She's fine. Fine. Getting on with her things as usual.'

'See what I mean?' she said, glancing at the lighted dash. Outside, an orange glare of street lamps only seemed to emphasize the dark. 'What Alice said was that everybody used to admire your mind; but you weren't exactly a social success.'

That was nice of her, I thought, remembering her legendary tongue.

My sister was trying to get the car into a gap between two white transit vans a little way down from her ground floor flat.

'Sometimes I do think it's a pity we lost touch,' I said.

'Really? It's a long time ago. Things are bound to be different. She seemed such a comfy motherly kind of person. Difficult to imagine you two arm in arm and walking down a street together, talking about metaphysical worthlessness.'

For the summer after she graduated, Alice had found a job on an educational program at the Brooklyn Museum. The experience visibly changed her: she'd bought herself a New York bohemian wardrobe, had let her hair grow longer and waved it. The other people working there had been such enthusiasts. They really believed in experimental art. The moment of Abstract Expressionism, Pop, Op, Minimalism, Conceptualism, the entire shooting gallery. Even the kids in their school parties seemed to be wild about it. Alice would say she really woke up in New York. She was used to adopting a canny reserve, but her co-workers didn't see the point of that. It was as if she were insulting them with her lack of superlatives. The whole thing had come as a revelation and release. She was going to become a curator. Back in England, she'd quickly found herself missing the excitement.

'Actually, she was a dedicated follower of poetry and painting. I learned a lot from her.'

'Like what?'

'Well, Joan Eardley … and Louise Nevelson … and Arp, Jean Arp: she was the first person I ever heard pronounce their names.'

'So it wasn't just her body you were after?'

'What? No: absolutely not. She didn't say that, did she?'

But that didn't deserve a reply, so after manoeuvring back and forth a few times, my sister got the Peugeot parked the way she wanted near the curb. Then she turned from the windscreen a moment and produced one of her parody daggers looks: eyes narrowed, lips pursed, head tipped to one side.

'Belle told me Alice had had an awful miscarriage. The baby died in her womb when it was already developed. The doctors knew, of course, and so did Alice, but she had to go through with the delivery anyway. Poor dead thing … a terrible experience, Belle said.'

There was a moment of blankness between us. The stillborn child had made her vivid in her life without me. My sister switched off the engine.

'Maybe I should write …' I was thinking out loud and unheard as I slammed the passenger door. 'You don't happen to have an address, do you?'

'No, though I could easily get one—but really, I'm not sure it's worth it. I mean she was quite interested in what's happened to you. But, you know, just so she could file you away. I wouldn't imagine you had anything very much in common with her, you know, even if you ever did.'

Now I couldn't help feeling a sharp twinge of irritation at the way my sister's words had seemed to write off that fretted fondness and desire, the mixed emotions starting up inside me, completely uncalled for and caught inside, like a puzzle with a missing piece.

'What's that supposed to mean, then—"if you ever did"?'

But by now Christine had the key in her blue front door.

'Well, honestly, I can't begin to imagine what she ever saw in *you*!'

CHAPTER 3

When I phoned her from the National that afternoon all those years ago, she gave me Isabel's address. Yes, if I remember rightly, it was Isabel's encouragement that brought Alice down to London in the first place.

Once in the capital, she quickly found a job as a Girl Friday for a professional photographer named William. Now Alice was working long and unusual hours on his shoots. The trains south of the river to where she rented a room in Sydenham were practically nonexistent after midnight, and on more than one occasion she found herself stranded in the West End, the last service from London Bridge long gone, with no alternative but to telephone Belle. A spare key for Alice was the obvious solution. The flat, so I gathered, was somewhere high on the Northern Line, but not far from the Tube station, easy enough to find … and if I had a problem?

'Well, you've a tongue in your head,' came her voice down the line.

'I'll be round straight after work,' I said. 'I'll bring the wine.'

'That'd be nice,' her voice returned. 'Oh, and make it white.'

The hour or so until clocking-off time would often be more or less empty of jobs: the clinics finished, inpatients accompanied back up to their wards, outpatients taken over to their nearby hospitals, or gone home with relatives more or less under their own steam. That day, idling away the last bit of time with some desultory chat, the morning's newspapers or weekly magazines, was more than my libido could stand. Now, expectantly ticking off the stops on its map, the Underground carriage deserted, I watched my face elongate and shorten by turns in the crazy house mirror of its glass.

Just the previous weekend, we had hitchhiked back up North for a birthday party at Jim and Veronica's rented terrace house. Our mutual, already-married friends had stayed on to begin research degrees. Both of us had been sent invites to the party and separately told we were welcome to stay the night. We found themselves alone together in the small hours of that Sunday morning with a mound of bedding in the half-cleared room where the gathering had been held.

We had naturally made up two beds on the floor. But lying there under the sheet, still chuckling over that incident from the party when Alice had gone into the bathroom only to discover Alison and Mick, sworn enemies from the year below, hard at it in the tub, the thought came over me: 'Well, why not?' After all, it wasn't as if the thought had never crossed my mind during our late-night talks at university. So, crawling over in the dark, I attempted to plant a kiss where it seemed her lips ought to be. I wasn't far wide of the mark, and, no, she didn't take offence, thank goodness, but put both arms around me and let things continue in their own precarious way.

I could hardly believe my luck, and our journey back South on that Sunday afternoon was charged with unspoken implications, possibilities and consequences. The chatty driver of an artic dropped us off where the North Circular meets the motorway and we took the Tube from Hendon.

Now, just five days later, as the West Hampstead station sign flashed past the window, I was still picturing her as she had looked round for her exit at the end of our weekend together. Through the sliding door, she had given me a glance that was as much as to say: 'Now look what you've done!' Suddenly another future beckoned like a crack in the surface of that curving concrete wall. Back in a seat with my train disappearing into a tunnel, I felt as if nothing could ever be quite the same again.

The house with Belle's flat in it was part of a renovated terrace. The entire street was lined with plane trees in full leaf. The land behind fell away to well-tended gardens and, beyond them, Hampstead Heath—where now the walkers with their dogs, the couples strolling, and ambling solitaries would be going their separate ways. It was getting towards the end of yet one more sweltering day, and still the heat clung to the city, appearing to soften its brick and asphalt like a bloom on the contour of the street. Way above the thick leaf-cover, the curves of shade, each intersected by paler arcs of pavement, some faint wisps of cloud deepening further the sky's full blue were just touched by a pinkish light.

Her flat was in the last house of its terrace. It was not a gable end. The absent neighbour must have been bombed or demolished, or perhaps it had never been built. The house itself seemed recently renovated: lintels, window frames and doors all painted a deep chocolate brown. Up the grey stone steps I went, and rang the bell.

And here was Alice now; smiling too, and showing me inside. A feeling almost like intense relaxation and tenderness suffused the whole of my body, as if from the hairs on my neck to the tips of my toes. It had started up uncalled for and gave such an intimate excitement to everything that would catch my eye. By the time I'd crossed the threshold and pulled the heavy door shut, she was heading off into the shadows of a long narrow corridor with gilt-framed ornithological prints the length of its walls.

'This way,' Alice called—her broad back and slightly turned out feet in brown crisscross woven sandals heading off before me, her lightly perfumed russet hair leaving its wake down the corridor.

Bijoux, I thought, meaning the contrast with my own accommodation, as she led me through to a living room on the far side of the house.

'Why don't I put that somewhere safe?' she said, taking my green bottle of mid-price wine wrapped in blue tissue paper.

'Quite a peculiar place, isn't it?'

'Peculiar?' she said, with a quizzical lilt, and moving about the flat where her friend had a bedroom and the use of facilities, from a certain James—unmarried, in his thirties, getting on. 'Belle says he's rather quiet, in a nice sort of way. Wealthy too, you can see by the décor. He's in the City.'

'Reprehensibly perfect,' I found myself quoting, and must have conveyed a trace of unease.

'Oh, no need to worry,' she said, responding to the glances with another of her smiles. 'Jimmy's away in Frankfurt, visiting the parent company's offices ... or something.'

'I'm fine ... I'm fine.'

'And Belle won't be back this evening,' said Alice. 'She's staying overnight at her parents' house in Wimbledon.'

Coming up the escalator at Holborn that morning, there seemed to be some hold-up connected with the usual works in progress. The hemispherical roof had all its panels removed; twisted intestines of wiring spilled out and hung down perilously near the heads of commuters being brought up slowly to the surface. Most mornings the southbound Piccadilly Line was packed with people on the platform at Finsbury Park. Hospital porters aren't paid a fortune, and to make a decent tour of the European galleries on savings from £27 a week involved putting away as much as reasonably possible. At the other end, whether Holborn or Russell Square, it was simplicity itself to pay the ticket collector the minimum fare for the shortest journey, five new pence, or nothing at all if nobody inquired. But that morning the crowd was filing out much more slowly than usual as I approached the barrier where a man in the booth was checking the tickets.

'And where've you come from?' asked the inspector in response to the small coin in my fingers.

'Caledonian Road.'

'Do they have automatic ticket machines there?'

Suddenly, prickling hot and cold, I found no answer forming in my mouth before the inspector started again.

'You didn't get on there, did you? Now, before you go inventing something I'm not going to believe, why don't you tell the truth? It's going to be easier.'

'But the machines were out of order.' The pitch of my voice was rising uncontrollably.

'Look, sonny, there's absolutely no point lying to me. You're in enough trouble as it is. What station did you start your journey from?'

'Finsbury Park.'

Then there was a silence while the inspector considered his options. As he did, I couldn't help noticing the man's shaving sores above his tight white collar and dark blue tie.

'So where were you going to?' he asked.

Again no answer came into my mouth, my tongue as if stuck to its roof.

'Do you work nearby?'

'The National Hospital for Nervous Diseases … I'm an outpatient porter.'

Then there was another moment's silence, the inspector still studying his hooked and wriggling prey—but now that bit more intently.

'You'll have to go and see my superior, young man,' he said, with a world-weary sigh, pointing towards the huddle of caught commuters, 'and when he asks the same question, you just tell him you're a male nurse.'

The inspector put his hand firmly on my shoulder and steered me over towards that morning's catch. There the senior inspector and his queue of offenders were flanked by two police officers. Members of the public were being ordered to pay the fine before a certain date, or expect a summons. I was sweating more profusely. Hands gripped clammily in front of my stomach, my muscles were involuntarily tensing and relaxing. Now this other London Transport official and, beside him, the tall police officers were examining the criminal: his shadowy two-day beard, scuffed white baseball boots, washed-out Levis, and a green tennis shirt to complete the uniform.

'Do you work locally?' the senior inspector asked.

'I'm a nurse at the National Hospital for Nervous Diseases,' I lied.

'And how much do you earn a week?'

'£27 after tax.'

The second inspector considered me a moment more.

'So how much was the fare you should have paid?'

'Twenty pence.'

'And have you got it?'

Automatically my hand reached into my pocket for the coins. The inspector was writing a receipt for the fare.

'Don't ever do this again, sonny Jim, do you hear? Right. Now, off you go. Or you'll be late for work.'

Out of the Holborn Tube station, into the sunny morning air, the flow and counter-flow of commuters moving in Southampton Row, the supposed male nurse tried to cool his pounding brain. The turrets and tourelles of Sicilian Avenue with its pretty collonaded screens went by, then Theobald's Road opposite the Liverpool Victoria Friendly Society Building. That morning the shock of being caught in a trap, only to be let off with a reprimand, baffled and befuddled me. Perhaps the inspector had done it out of pity for my apparent poverty and obvious youth, or out of solidarity at one remove for those in an overworked and underpaid vocation, or some other reason impossible to imagine. Unnoticed and unnoticing, I continued between hurrying business people, their faces set in masks of purpose, habit, disturbance, abstraction—at the start of one more stifling summer's day.

Standing beside me in an alcove of the kitchenette, Alice

was dressing the salad, and turning to talk. Things seemed to be going as well as I could hope—though my story of the encounter with the Underground inspectors, told as if to recruit her into a version of life for underpaid care-workers in the capital, had not produced the wished-for result.

'It's your own silly fault,' she said. 'You can't expect me to have any sympathy for you when you try and cheat them out of twenty pence, for goodness sake. And it's not the money either: it's the feeling that you somehow have a right.'

'So why do you think they let me off?'

'Well,' she added, with a minimal smile, 'what if "male nurse" were a sort of code word for one of their kind?'

'What? You don't think …'

But now she was positively laughing.

'No, you obviously don't.'

Crestfallen and doubly upset, despite her seeming immediately to forget all about it, I was taking in her latest look. All through university she had worn her hair in a bob. It was naturally straight and an auburn colour. Now she'd let it grow almost to shoulder length, had it permed into tight springy curls, and hennaed a rich chestnut brown. She kept running her fingers through the soft washed locks with a smile of satisfaction. Alice was blossoming: such a lovely young woman, fresh-faced, calmly confident of her attractiveness and worth. Her solidly-built figure was moving between the stove and sink, silhouetted in a sash-window's fading light. There were traces of Edinburgh in her accent still, a warm contralto that rose from the chest, usually with something decisive to say. A semi-circular scar marked the back of her left hand—as if someone had put a scalding pan down on it by mistake—and there was a white crescent moon below her right eyebrow.

The mass of that red-tinged hair enlarged and softened the outline of her head, turning now to speak in the large painted frame of the window.

'Take the salad to the table, will you?'

She was so lovely and bonny, her well-defined features, blunt nose and narrow mouth expressing the congruence and firmness of a person who had thought quite a bit about exactly who she would be. It was someone whose self could be directed against other people's by the mouth quickly lifting at one side—an accompaniment to some piercing witticism. Those lips might, though, with luck, break into some cheerful laughter. Her eyes, which could hold you with their even gaze, would also glint wickedly as a confidence was offered, or when, with an epigram, she summed up a person's character and weaknesses. That glint had sparkled against all of us in her circle at one time or another. It too constituted part of the excitement: how to keep on the tender side of her tongue.

Turning my too attentive eyes from her a moment, I glanced again round the room. It was all done in a dark, neo-Victorian manner, cluttered and eclectic. Hand-tinted prints of rare flowers behind glass in veneered frames were hung against the bottle green Morris-style wallpaper. The original fireplace had been retiled. Arranged on the marble mantel stood a collection of vases with leaf-shapes set into them. They grew out from the shoulders, tinted with earth or vegetable glazes. These, Isabel had warned, were James's prize possessions and extremely valuable. The entire array was doubled by reflections in an enormous mahogany-framed mirror with speckled foxing at its edges that had been fastened to the wall immediately above the mantelpiece.

'Do be careful with them,' she was saying. 'He's obsessed with the jugs.'

'Smashing place for a party!' I heard myself exclaiming, and immediately regretted it.

Alice frowned a dismissive frown. An enormous livid peacock feather curved from the full mouth and slim neck of one of those pots, brushing the mantel with its plume. Isabel's dining table was set against a window that gave onto a pampered garden. Deepening shadows extended from the trunks of great elm trees. Over the Heath the sun glowed like a dying ember. Its colours came flooding through the window's now almost dark rectangle where our two heads were surrounded by the broad leaves of the garden's sycamores. Threads of pale grey cloud were strung above the thick foliage.

That piercing fondness when she opened the front door returned more sharply, more persistently. She was so appealingly self-possessed, so absorbingly different and separate. Which is why there would always be that healthy resistance: as if the idea of us together might spoil a conversation, or make me lose track of my thoughts.

She offered me the bottle of Frascati to uncork, brushing lightly against a shoulder as she passed back into the kitchenette for two chicken breasts. They were sizzling underneath the spotless eye-level grill.

'You know,' she was saying, 'I've never really thought of myself as your type.'

From the age of about thirteen, at the growing consciousness of my involuntary eye movements while walking back from school, it was true I had become aware of being attracted to a certain type of girl. She was petite, though preferably with generous breasts, dark hair and small features, a sun-tanned or Latin complexion, ever so slightly eastern-looking—a composite personal temptress, as it were, like the nurses at the *Ospedale Italiano*. This comment of hers, though, was my first encounter with the idea that other people might have opinions, and determined ones at that, about my attraction to the opposite sex. But then again, perhaps what she meant was that she hadn't ever really thought of me as her type?

Now she was carrying our plates over to a table pushed against the large back window—laid already with condiments and cutlery on a dark blue cloth.

'So what is my type?' I said. 'I ask merely for information.'

'Oh Algy,' said Alice, replenishing our glasses. 'And don't you dare take me for your butler, either.' She had casually sloshed the pale green liquid out of its bottle, filling each glass to the brim.

'Would I do a thing like that? No, not even for ready money.'

'All right, then, I'll tell you. You're the sort of person who marries late, when you've got yourself established. It'll be to a girl of about our age, one of your students quite likely, a slim blonde, fairly short, so she can look up to you, the older man, the sugar daddy; someone who'll take you on your own terms—a pretty art student, somebody like that.'

'No, definitely not,' I said, uncertain where the sentence would go. 'I've fancied you for ages, and when we talked at university, when we were "just good friends"'—making the rabbits with my fingers—'I couldn't help thinking how much more we might have been.'

The clumsy phrases out, I looked up from a slice of chicken breast and let my eyes wander over towards the window, by way of her face, in the hope of glimpsing the impact my words were having there.

'Well, then, you were the first to think of it,' she said. 'I thought of us as only just good friends—if you see what I mean. After all, it seems like you've always been with your quite contrary one. It wasn't until you said those things, before I left the North, remember, that I even had an inkling you might have other ideas … which is when I began to think about you differently and to feel, to feel, to feel the way I do now.'

On her last day up North, we had met at a Kardomah. It was a miserable, late autumn afternoon. Raindrops were coursing sluggishly across the panes. Heads over the coffee cups, we were warming our faces with the steam rising from them. She was rummaging in one of her large paper shopping bags with its coloured rope handles.

'Can't imagine leaving the North … I'd lose what shred of identity I have.'

'One thing you'll never lose,' she said, as if foreseeing the other things, 'is your Northern-ness—and especially if you go away.'

'But what makes *me* so provincial then?'

'Asking the question! What doesn't?' she laughed.

'Well, you know I'll miss you.'

'And why is that?' she asked.

'Oh because, because …

Above the steam, across the Kadomah's window, rain

droplets merged and parted as we talked. Staring out at shop displays blurred and confused through the globules of water, I heard myself fibbing about the reasons for expressing that suddenly urgent thought.

'... because you don't mind telling me the things I need to hear.'

Better not press her about how she feels now, I thought, arranging the knife and fork in a vertical direction on the plate and still worrying about her reaction to the let-off at Holborn. So instead I let my eyes drift back to the all but finished bottle; once more glancing at her face, the cheeks rising and falling slightly as she chewed and swallowed a mouthful of salad. Her blue gaze seemed a little fuller, her face composed into a smile as she put down her glass.

'I'll make some coffee,' she said.

After a few minutes absence, she came back over to the sofa with a tray. Sitting by the fireplace, examining the ornamented screen placed in front of it, her eyes widened and glanced away. Then she crossed her legs. The newly red-painted toes were glistening above the leather of her brown summer sandals. The pattern of their weave was imprinted onto her feet in the negative by all that sunshine we were having. As I turned my head slightly to look at her, my eyes were drawn to and held by the right lobe of her ear. There was an amber earring attached to it. As if to reveal the thing, she had brushed her hair back with a casual combing action. She was looking at her toes as well, wiggling them to see how the light of the table lamp glinted on each one, and how the tiny glimmer shifted as she moved.

The window opposite, its curtains not drawn, still showed the dark curve of the Heath against the blue dark of the night. A lamp glowed warmly through its treated paper shade that seemed like luminous skin. Then the two of us became aware of the other's gaze directed at the wiggling red toenails. And as if there were nothing else for it, I leaned my head towards her and she didn't pull hers away. We would prove to each other that we were equal to each other's desires, equal to being desired. We would try to satisfy, try to be satisfactory. For now it had became obvious that the sofa was far too uncomfortable. Twisting around as we were, holding each other with a passionate firmness, kissing and being held and barely talking, sometimes just gazing off through the window at the dream-like dark outside, we were, we were doing our best. Then she simply stopped and whispered what seemed like words of love to me—

'You know you have no right, but you can if you want to.'

James's bathroom was a sultry cube. Three wall mirrors multiplied the cramped space, offering innumerably varied aspects of the features reflected and receding in every direction. Each one of them leaned forward slightly and peered at the selves to identify a blemish that might be there inside what was then my hairline. At that, a multitude of hands reached out to touch with an infinite number of distinguishable disbeliefs the olive-green, flock wallpaper.

That first temporary job in Park Royal, the one the Manpower Agency found me, was at a metal rolling warehouse. It was exactly the time of the Moorgate Tube disaster. Why had a train failed to stop on a terminal line? The dead man's handle should have halted it. The Underground's worst ever accident, the papers said, with their grainy grey photos of corpse-filled, mangled wreckage. It made compelling reading for the blokes with head bowed over sausage and chips in the tiny works canteen. There were columns of speculation about mechanical failure or human error. Had the driver been suffering from a nervous disease? For the dead man's handle not to operate, he would have had to drive his train into the wall.

At the warehouse, my first job was to help making up orders of copper piping. The stuff needed collecting into bundles, tying together, then loading onto the back of a lorry that would take the orders somewhere in the Midlands. My work mate's conversation was all about exploits on days off, holidays, at weekends, and always with different girls. He described a trip to Brighton that involved a swimming party, intimate details of acts performed underwater, and the views of massive breasts in drenched dresses and wet T-shirts. But despite all the details it sounded like his sex-life was a work of fiction—as if he spent his spare time in a Pirelli calendar.

Then, just when staying there would have obliged him to yet greater flights of fancy, I was transferred to the presser. This was a vast machine that took blocks of metal and squeezed them into great flat sheets. It was an enormous mechanized rolling pin. The trick was to walk the metal, keeping it in place on the rollers. The work pieces needed to be kept moving on the conveyor belt until they slid off the machine and down into a trolley. This vehicle then transported the flattened sheets to the next in their series of processes. Also working on the machine was a short, red-haired guy who controlled the switches from a gantry.

'Let me have a little feel of it,' he said, 'just a little feel.'

He'd strolled into the lavatory after me and was staring directly south towards what I had in my hands.

'I'd prefer it if you didn't,' were the strange, ungenerous-sounding words that came out of my mouth.

'Oh go on, why not?' the redhead persisted. 'You'll like it if I do.'

Onto the inside of my hastily buttoning up flies, a last trickle of pee expressed itself. Another employee, one of the foremen, had come into the toilet, putting a sudden stop to my new workmate's advances.

'Get your maulers off his dick, you filthy pervert,' said the other, with a joshing sort of familiarity.

From that day on I only went to the toilet when I was sure that others were on their way to have a slash, which didn't look unsuspicious itself. By the end of the week, what with the man on the presser, and the others' fantasies and jokes, I asked for my cards. Then there followed a desperate month, a month of phone calls from booths and interviews terminated after barely sitting down with 'You don't really want this job, do you: and, in any case, you're way over-qualified'—a month which inexplicably produced that more suitable niche in the Outpatients Department at the National Hospital for Nervous Diseases.

No, perhaps James wasn't ... because there was an Ingres odalisque, a turbaned nude framed in varnished wood, hanging above the bath. All of their heads turned back on long, sinuous necks, plump but coolly seductive, seeming to follow those selves of mine around the bathroom, and proving frankly nothing.

Cleaning my teeth with the usual staccato movements, toothpaste foam spilling out of one side of my mouth, I was still worrying about my being attractive to the opposite sex, about finding myself pressed into service as an object of desire for a member of my own.

A prize fish balanced on the cistern in the bathroom. It looked about a foot long, a silvery brown colour, and had its mouth slightly open so that the two tiny rows of teeth could be seen. The fish's tail was turned towards the front, as if it were still propelling itself through the water. The taxidermist had mounted it in a case with a wooden base and backboard, the other four sides being made of glass. He'd painted the distance to resemble a riverbed, placing a few small stones and bits of gravel on the base.

Leaning forward to study more closely the detail of the artist's brushstrokes and the stuffed fish's insensate eye, I pulled automatically on the handle to flush the toilet. At once a fierce pain started at the second joint of my right middle finger. Blood was flooding from its side, threatening to stain James's bathmat. Stepping back in horror, I turned on the cold tap. Running the cut under it a moment to get the sensation of pain in perspective, I found that the bloody thing wouldn't stop bleeding.

'Oh God, oh God!' all the mouths exclaimed at once.

I sucked at the side of my finger to try and control the flow; then, raising my hand, its wounded finger pointed at the sky, I came running from the bathroom calling Alice's name.

She stepped out of Isabel's bedroom wrapping a lemon-yellow bathrobe around her otherwise naked form.

'What's happened? What's the matter?'

'I've gone and cut my finger!'

'How?' She seemed to wince and smile at once. 'How did you manage to do that?'

'It must have been a sharp edge on the handle ... or something.'

'Come into the kitchen,' she said, taking my hand in hers like a mother with a son in the wars. 'Here, take this tissue to wrap it in while I look for a plaster. Oh, mind the floor. Let's see if I can find some antiseptic to put on it.'

Now she was rummaging rapidly through the kitchenette's cupboards and produced some lint, some cream in a tube, and a plaster. She held my hand beneath the tap and inspected the shallow, half-inch gash.

'Nothing to worry about here,' she said, and, squeezing a little ointment onto the lint, set it against my stinging finger.

'Hold this while I put the plaster on.'

'Oh God, oh hell,' I sighed, embarrassed and anxious about the effect my mishap might be having on her mood.

But there was no need to worry, not yet awhile at least, for we were already sloping off towards Belle's bedroom.

Porters on day shifts at the National were expected to clock on by eight thirty sharp. We were both awake and up by seven. Swathed once more in the yellow cotton robe, she was filtering some coffee and heating up a couple of croissants in the oven. She'd been given the day off from that Girl Friday job of hers in Fulham. William the photographer was young and keen to make it in the Capital—which meant that because he didn't get the work he aspired to, he had to put up with establishing a reputation by taking the pictures to go in crystal chandelier catalogues and the like. For that particular one it was her task to fiddle with the placement of the spots so as to get the glints in the right place on each and every glittering piece of glass. By no means the life you might imagine, she had said, endlessly having to run errands for a perfectionist. The previous day she'd spent the afternoon painting glazes over prawns for his shoot devoted to a plate of spaghetti with a fancy sauce. William couldn't make his mind up about whether he wanted a droplet of light gleaming on each of the prawns, or whether the horrible pink things wilting under the spots should merge more into the whole ensemble. Relieved not to be at his beck and call for a whole twenty-four hours, she would make her way, in leisurely fashion, back to the flat she shared near Crystal Palace after some window-shopping in the West End.

The night had been no less sweltering than usual. Barely room for both of us in Isabel's single bed against the wall, she must have got too hot lying cramped up there. At some point in the night she had taken a pillow from her side of the bed and stretched herself out naked on the floor. Waking in the small hours, finding her not there, I rolled across, about to get up and look for her. But there she was lying fast asleep on her stomach, the wide expanse of her sun-tanned back peeling around the bikini-shaped white areas, semi-transparent flakes of skin lifting along the ragged curve between her shoulder blades.

'I don't much like relying on Belle like this,' she was saying between bites at her croissant. Alice wasn't alone in the bedroom at the little flat she shared, and I would only once visit that place above a sweet shop not far from the Crystal Palace. Such practicalities threatened to render our thing impossible too, and before it had barely started.

'No, I know; but what can we do? The Seven Sisters Road's no good. I'm not supposed to have anyone in the cupboard. It's against Mr. Power's rules and regulations.'

'As if anyone else would fit,' she smiled.

'Well, look, why don't we take off somewhere together when I quit the National.'

'Why not?' she said, but in a tone that implied she had a list of reasons as long as her smooth freckled arm—which was just then reaching towards a drained coffee mug.

She placed the crockery in the sink on top of last night's plates and glasses.

'Don't stare at me like that!' she exclaimed. But she was talking to the sink. 'I'll deal with you lot later.'

'Sorry I haven't the time to help.'

'Don't even think of it,' she said. 'But I thought you were going to be gadding about with Miss Quite Contrary in Italy when you stop pushing the nervous around?'

'Well, yes, I am—or we are.'

'And everywhere that Mary went,' sang Alice, 'the lamb was sure to go!'

'It's been arranged for months; but that doesn't stop the two of us taking ourselves off somewhere else first, does it?'

'Well no, I don't suppose it does,' she said. 'What did you have in mind? A dirty weekend in Rottingdean?'

'No, obviously not: I just thought it was a good idea. Rotterdam, more like. Maybe we could talk about the *where* and *when* next time.'

'Richmond Park, Saturday?'

'No, sorry, can't Saturday. There's that party of Mary's cousin's we're supposed to go to in Denmark Hill. How about Friday night?'

'Sure,' she said, holding everything in reserve.

'Let me just go and clean my teeth …'

'You want to do that now?' she asked, surprised and

sucking her own. 'I like to keep the taste of my breakfast lingering a while.'

So, postponing the teeth cleaning, stooping instead to thread up the laces through the top eyes in my pair of mucky white baseball boots, I caught myself remembering the peeled flakes of skin across her back.

'Let's meet for a drink before then. How about tomorrow, after work, at the Lamb, if you can get away from William?'

'I'll see what I can do,' she said, and looked away through the window towards the now not-so-dreamlike Heath. 'Maybe I can come up with a *where*.'

Then she caught me glancing at the empire clock nestling amongst those precious vases on James's mantelpiece.

'You're late, you're late,' she said. 'Oh your paws and whiskers!'

Beyond the back window, sunlight already filled the sloping garden. It was gleaming brightly across the glass, almost effacing the lawn and trees. Today would be another of those seemingly endless summer days. Already mid-August, for weeks the radio news had been warning us to save water. In Cornwall, standpipes were reported to be operating, and no rain forecast for at least another month. Muted, remote, somewhere in the blue above an opened window, one inbound jet for Heathrow reached my ears—the various birds of the garden sycamores lifting and swooping as if in response to its roar.

'So you're thinking of leaving her then?'

'Can't exactly leave someone you're not living with, can you?'

'You know what I mean. Don't prevaricate,' she said.

'Things haven't been going that well between us lately.

Not since we came down to London, in fact.'

'Never struck me as the passionate type,' she said with a grin, 'a dead hake between the sheets, if you ask me.'

'Certainly, he that hath a satirical vein', I remembered, 'as he maketh others afraid of his wit …'

'… so he had need be afraid of others' memory,' she added, completing the phrase. 'But, darling, I even give you your best ammunition.'

As a kind of *memento mori*, she had neatly inscribed that sentence of Francis Bacon's onto a piece of white card and sellotaped it to the wall beside her first-year college-room bed.

'She's using you, you know,' she said, changing her tone.

'Using me? How do you mean?'

We were dawdling along the shadowy passageway, reluctant to bring that brief chance of being in the same place at the same time to its inevitable end.

'Don't you see how possessive she is, you're her vicarious culture.'

'There goes your satirical vein again,' I said, thinking how much better it would be if we stuck to discussing the light spots in Vermeer.

Nonetheless, adopting the look of a person allowing an important point to sink in, I lifted and spread my shoulders in an inquiring shrug. Alice reached out a hand. The chocolate brown door was open once again, then we were standing on the top step looking out across another North London summer morning, all the world before us, or so it seemed. I leaned and kissed her on both cheeks, like a foreigner. She kissed me on the mouth, like a lover.

Down into the street, relishing the fresh warm air, her hospital porter turned to wave. She was still standing there, a lemon yellow shape in the brown rectangle of the porch. But instead I just rubbed my chin, unshaven again that morning: a three-day beard, there was so little growth it didn't really matter back then. Alice gave me a wave, and stepped back inside behind the closing door.

CHAPTER 4

Porters at the National only had to be one minute late by the punch-card clock and fifteen minutes pay was docked, but this couldn't prevent them arriving after half past eight. It was true that four minutes on four different days was an hour's less pay for the holiday savings, but, what with the traffic in London, there was often nothing to be done but make the best of it. Sometimes, sick of the Tube, I took the 19 through Highbury and Islington to the stop opposite Boswell Street, then got off and walked through to Queen Square. But if the rush-hour was a bad one, as it frequently was, then the bus would get stuck, and with only ten minutes still to go as we passed Sadlers Wells, there wouldn't be a hope in hell of making the punch-clock by eight thirty sharp. So, seeing as there was now the time until eight forty-four, why not get off to have some coffee and a bacon sandwich in one of the espresso places along the Holborn side of Theobald's Road?

That Tuesday morning in mid-August, the unfamiliar bus had trundled down from Highgate, crossed the Euston Road and was heading along Southampton Row. There were construction workers up on scaffolding. Leaning over in silver hard hats, they were calling down to one of their mates on the pavement. He was unloading a bucket on a winch. A group of secretaries came out of a sandwich bar. As they emerged from under the cage of steel poles and wire, sunshine showered their pale-coloured blouses with a dazzling light. Wolf-whistles pursued them down the street. The bus shuddered forward. Perhaps Alice would already be heading towards Knightsbridge, and you would be arriving at Great Ormond Street. We were to have lunch that day.

The traffic had fouled up again: jarring shrieks and hoots of horns and the hiss of airbrakes …

Already late, I swung down the bus's stairs, trying to keep the bandaged middle finger straight and away from its rail. The lights had just turned red. I stepped off onto the pavement. Young women in nurse's uniforms came swarming around and went by. Tourists, foreign students, businessmen in their shirtsleeves, the puzzled and determined pushed along the street. The voice of Frank Sinatra emerged from a hi-fi shop doorway already open against the coming heat: *To every word of love I heard you whisper, the raindrops seemed to play a sweet refrain.*

I didn't know the song back then. But I needed to feel alive and loved, too, like everybody else: the patients in their wheelchairs, shop assistants gazing off into distance without customers to help, a petrol pump attendant down on his knees, and you, you as well, of course.

And there was Steve, my fellow porter, an even worse timekeeper, emerging out of Boswell Street on his Honda 250. Beyond the plaque recording the occasion when Princess Alice had opened the New Wing on the 30th April 1937, a Spanish girl was disappearing into the entrance marked RESEARCH. She worked in the kitchens. This morning she was wearing a sleeveless white cotton blouse that revealed the side of her pale pink bra and armpit where a black tuft sprouted. She'd been fastening her hair back with a green rubber band.

The morning stretched out before us: first, we would have to unload the cleaned laundry through the entrance marked HEALING—a trial for my middle finger wounded in love. We were to bring down the lab samples, then go up to x-ray and the wards or physio, then the Homeopathic or Italian for that day's patients.

Going in through the front entrance would mean saying a bright 'Good morning' to the head-porter at Reception. He was likely to produce another of his black looks and a meaningful glance at the wall clock. It was easier and safer to walk round past the Homeopathic, down Great Ormond Street and in the Powis Place entrance. Just cut through the underground passages to the porters' locker-room, throw on a white jacket and clock in exactly fourteen minutes after eight-thirty. That wouldn't hurt the holiday savings too much. Night nurses were just going off duty, stepping down from the main door. A taxi halted by the entrance. A crumpled figure in a fur coat was lifted out from its rear seats: a venerable old lady with a badly curved spine and a head her neck seemed no longer to fully support. The taxi driver strode into the front hall and now a porter was coming down to help with the lady. Up the steps she climbed in evident pain, towards the double doors that another porter was holding open for her, as I disappeared round the corner and descended into the bowels of the National Hospital for Nervous Diseases.

'She makes me so sorry for her,' said Pilar Bistouri, standing outside the kitchen cubicle that lunchtime. She was wearing the dress with narrow pink stripes which distinguishes auxiliaries from the nurses in their blue ones, a white folded-paper cap perched on the back of her tightly wound hair. Pilar was one of the many thousand migrant workers who help keep the National Health Service going. She'd no wish to return to the Philippines, because she was afraid of Marshal Lo. He was showering a confetti of torments on her homeland, she said, paraphrasing some of the dissident exiles' protest literature.

'Who is this Marshal Lo?' I asked.

'Who? *Who* is Marshal Lo? No, *what*?'

'Oh, he's so bad he's a thing, is he?'

'No, not he … it's a thing. You mean you don't know what *martial law* is?' she asked, saying each word slowly and loudly, as if speaking to a tourist lost on the Underground.

'Oh law, yes, right, sorry, sorry.'

Her English was practically flawless, except for the pronunciation, and we found ourselves standing there, blushing face to face, strangers to each other—neither anything like at home in that moment. It took me more than a few days to get over this foolishness, and the ignorance it revealed about what was going on out in the world. In fact, looking back, I don't suppose we ever did get over it. Certainly Pilar soon stopped making any effort to confide in me.

'You know I am really so sorry for Gran,' she began again that day. 'All the time she works and nobody will talk with her. Nobody can even make a joke to her. She thinks you are criticizing.'

The old girl we were talking about also wore the pink striped dress and white apron of an auxiliary. An epileptic with a limp, Gran, as all the regulars in Outpatients called her, though not exactly affectionately, must have been approaching sixty-five. She'd been employed by the hospital for the past seventeen years.

'Hell of a long time,' said Steve, towards the close of

one more seemingly endless afternoon. Our ginger-haired Honda 250 biker was a temporary porter like me. He planned to go grape picking in France come September.

'Someday you'll have to settle down,' said Jack, the senior man and our union rep, 'spread sideways, take root, become part of the woodwork.'

Jack, a short man with a long grey beard like an Old Testament prophet, had been at the National man and boy. Nervously unsteady eyes and an indecisive syntax belied the daily efforts he made to assert his authority. Jack tended to do better at being fatherly with the likes of Steve and me—who presented rather different challenges to his precarious self-esteem.

Steve was in the habit of defending himself with an infectious, broad grin. Not long out of school, he must have been three or four years younger than me. London was his town, though, and he would offer me the benefit of his greater street wisdom. Steve treated Jack's ingrained respect for the conventions and practices of the National with an undemonstrative bolshiness.

'Stuff this for a game of soldiers,' he would murmur, as we idled away the last few minutes before clocking-off time.

Gran had certainly taken root in the place. The colour of the hospital was in her hair: a whitish-grey. She always wore an elasticated bandage on her left leg. One day she fitted and fell so badly she suffered a fracture. The glistening look in her eyes wasn't tears, but the medications she took for her epileptic condition. The pink glasses she wore had a tiny wing on either side.

The National was the only home Gran had left. She already looked like a subject for treatment all those years back, and the many quiet moments allowed me time to scribble down notes about her, and the complaints she attracted, on the backs of torn up heart-rate print-outs. Turning over my smudged and faded pencil scrawls these many years on, I can only think she must have died, and maybe Jack as well.

Steve, though, did cross our path again by chance one blustery afternoon. We happened to be walking in opposite directions half way between Queensway and Notting Hill Gate. You were with me, remember, and seemed to recall him too. But it was one of those tricky encounters when you know the moment recognition occurs there's really not much you can say.

'Have a nice rest of your life!' Those were the words he as good as shouted over his shoulder after we parted on that late spring afternoon. It must have been ten years or more after that sweltering summer, and that September in the nineteen seventies.

There was no shortage of quiet moments through those months in Outpatients. I never like being caught at a loose end, and anyway needed to keep a nose in the Courtauld reading list. So I'd make sure to have something with me for the journey to and from work, for the lunch hour, or when our routine of jobs slackened off in the late afternoon. Most days there would be a thick paperback sticking out of the right pocket in my white porter's jacket. The only thing bothering about this was that people could mistake it for a sign I didn't actually think of myself as a porter, as part of the team. But then, let's face it, I wasn't.

'Just warn me when you're about to say something,' said

Steve, glancing at the Cubist cover, 'and I'll go and fetch a dictionary.'

Yet often the impulse to semi-licit study would evaporate in the limbo of Outpatients, with Jack unsmilingly tolerant of his porter being buried yet again in a book. That day, there were the latest newspaper reports about a playwright's break-up with an actress, seemingly caused by his affair with some aristocratic writer. The usual photographs showed harassed figures emerging from swish residences and the insinuating speculative comments, the usual pocket biographies like interim obituaries.

While waiting for the next bit of work to arrive, Steve was interrupting those articles with some chat about this brilliant chick he had his eye on in Physio.

'You should see her do the massages,' he was saying, with a parody of a leer.

'But I thought she worked in the Dispensary.'

Steve was also killing time in a protractedly hopeless flirtation with the blonde chemist there.

'No, not her; that's my other one.'

'Oh, your other one?' I said. 'But she's got to be at least five years older than you. Haven't you noticed her chatting up the junior doctors?'

'So?' said Steve.

'She's a chemist. You're a porter.'

'And so?'

This time the question seemed to be asking why anyone should care a damn what he did to get through the summer's duller moments. What did it matter if he was wasting his time? Steve enjoyed being flirtatious; they, at least up to a point, enjoyed finding new ways of sending him packing. Which still, despite the convenient assumption that 'No!

No! No!' means precisely its opposite, made it baffling how Steve could convince himself or pretend to think that 'Get away with you' might be taken as a come-on.

Now we'd been joined in the empty patients' armchairs by some of the staff nurses drinking cups of tea, and our talk drifted back onto Outpatients' perennial complaints about Gran.

'You know she hasn't had much of a life,' said Martha.

But Pilar, still at a loss, was taking a different line.

'I know we must pity her for the life she lives,' said the auxiliary, 'but sometimes I want to cry at the anti-social things she will say.'

The kitchen cubicle where Gran worked was not quite a room, more a space partitioned off near the rear entrance. Its walls were painted white and it offered, at times, the only respite from all those quiet, or occasionally not quite so quiet, private tragedies crowding Outpatients during treatment hours.

While washing up some pots, Gran asked if I would go and buy her the *Evening Standard*. It was her little conspiracy: the conspiracy of being liked by someone. That had a history too. Everyone had a history, like everyone had a mother, difficult though that might be to imagine with some people who give the impression that they were born old. Gran's name was Enid Warburton. She was from Kings Lynn, and her mother was still alive somewhere out in Essex.

'The old girl's ninety-four, and gets upset by the sight of Gran,' said Martha, 'and her elder brother tries to keep her from seeing the dear. She's terribly isolated.'

'Oh thank you,' said Enid as she tucked the newspaper inside her shopping bag. 'I've got no one but you to do anything for me here. You're my only friend. I haven't had a word from my brother since my birthday in June. And you see I get so tired. The drugs I'm on do tire me, and it's worse if I've had no breakfast.'

Matron in the National Hospital for Nervous Diseases was a distinguished-looking lady of about sixty, dressed in black, who walked with the aid of a telescopically adjustable aluminium stick.

It was her policy to employ epileptics as auxiliaries. The staff nurses and SRNs in Outpatients knew that when Gran had a hair-do, she might well fit the next day. She was going for a holiday to Margate on Wednesday next. She had arranged with Matron to have her hair waved on the Tuesday morning.

'It'll be all right here in Outpatients, won't it?'

Jack said that. He's been here even longer than Enid. He's worked here for twenty-two years.

'The way you porters stand outside our windows and stare up at us girls, it's disgusting!' Gran said a few days later from beyond the kitchen cubicle door. 'No, it's not so bad just now, in the summertime, with the leaves on the trees. But every winter you can see right in. And a body needs her privacy. I hardly dare undress and the room gets so hot, what with the central heating pipes and all. I just want to open the window, but, I ask you, how can I? You never know who might be standing outside!'

'Do you mean in the freezing cold, on a winter night, outside your window?' asked Steve, with genuine-sounding curiosity.

Gran had lured him into her kitchen cubicle on the

pretext of asking if he would run an errand for her. Now she'd cornered him there and he was allowing the endless stream of her complaining to be vented in his ears. But soon Steve too would start to look round for some work to do, or Jack would rescue him with a task he could go off and pretend to fulfill.

There he goes, sidling furtively away, just glancing in my direction with one more of his conspiratorial smiles.

'And just who were you staying with last night?' you asked me, stumbling about amongst a crowd of withered pot plants on a back garden terrace. We were alone under the stars, with a half moon casting down its borrowed light; there were three hollyhocks pitching slightly in the breeze that flurried your white party dress, made faintly luminous by that moon. At last you sat down on a wooden bench by the French windows. '*Oh it might as well rain until September*'—the record's sweet refrain came drifting out into the thick rhododendron bushes whose leaves reflected more splashes of moonlight at the borders of an un-mown lawn. Beyond those borders, some hardy perennials survived the student neglect.

'Go on. Tell me. Who were you staying with last night?' you repeated, staring out into that wilderness.

'What do you mean?'

'The toothbrush,' you were sighing, 'the toothbrush!'

Your voice, saddened as if by expectations finally confirmed, echoed across the forsaken garden.

'Oh come on now, you know you're a hopeless liar.'

So there went my plans to keep that summer fling a secret: jacket hanging open, the brush protruding from my inside pocket, its worn bristles first.

'Why don't you come in and join the dancing?'

It was Emily, our hostess, appearing through the metal-framed French windows to interrupt the silence.

'Why so long-faced? Come on. Enjoy yourselves! Have another drink!' exclaimed inebriated Emily with yet another laugh.

'We'll be there in a second.' You had managed a smile. 'It was too hot inside. We thought we'd try your garden for a moment, didn't we. It's nice and peaceful out here.'

'Not much to look at, I'm afraid!' said Emily, skipping back into the flat.

One of the rooms was crowded to the door with dancers, its stereo turned up to full volume, and, as you implied, we were both such choosy beggars when it came to dance music. Another room was pitch dark, filled with intertwined couples. Which left the kitchen. It too was crammed with the partygoers, but here they were rifling through a sink filled with empties searching for one last drink. There, and in the crammed passageways, you couldn't hear yourself think above the wild exchanges between drunken friends, acquaintances, and strangers who sounded on the point of picking a fight.

'Why don't we go for a walk round the block?' I shouted it into your ear.

Cooler than Emily's party, the empty streets nearby were still warm from the day, the heat slowly fading out of them, dying away in the darkness. We walked past bleak three-storey Victorian houses with small front gardens behind low brick walls—their shiny privets glinted in the moonlight.

'I was just staying overnight with Alice.'

'You know, I thought it was something like that.'

'Like what?'

'You tell me.' You had stopped beside one of the low stone-capped walls that separated the front gardens from the street.

We were already half way round the block and in danger of arriving back at the party too soon. You took out a handkerchief, dusted the grimy stone and, catching the skirts of your white dress up under you, sat down on the wall.

'How long has this been going on?' you mumbled, as if echoing the distant stereo system; sun-parched leaves crackled faintly in the breeze.

'It just sort of happened that weekend when we went up North.'

'Oh really, that weekend ... and were you going to get round to telling me?'

But then you couldn't stop yourself from moistening at the eyes, still staring straight ahead across the deserted suburban street, into the shifting branches opposite. 'And don't you dare think I'm clinging,' you added. 'That's the last thing I want!'

There was another nasty silence in the deserted street, a sharp sense of unforeseen loss and disorientation figuring itself in the contrasts of leafage and brickwork.

'All right then: why don't we just stop seeing each other?'

Nothing came to mind, and so I said nothing. You had turned to look at me, with eyelids glistening—your lips slightly parted, and quivering from the disappointment, the rage.

'Honestly, I wouldn't have minded so much if it had been with someone I'd never met,' you said. 'But you must have been talking about me behind my back, making assignations even when I was buying a drink for you both, like the other day at the Lamb, or when I went to the toilet. And I thought we had no secrets from each other. I thought we could talk about everything.'

'Really, well, anyway, every one has secrets.'

'They do? All right, why don't we just stop seeing each other then?'

'But why should we?'

'Because I don't want to be compared all the time: it makes everything impossible. Don't you see?'

'That must mean you expect to come out worse from the comparison.'

Your reply to that was a look of cold contempt.

'Didn't I let you get on with it last year when there was somebody else? You know, what's his name? I went away for the weekend so you could be with him, didn't I?'

'Except that he didn't turn up!'

'But that's not the point, is it? Did they ever make any difference to us?'

'No, because you never met any of them.'

'So what?'

'So I thought her and me were friends.'

'Better be getting back to the party,' I said. 'Emily will be wondering.'

'You've got to be joking—I'm leaving—I'm going home—I'm going home right now.'

You got up off the wall, dusted down your party dress, remembered to pocket your handkerchief, and began walking slowly away. Then you stopped and glanced around, as if trying to remind yourself who this person was—the one who had met you after your shift, travelled down to Denmark Hill, talked on the Tube about our holiday planned for September, the one you had lived with for two whole years in St Luke's Square. Me, the one still standing in the silence of that street, he was evidently not. On your face was an expression of what looked like contempt and sorrow commingled. As if that person had gone forever.

'Look,' I said, 'why don't we meet up … meet up and talk about things quietly, over a meal or something?'

The following Monday in Outpatients I was sitting amongst the crowd of visitors attending for their treatments, flicking over pages of *The Illustrated London News* and waiting to be commandeered for my next job. That day it was Parkinson's disease. Most of the staff didn't pay any attention to the roomful of shaking people. Then a pungent old woman wearing a faded moss-green headscarf occupied the armchair next to mine. A glance confirmed that she must have been one of those people who regularly sleep rough in places like the Gardens of the Savoy. There was a layer of dried grey mud on her sloping-heeled shoes, her face and hands engrained in dirt. She had two plastic bags of possessions, one from Sainsbury's and the other from Top Shop.

'Who do you bloody well think you're looking at, you great fat loon?'

'Pardon me.'

'Pardon me! Pardon me!' she jeered. 'I bet you think you're a right fool clever dick, reading that pornography there. You ought to be ashamed of yourself!'

'Sorry?'

'Sorry, is it?' Who's sorry now, that's what I'd like to know. Did you hear that? Sorry, he says, the silly little idiot. And I know you're only thinking "When can I stick it up all these pretty little nurses". Shame on you! Don't lie. Don't lie. I can see it in your eyes!'

Martha, responding to my silent appeals for assistance, hurried over and squatted in front of her.

'Come on now, Maggie, don't go picking on the poor boy like that. He's new to us here, and you know he can't answer you back.'

'He's got a filthy mind, that one,' said Maggie, confiding in the staff nurse.

Yes, there were more than a few reasons to be grateful for Martha's presence in Outpatients during my time at the National. She had recently given someone the push, an interior decorator that didn't want to get too involved. 'So I let him get uninvolved,' she said, not seeming in the least bit bothered.

'So he's got a dirty mind? Of course he has! Nothing wrong with him,' she replied, laughing as she did. She looked at me. 'Gran's just this moment told me she needs you in the kitchen. You'd better go and see what she wants.'

It was Martha who later explained that Maggie the bag lady had been a patient at the National before the war. She'd got the worse of an early frontal lobotomy operation.

'I like Maggie a lot,' she said. 'You see she just comes straight out with what most of us think all the time. Of course, she knows everyone here. When the operation went wrong they couldn't get rid of her. She just kept coming back. Officially, we're not supposed to let her in, but what can you do? She's one of our failures, but I don't think we should fail her twice. There's no point sending her away, and Sister just turns a blind eye.'

It must have been about then I asked Martha why she didn't seem bothered about dumping her interior decorator chap and discovered she had designs on a senior houseman in Neurosurgery.

'Very very dishy,' she told me, and either to boast or repay her trust, I naturally reciprocated with a little glimpse into my own love-life dilemma.

'Well now,' said Martha, 'can't say I ever had you down as a love 'em and leave 'em type.'

'But I'm not, I'm not,' I said—quite redundantly, as her face confirmed.

CHAPTER 5

Despite everything, you agreed we could meet up again on the Saturday after that party. We were to eat at an Italian restaurant behind the Gate in Notting Hill and, presumably, have the whole thing out.

The *Tivoli*'s tables were designed for lovers, each couple in a separate booth; but its rustic, carved wood screens would serve for a low-voiced argument too. It wouldn't disturb the other diners. I was doing my best, being fussily attentive to start with, asking you about the menu, replenishing your water glass, overacting, as people often do when they're about to betray themselves. You ordered the trout. For me it was going to be *pollo sorpresa*—which the waiter explained was a boned chicken leg filled with butter and olive oil then fried in a coating of breadcrumbs.

'So where's the surprise?'

'Try one and see,' said the waiter, his role assumed to perfection.

'Well then?' you were asking, as we waited for the starters to be taken away.

'She and me, well, we've decided to spend a few days in Amsterdam together looking at paintings. So then you and I can meet up somewhere afterwards. And we can hitch-hike down to Italy together as we planned.'

'You worm,' you muttered. 'You absolute worm.'

The waiter arrived with our main dishes. You were sitting with your back to the wall, eyes stinging above the untouched trout in its ring of cream sauce.

'But what about the plans we made for Italy? We really

can meet up in Holland after she's left, why not? And then hitch down to Italy together.'

'Tell me, what does *she* think about this particularly brilliant idea of yours?'

'Don't know. I haven't told her yet.'

'Oh really. I bet she'll be overjoyed. Well, as far as I'm concerned, you can forget it,' you said.

'But why on earth should I? Why should we?'

'Then go with *her.*'

Think how different all our lives might have been had I gone and done exactly what you appeared to be suggesting. Not that you were, of course, not really.

'But we agreed to go together.'

At the next table, above the partition, a waiter was lowering an enormous pepper grinder, smiling obligingly and twisting the top, then shaking the contraption with a flourish.

'I can't bear it,' you were saying. 'Just chuck her ... or chuck *me.*'

Neither of us seemed to be eating anything, so the waiter invited reassurance that the courses were to our satisfaction. I attempted to appease him with a couple of symbolic mouthfuls and mumbled insincerities.

'You make it sound as if I were two-timing you,' I went on. 'But we're not at school now, and we're not living together because we couldn't find anywhere, and that's all there is to it.'

'Not living together any more, is it? You bet we're not!'

Then, as if on impulse, you simply stood up and walked away. Despite the booths, your sudden exit had disturbed some of the diners nearby. A few were turning their heads to see me leave some money on the table and abandon my *pollo sorpresa* with the hot butter and olive oil still leaking from its wounded side.

'Don't be so upset,' I gasped, managing to catch you up on the pavement. 'You know I want us to stay together.'

It wasn't untrue. After all, I didn't really know what I wanted or thought. You had stopped at the head of the steps down to the Notting Hill Tube.

'And anyway, the trip to Amsterdam will just round things off with her. Maybe it was a mistake, what happened; but it did, and you know I've always liked her. So, look, then we can go on to Italy like we planned, and everything will be just the way it was, you'll see.'

'But how can it ever be like it was? How could anything ever again?'

We descended into the bowels of the Underground following the direction of the rushing cooler wind and train noise.

'Things have to change,' I found myself quoting, 'if they're to stay the same.'

'*Book*worm!' you said, and disappeared round the corner towards the westbound Central Line.

CHAPTER 6

Some days later a message came down from the private ward saying they were having difficulties with a very important patient who couldn't be sedated. He needed constant attention. Steve had been sent up to keep an eye on him, and had already been there for more than two hours.

'We've been asked to supply cover,' Jack explained. 'Go and stand in for your mate, Ginger, so the lad can have his lunch break.'

Off I went, bounding up the flight of steps that led into the main hospital building and on to the corridor past the well-stocked patients' library. Jack was always telling us never, never, *never* except in the gravest emergencies, to run inside the hospital. It gave a bad impression. Still, I couldn't help youthfully leaping up those two or three steps at a time, especially with the sense of release after struggling down from the wards with the deeply depressed patients who came to Outpatients for their ECT.

Most of these victims were middle-aged in-patients, but a few arrived each week for the preliminary talk with a doctor and then the electric-shock therapy. There was an old lady who came for her treatment every Thursday afternoon. Recovering, she would be seated in the outer curtained-off room. Then each week she would begin:

'Where's Denis?'

It fell to Martha, since she was so good at it, to sit beside the distracted lady, responding to her plaintive demand.

'Where's Denis?'

'He's coming as soon as he can,' she'd say—Steve disappearing through the curtains into the main waiting area to hide his tears of laughter, heading towards the stairs and the labs for specimen results, back to the wards for another patient, or to X-ray for their dark transparencies.

'But where's Denis?'

Denis was the old lady's middle-aged son. Dressed in a dark blue, pin-striped, three-piece suit, he brought her to Outpatients at exactly the same time each week, then collected her, regular as clockwork, just two hours later after trading in the City.

'So where's Denis?'

'He's been held up in traffic—but he's on his way, he's on his way.'

'Where's Denis now?'

'He's looking for somewhere to park the car,' Martha ad-libbed. 'Go on, have a biscuit, have some more of your tea.'

And so it continued, with her helpless litany compelling Martha to ever more elaborate stories.

'Why isn't Denis here yet?'

'He's talking to the doctors now about what to do for the best. He'll be here in just a minute. Don't forget your biscuit. Any minute now, any minute.'

Finally, as if summoned by Martha's words, Denis himself, a balding, overweight businessman, suffering from the heat as his moist pate made evident, arrived through the screen curtains, and took his distracted mother away and off our hands for one more week.

Every Tuesday and Thursday the porters would be sent up

onto the wards where the long-stay patients lived. Usually they were so heavily medicated they'd partially lost control of their legs. Steve and I helped them shuffle along. Some could barely lift feet off the ground. Painfully slowly down the main hospital corridor we would go, the ladies in their pastel shades and dusty pink slippers or mules clinging for dear life to the wooden rail that ran along the wall, Steve generously chatting them up as they went.

'There you go now. Mind the gap. Stand clear of the doors,' he'd say. 'Just one more step, one step at a time. And keep your pecker up, sweetheart.'

Beyond the second set of screening curtains was a black leatherette couch, a sterilized trolley with short plastic airways to prevent patients from being choked, and the apparatus to induce artificial epileptic fits. The medical profession had been delivering electric shock therapy for almost two centuries. What good did they imagine it could do?

One Egyptian woman we helped down twice a week appeared entirely immune to it all. Martha told me she was once a doctoral student working on Proust at the University of Cairo. But everything had to be abandoned when her fiancé, in a maddened attempt to wound her, shot and killed her sister instead. This student of *À la recherche du temps perdus* had attempted suicide many times. Poor soul, she was nearly shapeless in her light middle-eastern robe, clinging to the corridor rail. Once in a while, as she crept along between one of the porters and the wall, Mr. Roger Bannister, the former four-minute-miler and consultant at the National, walked thoughtfully by on his way to a ward round or a meeting with hospital governors.

One unsteady step after another the Egyptian lady

went, struggling down into Outpatients, a white-jacketed porter in attendance. We would help her to sit down in the screened-off outer treatment room, and there she waited for her artificial fit. It was believed to release a chemical in the brain that made real epileptics elated after their episodes. Lowered into an armchair, the one-time research student would be engaged in painfully stilted chat by the staff nurses.

'And how are you doing today then?' asked Martha. 'You're no better? Oh dear. So where are you planning to go for your holidays? I hear Lisbon's nice. No? Well, what have you been reading?'

Brought down twice a week, each in their turn, the patients were put on a respirator and given a paralyzing drug. Jack and a nurse, one on each side, would then help to restrain the person on the couch while she, or occasionally he, shook violently. On one occasion, when a staff shortage took Jack elsewhere, I was called in to perform that task. There the patients lay, a doctor holding the heavy contacts that transmitted the shock against both temples of the papery-skinned, unconscious, violently shaking patients. As they came round, the doctor would encourage them with enthusiastic words about how they were feeling so much better now, remember?

Towards the end of August, our Egyptian scholar suddenly stopped coming down for treatments. Wondering why, Steve asked Martha if she'd got better or something. With relief at another's prayers answered, Martha explained how she had been transferred to University College Hospital for yet more tests. Once there, she had managed to heave herself out of an eighth-floor window— and anywhere, anywhere out of the world.

Dressed in a loose green skirt, with an embroidered white cotton blouse, the young doctor from psychology, a little department in a wooden shack up on the roof, was paying her weekly visit to give our electric-shock patients their aptitude and memory tests. I asked what her questionnaires were intended to show.

'That they don't have much left of either,' she said, and it was as if the ghost of those researches into lost time echoed a moment in the air around us.

One Friday in late August, Tina, the girl who shared that bed-sit near the Crystal Palace, gave Alice a nod and a wink: she wouldn't be back till the following afternoon. Here was at least one more chance to be together before September.

Dusk was beginning to close in as we strolled back from a café across some unkempt parkland, behind tennis courts and a community hall. The sky was strewn with white cloud-tails above roofs of semis, the houses' green paintwork glinting at a distance. On ahead, the parched grasses sloped away across a playing field to rows of small houses down in a hollow. There was some washing fluttering on an aluminium clothes dryer that looked like a large raised umbrella with its covering replaced by the waving white pieces of cloth—so many flags of surrender in the breeze.

Alice had bowed to the inevitable and would, if accepted, be starting a teacher-training course at Bristol in the autumn. She was back from a visit to see her old tutor up North, to talk over plans and pick his brains about the pros and cons of going into teaching. But he had been busy and evasive. Now she was confessing to me her infatuation as a means of distancing it—a little ashamed of having imagined that attachments formed in that strictly limited space of time might be such as to last beyond it, and expressing an unexpected disillusion with her undergraduate idol. He had, of course, agreed to write the reference, but the valve of his charisma and projective enthusiasm regularly employed on female students had now been abruptly turned off.

'Made me feel like an unsold, end-of-line bargain,' she said.

'I suppose it's bound to be like that. He can't get off on the infatuation any more, so he has to move on to the next batch, and then the next, and so on, until he retires.'

'I think we were all a bit in love with him,' she said. 'You know, he's such an inspiring lecturer, and has done so many exciting, creative things with his anthologies. You know the cover of the most recent one, the Louise Nevelson sculpture-assemblage—did I mention I saw the original in New York?'

The sky was offering an unusual range of cloud forms that evening. Most peculiar was the fact that the different shapes appeared to be moving in contrary directions. So if a pink one was rising above the darkening trees and going approximately north, across the Thames, then those few trails of cirrus had to be heading west towards Heathrow and the sunset.

She must have picked up on my faintly jealous irritation, because she switched the direction of talk by wondering mildly what might happen when we were back from the five days in Amsterdam. After all, London to Bristol was not an especially difficult commute.

'Well, I promised I'd go to Italy, but I can't see it working out really. She's bound to get bored with the galleries and stuff. Then that'll be that.'

'But why Italy?'

'Always wanted to go,' I said, not fully answering her question, 'and now I've got to see the frescos at first hand if I'm going to be doing this MA at the Courtauld … and my dad was there during the war.'

'Oh, your dad again, is it? You're always on about him, but you never so much as mention your mother. Now why *is* that?'

We were standing on the slope of yellowed grass. The drift of her words had brought back once more a trace of the childish urge to run home, home to one of those houses, past that washing on the dryer, back across the road from scouts, back to mum with my sister Christine almost a teenager and just starting high school. How many years had it been since Dad had keeled over in front of his class with a heart attack? Just for a moment I couldn't remember. The doctor who examined him said he couldn't have felt a thing, dead before he hit the classroom floor. After that, Mum was obliged to go back to teaching herself, a career she'd never exactly chosen. Mum would get through periods of depression and the medication prescribed for it. There she would be, sitting in the lamplight of our living room, curtains not drawn, front garden shadows looming, feet on the coffee table, and a toppling pile of English essays for marking on the floor beside her.

All around now the dusk was deepening, the neon lights coming on as we strolled back to her flat above the sweetshop. There was just a trace of something like fear to be sensed in that thickening darkness—as if the street lamps had caused it, blinking on pale in the sunset.

'What can I say? My mother … She's a mystery to me.'

Then Alice turned and looked me square in the face. She seemed about to speak, but merely smiled instead. We walked on a few yards further.

'I suppose you must feel terribly guilty,' she began again. 'You never said goodbye to your dear old dad, and you don't think you loved him as much as you should have. Then again, you're probably afraid you love your mother just a little bit too much—so you never talk about her, and generally give the impression of being completely un-filial. I shouldn't worry about it, though, darling. It's really quite normal.'

'Look, just because I don't talk about my mum all the time doesn't mean she isn't important to me.'

'Oh, poor Rich!' exclaimed Alice, with such a knowing look—as if needing to underline what life as an oxymoron might feel like.

No, running home to mum was not the answer. And picking up on the uneasy silence that followed, Alice let the topic drop. There and then, in the empty street, she took my arm. Side by side, as lovers do, towards her room, we walked—me gratefully taking a last glance back towards the houses, their laundry waving its offered surrender, and the street lights' globes of amber on their arching concrete poles.

As I say, a message had come down from the private ward to the effect that they were having difficulties with a very important person, so I stepped with excited anticipation into the lift and pressed the button for the private ward.

It would be the first and last time I ever went there. At the reception desk, Sister and a cabal of consultants were confabulating around the phones. One of them had a sanatorium on the line, and was explaining that their patient was suffering from a pre-senile dementia, but that it could be significantly retarded with the right cocktail of drugs. The patient, a managing director of some big electronics firm or other, would soon be able to resume his post, regardless, and for many years to come. The hospital had admitted him that morning in a condition dangerous to himself and those around him. At this discreet sanatorium, somewhere in the Home Counties, the drugs could be administered; and this very important person would be nursed back to socially useful lucidity. An ambulance had been ordered for early that afternoon.

'Good,' said Sister, turning from the phones. 'You must be the replacement porter.'

'I'm afraid he was rather hyperactive earlier in the day,' she said, as we set off down the spotless corridor with its rows of private rooms, their doors all firmly closed.

'They said in Outpatients that he could be violent?'

'No, not really,' Sister replied. 'He settled down once we gave him something, and I don't think he's been any trouble to your friend here. However, I would recommend that you keep a healthy distance. Agree with whatever he tells you. Don't be doing anything that might at all upset him; and don't, whatever you do, try to restrain him if he does become agitated. Call for assistance. There's an emergency bell on the edge of the bedside cabinet—on the right as you face it. If you think he's becoming even the slightest bit out of control and you're getting into difficulties, use it. We'll have an ambulance here for him before you can say

Jack Robinson. But I don't think you need expect much of an ordeal.'

Sister opened the locked door to a large, well-furnished room. Steve was standing over by the windows. They were open, for the cooling breeze, but caged in with close wire mesh to guard against suicide attempts like the one that had offered a release to our student of Proust. Turning as he heard the two of us enter, Steve came striding towards the door.

'See you later,' he said to a large man in loose-fitting winceyette pyjamas who was pacing restlessly back and forth about the scrubbed and polished floor. Then Steve gave one of his infectious smirks, and a wink as he slipped out of the room for his lunch break. Sister also proffered a reassuring smile and closed the door, leaving me alone with this very important patient.

'Come over here, young man,' said the dementia sufferer. 'I want to show you something.'

He was stoutly built, with thin grey hair that must have usually been combed back over his head in a controlled wave. Today, it fell sideways in the shape of a ski-slope over one ear. He had small, but well-defined features. The sagging skin of his face showed broken blood vessels flecking the upper parts of his cheeks. On top of the striped pyjamas, whose trouser bottoms fell in loose folds over his slippers, he was wearing a white towelling bathrobe.

'You are a doctor, are you not?'

'I am, yes ... I am.'

'May I ask you what kind of doctor? You certainly don't look old enough to be a doctor. You must be completing your training. Tell me, precisely how many years does it take to qualify?'

'Oh, about seven,' I guessed.

'Whatever you do,' the patient continued, 'don't become one of those pill doctors. They don't do you any good at all, and I should know. Damn pill doctors for drug addicts wasting the public's money, that's what I say. Take my advice, young man, do you hear, go into surgery. You be a surgeon. They're the only *bona fide* doctors. You are a doctor, aren't you?'

'Yes. I'm training to be one.'

'Well, come over here, then, my good fellow, and let me show you just what's been driving me right round the bend!'

Warily, I advanced a couple of steps as the important patient strode over to the window, leaning out as far as he could until his forehead was touching the wire-mesh cage.

'A surgeon is exactly what I need, of course. Had enough of these tuppenny ha'penny pill pushers. They're no damn good, the lot of them. What I'm here for is my operation. I'm waiting for my operation. You're aware of that, are you not?'

'I am, yes.'

A faint breeze from the open windows caught the disordered remnants of his hair.

'You're not lying to me, are you, young man?' he said, his voice beginning to rise. 'You're not one of those pill doctor fellows, by any chance? No good to me, if you are. Let me tell you, you might as well get right out of here this minute if you're one of their sort, you hear me.'

Down in Queen Square the thick layers of leaves above its garden barely stirred with that faint breeze. The August sun was at its height, the narrowest of shadows outlining the tiny bodies stretched out on the grass below. Between the leaves I could intuit the outlines of secretaries and nurses who had raised skirts well above their bare knees to improve and extend the tanning of their legs. There were some doctors sitting talking in shirtsleeves, ties loosened, top buttons undone. Technicians and porters lay on their backs, some with their shirts removed, making the most of that scorching lunch hour. An ambulance arrived. Two porters were carrying another stretcher up into reception.

Pigeons and sparrows were alighting around the fountain with its water UNFIT FOR DRINKING. And there you were sitting on a bench nearby with your high rounded forehead, the determined expression of your mouth in repose, your dark brown straight hair, parted in the centre and falling to your shoulders. You were finishing your packet of homemade sandwiches and dusting the crumbs from your flowery smock. Birds were pecking at the few scraps you threw them, coming up close to you, no distance at all, almost eating from your hand. By then I knew you had given in, had agreed to meet up in Brussels after my week in the Netherlands. But why had you agreed to that? Maybe you thought it wouldn't last with her, wouldn't even survive the week in Holland. No doubt you were giving me one last chance. And, in a way, I suppose that's what I got.

Others might say that the best thing in the circumstances would have been a clean break, but, of course, there's no such thing. The hurt to come from not breaking up was something that nobody could have predicted, though with hindsight this plan of mine looked crazy enough to deserve some foreboding. But the trouble with being young is you think you're immortal. I should have known better.

I should have known better. But now you were glancing down at your watch, twisting your wrist round to see the face at your pulse, the thin black ribbon you used as a replacement strap quite visible. Then, your lunch hour over, you stood up from the bench and set off in the direction of Great Ormond Street. As you did so, always a great devourer of crime, you dropped a green Penguin Marjorie Allingham who-dun-it into your embroidered shoulder bag.

'Just look at that! Look at that laziness! Get back to work right now, will you?' It was the chairman, leaning out as far as he could, shouting through the cage, shaking his fists, as if the sunbathing hospital staff down below could hear and would take notice of him.

'Get back to work, I tell you,' he yelled. 'Would you be so kind, young man, as to go straight down to the shop floor and order those wastrels back to work?'

But who did he think he was talking to now? Yet no sooner had he uttered the words, than the chairman seemed entirely to forget them. His head had been pressed so fiercely against the window cage wire that its mesh was lifting in red lines across his wrinkled brow. He turned back to the scene below.

'How many times have I said it? Just tell me how many? What do the shareholders expect me to do? We'll never meet our deadlines if I don't get an agreement from the workforce. The workforce, you call them? They're ignoramuses. They don't even know the meaning of the word. AEG are moving in. They're just waiting for their chance. Breathing down my neck, by God. And I'm telling you, they'll do anything to avoid a decent day's work. What do the shareholders expect me to do? Put the stuff on to the wagons myself? Only look at them now! Believe me, it has to stop. I'd go down myself, but there's a young man with me here who's training to be a surgeon. Put me through to Harold immediately. No, a meeting with him, an hour will do, any time early next week. Just now I'm waiting for my operation. An hour is all I need with him to sort this whole mess out once and for all. I've been telling him for months. Telefunken are strong. They've got something new up their sleeves. But what has Harold ever done about it I'd like to know? Can't get them back to work either, whatever he tells the country. Just give me an hour with the PM. I'll make him see sense, let me tell you. Can't match their delivery dates. All because you scum down there won't lift a finger, scroungers and yobbos the lot of you. Something for nothing! All they want is something for nothing! Get back to work, why don't you? This young man I have here with me, he's got the right idea. He's going to be a surgeon, a real doctor, not one of your pill-pushers wasting the public's money. We need more people like him! Yes, just get Wilson on the phone right now. Go to the top, young man. Believe me, it's the only way. Don't, whatever you do, get tied up with the secretaries. Tied up with the secretaries! Get back to your posts! Get back to your work places. For God's sake, why don't you? They should take my advice, do you hear, young man. Get rid of these foreign pill-pushers. Look at them down there, flat on their backs. Having sex, is it? Is that what they're up to now?'

CHAPTER 7

At the very end of August, on my last Friday at the National, I took all my savings from the Lloyds Bank in Great Ormond Street and closed the account. There was time enough during my lunch hour to visit the Barclays with a foreign currency counter on Southampton Row and change a portion for the week ahead. The Dutch money was brightly coloured, as if by a De Stijl designer, with bold angular shapes and portraits of famous Dutchmen like the poet Vondel, or Spinoza the philosopher. It had a crispy feel and a cheerful look—as if it wasn't really money at all.

Leaving the hospital meant giving up my cupboard in Finsbury Park. You had moved into a home for juveniles in Paddington. Reluctantly, though doubtless with your own hopes in mind, you were letting me, your practically ex-boyfriend, spend my last few nights there before leaving. It might have seemed I was simply using you, but here at last, and maybe not too late, was a flat big enough for the both of us to fit in.

From your kitchen window I could see the flyovers, underpasses, and skyscrapers stamped with words. The early sun cast strong, sharp shadows across the area's concrete pillars and frontages. Traffic on the Westway was at a standstill; silver-grey Metropolitan Line trains were clattering on; an Intercity express was heading out west; a barge moved away from its moorings beside the gardens in the Little Venice Basin. Heaped in the corner of your living room were my winter clothes, a pile of books, boxes of paints, filled sketchpads, and two files of assorted art history notes.

You hadn't been at the place long enough to make up your mind about the new job yet, though the way you'd been greeted on arriving, you told me—well, it was hardly promising.

'We're so glad you're joining us,' the director announced as you stepped through the blue street doors.'The previous girl ran away. I expect you'll be of immense value to our little team, though. Poor Sharon, she had a very tough time of it, but I'm sure you'll cope. We had to let her go. Never mind, never mind.'

Your flat was on the fifth floor. The senior social worker, Danny, had rooms on the same level as the children, but he was usually sleeping somewhere else for amorous reasons of his own. The inmates, mostly teenage boys, were from broken homes in estates across the Edgware Road. The aim of the institution was to help the younger children get some schooling, and the older find work and a place to rent.

'What'll you do when you grow up?' the director asked a boy called Justin one day.

'A bank,' said the lad, laughing into his face.

It was no joke. At that very moment, over the insistently lifting beat of a Bob Marley record, banging noises came up from the children's living quarters. The kids were obviously hurling things around the room. You had advised your maybe still boyfriend just to ignore them. But that was easier said than done. As the morning wore on, those crashes and rumblings continued unabated from the floor below.

'Best not over-react,' you said, and tried to illustrate how not to do so.

A little while later, and as if to prove your point, you decided to slip out a moment to your new bank in Westbourne Grove. Not wanting to be left alone with the kids, I volunteered to keep you company. Once beyond the Settlement's doors, we turned left down Warwick Crescent and walked briskly along beside the Regent's Canal in the direction of its black iron bridge. The grass in Rembrandt Gardens was all but shrivelled away, and had been kicked through on the traffic islands to the grey dust beneath. That summer, every day's weather exactly like the last, it had been easy to lose track of time, to assume that August would go on forever, that September could never come. Barely any clouds crossed the sky above to variegate the yellow grass or grey pavements with shadows. We crossed the iron bridge and went on past a French restaurant, the Warwick Castle pub, and one of your favourite antique shops. In its window hung a Persian carpet and, like make-believe homemakers, we paused a moment to admire it once more. When we got to Warwick Avenue's tree-lined dual carriageway, you led me round to the left and down towards the Tube.

'Be careful,' you were saying, as we passed by the ramshackle newsagent's stand, its shutters down—as if drained of the meanings which issued from it day after day, attaching themselves for a moment to those surroundings, a capital city on the cusp of earliest autumn.

'Careful of what?'

We were waiting at the zebra crossing.

'She's toying with you, you know.'

'Well, I don't know ... is she?'

'Just be careful you don't come running back after this little fling of yours asking me to pretend that nothing has happened,' you said. 'You might very well find I'm not there any more.'

Oh if only I'd taken you at your word. You should never have agreed to meet me in Brussels. Experimenting too, I must have thought that the rules had been changed for everyone, or, if not, that they should have been. But perhaps every generation believes it can get away with anything, as if the rules of previous ones somehow no longer applied. That summer it had really got far, far too hot, though Italy I knew would be hotter. So it was a relief to be out of the sun and inside the bank. Up at the heavy wooden counter, you found your blue passport in the shoulder bag and presented it to the cashier.

'I'd like to change ten pounds into Italian money, and to have forty pounds of travellers' cheques, please.'

The teller was a well-dressed, neatly made-up woman wearing a badge. Her name was Mrs. Joy Worthy. She had freckles across the bridge of her nose, and there was a mole on the side of her chin with a single fine hair sprouting from it.

She was handing you a rectangular booklet under the glass screen. Up above her on the wall the day's date was shown on a rotating display: Thursday 4 September 1975.

'Have you ever used travellers' cheques before?' she inquired.

You hadn't. Now she was asking you to sign them.

'You'll have to countersign them in the presence of the cashier when you change them, and don't forget to make a note of all the cheques you cash. If they're lost or stolen, you must telephone this number in London immediately.' She pointed at the slip of paper showing their numbers and a list of contact addresses.

Then you wrote a small cheque to 'Self'. You folded the Lire and traveller's cheques into one compartment of your purse. The five pounds for the next five days were squeezed into your jeans' back pocket.

There was a portable fan set up behind the bank tellers' counter. It made a faint whirring sound. Even so, the cashier could be heard complaining about the weather as we stepped out into the late summer light and unremitting heat.

Hurrying back across the iron-bridge, you were glancing over at that great white house, the children's home, which commanded its far corner of the Paddington Basin. The building containing the private welfare centre had begun the century as a hostel for music students—one of them Katherine Mansfield, you told me. This patch of London was also George Dixon's beat in *The Blue Lamp*. The night before that old black and white film had been on the TV, and we'd sat seeing parts of the world outside your window bisected by Flying Squad cars. Their alarm bells rang out as they chased a youthful, delinquent Dirk Bogarde with his handgun through pieces of an urban scene barely still surviving between new developments all around.

That day, half a dozen red and green barges were moored in the basin. Pot plants along the cabin roofs were sagging in the sunlight. White façades of grander terraces gleamed beyond the shimmering water and the curving wall to the bridge. The weeping willows on their tiny island trembled in the currents of warm air. Another barge was chugging steadily past it, slipping under the bridges on towards Camden Lock. I too was gazing around as we re-crossed the little iron bridge, looking out past the white house by the water, another fast train leaving from Paddington, on the elevated flyover a car heading eastward ... when suddenly a loud splash came echoing from that part of the Regent's Canal.

Clutching the shopping bag under your arm, you set off at a run towards Belle View House, your eyes lifted to the fourth floor windows. A coffee table and wooden chair could be seen being shouldered from the children's living quarters. The institutional sticks appeared to drift lazily down through the air, before splashing brightly into the glistening water below. Exasperated, and seemingly helpless in the face of it, you were hurrying past the moored barges as fast as you possibly could to put a stop to what was going on. For now your wayward charges were defenestrating their furniture, and you'd been left alone in charge.

You stepped in through the front door and began running up the five flights of stairs. More slowly, in two minds about whether to continue up to the flat or satisfy my curiosity, I was following close behind you. Alice might well have been right about me being your vicarious culture, but here was some more of my vicarious life. You had dropped your shoulder bag at the children's door, assumed what must have felt like an air of authority, and stepped directly into the communal living room.

There was Edwin confronting you, with his Elvis Presley haircut, a chair arm doubling as his customized guitar.

'You can do any*thing* ...' he crooned, his spindly legs and small hips waggling. It was a good imitation, showing parody for parody, farce as farce.

The chair arm had been torn from a piece of furniture that Justin was hurling through the window at that very moment. He was leaning out, looking down at it and giggling as the chair plummeted into the canal.

'Stop that!' you shouted.

'Piss off, girlie,' said Sylvester in a stage whisper, too close to your ear, and, as if it were addressed to me standing in the doorway, 'You know what I do to whitey cunts.'

Edwin, copying the older ones, had picked up a metal waste paper basket and was lobbing it after the armchair. Althea, an anorexic, and her friend, the spotty anaemic Tessa, were tearing lurid curtains from the windows, bringing the rails down with them.

'We could just set these on fire!' the girls sang and danced around the room. 'We could just set these on fire!'

'Get on with it then,' you were shouting at the lot of them, 'and chuck the telly in while you're at it.'

You were trying the paradoxical injunctions, knowing they would never chuck the TV out. Beyond the partly eaten crisps stolen from the storeroom, scattered across the floor, and then ground into the carpet, there it would remain; surrounded by wallpaper hanging in strips, half torn from the scribbled-on walls, bits of it charred or smeared, alone there, in a corner of the devastated room, there'd be the television, the sole remaining item of their furniture.

Then, just as unexpectedly, you turned on your heels and, with a look of anxious responsibility, strode back towards me and the door. Mustering all your composure, you grabbed your shoulder bag as you went by, hissing 'Upstairs!' into my ear.

'Piss off, girlie, like the rest of them!' Sylvester was leering.

You locked the flat's front door behind us, dashed to

the phone and called Roger, a fellow worker, at his home number. He was just going out.

'What do I do? They're throwing all the furniture into the canal.'

You listened for a moment.

'Should I try to stop them? ... Well then, what about calling the police? ... Can you come in, Roger? ... Sure, fine, good idea ... but what do I do now?'

'All right then, yes, see you tomorrow,' you were saying, slamming down the phone and gasping, 'Bastard.'

'So what did he say?'

'He said I should learn to cope on my own. He said it was character building. Then he had the nerve to admit he couldn't come and help because—you won't believe this— he has to be there for the opening of Captain Psycho's cabaret at the King's Head. The sod's their agent. And did I want to ask you if you'd like to make up a threesome before the show closes?'

Rolling my eyes towards the ceiling, I attempted what was meant to be an expression of pained and sympathetic disbelief.

Early next morning, after trying to kiss your forehead in the dark and missing, I slipped from the flat as quietly as possible, hurried down the flights of stairs and past the inmates' living quarters. Their door was standing ajar, the room empty of furniture except for the one large television set in its corner. On the floor below were the Belle Vue Trust offices, then the classrooms of its Adult Literacy Scheme. Down two more staircases, and it was simply a matter of slipping the catch on the heavy blue front doors to be out into Warwick Crescent's bright, deserted pavements. London was still sleeping, the Friday morning silence intensified by a distant car changing gear, accelerating away, and then nothing but the last of the birds' morning chorus. Underneath the Westway's flyover towards Royal Oak, the earth was a powdery grey.

I bought a ticket for Liverpool Street, descended to the empty platform and, sitting down on one of its benches, dropped the army surplus rucksack onto its grimy floor. Thick moss and grass were growing out of cracks in the opposite cutting's concreted walls. Alice would be arriving in Amsterdam the following day. While you were waking and readying yourself for the second twenty-four hours of your shift, my ferry would be steaming out past Harwich's piers, heading for the Hook of Holland.

Could I imagine living in the Netherlands? It was certainly the country whose landscapes were among my favourite haunts in galleries. What about stopping overnight in Rotterdam with its forests of masts and derricks, the ferries moored right on the doorsteps of houses? There was the Boymans Museum to revisit. But then there'd be the risk of missing my rendezvous. At last a faint movement in the lines began, a humming which signaled the arrival of a train. The silvery Underground carriages slowed to a halt. A purple line map appeared above an entrance opposite. The doors slid open before me with a thud.

CHAPTER 8

Reaching the Dutch capital late that Friday afternoon, I followed the signs for the Museumplein and Paulus Potter Straat. The Hotel Kok, where our seminar group had stayed three years before on an art-history study trip, was somewhere nearby. It was a reasonable place much frequented by American students doing Europe on five dollars a day, but would be no good when Alice arrived. It was organized like a youth hostel with the sexes in different dormitories.

Her boat train was due some time after one o'clock the following afternoon, and I spent much of the next twenty-four hours dreaming in various squares of cream-coloured gravel, squares edged with trees, parked cars, and, beyond, the street doors to small businesses, shop fronts, and bars—above them the windows of higgledy-piggledy apartment houses. Sitting down on a public bench, taking out one of my reading list paperbacks, opening the volume at the book-marked page, I would lose my place and drift off into memories of that first study trip we had made through the Low Countries.

Dr. Green had made no attempt to disguise the fact that he had his favourites, and he didn't get on well with the girls in the party, especially Isabel. There were outbreaks of gossip and backbiting as we travelled to Antwerp, Brussels, then Amsterdam, Haarlem, The Hague, Delft and Rotterdam. At Antwerp we stayed in the Seemanshuis and one evening, for a breath of air, I wandered off alone in the opposite direction from the town centre, Rubens' house, the churches and galleries, to the docks on the Scheldt, where the lights of coasters and fishing smacks rocked in their rigging. After a while I went into a bar. It was a very modest place with just a few wooden tables and chairs. Two men were playing with a red and yellow plastic cigarette dispenser. The thing would stick every time they tried to use it; the men's stubborn determination, the attention they were devoting to the thing, seemed only to humiliate them all the more. The cheap little object was like a Christmas present that breaks the first time you play with it—and however much you're told it's the thought that counts, something has been irreparably stolen from the thought.

That same night in a student bar our group played Dr. Green's guessing game: which famous reproductions did we each have pinned to our bedroom walls? Others were caught out with Breughel's *Icarus*, his *Tower of Babel*, Piero della Francesca's *Nativity*, Vermeer's *View of Delft* and such like, but all the paintings attributed to me were met with a definite shake of the head.

Then Dr. Green exclaimed: 'I bet he has his own daubs up on the walls!'

My blush at the acuteness of the remark made it clear our lecturer had guessed correctly.

'How pretentious of you!' Isabel said.

'Why so?'

'Because it's your favourite word ... and you're always using it about other people.'

'Which is rather pretentious in itself,' Dr. Green added for good measure.

Sitting alone in one of those tree-lined squares, book open on my lap, another memory from those three years before came back, a memory of Isabel curled on the deck of the ferry home to Hull. She was petite, with auburn hair cut just to shoulder length, parted in the middle, a tiny upturned nose, aquamarine eyes, and a vulnerable smile— surprisingly vulnerable considering her subsequent career as a child psychotherapist. The ship's steel decking was painted a dark emerald green; Isabel had become horridly seasick and her face turned a green much paler than that of the deck. Wearing a short grey coat, and pair of jeans, she was lying in a foetal position on the floor with a strong wind blowing and the white wake of the ferry widening behind us, seagulls scurrying above the lifting stern. It was the two shades of green brought her back. Isabel had matched her surroundings—as if they themselves had made her ill. Dr. Green stood fussing over her, wondering was she all right or should he call a steward?

I spent that restless night of high anticipation at the Hotel Kok, paid my bill the next morning and dawdled the time away exploring the Nieuwe Herrengracht's environs, the Plantage, and Waterlooplein—arriving only too early at Amsterdam's central railway station. In its buffet, a Borussia Dortmund fan wanted to discuss his favourite soccer teams in German. Escaping from that fix once our minimum of common language was exhausted, I waited impatiently by the timetable boards; then there was Alice stepping off her train, looking around, and now walking towards me.

'Great to see you,' I said, to acknowledge the fond feeling inside.

'Great to be here,' she replied, and kissed me Euro-style.

Outside, in clear sunlight, her firm features and usually animated mouth seemed drawn, her cheeks slightly puffy from lack of sleep. She put her travelling bag down and ran both hands through the thick hennaed hair, drawing it tight as she stretched, her neck curved back and eyes squeezed shut. She had freshly plucked her eyebrows.

'Something to eat?' I asked.

'Did you find a place to stay?' she came back, recomposing her features and granting me a smile. 'I'd very much like to wash off that journey.'

Emerging from Amsterdam's station, I had to admit that I hadn't. But we immediately noticed a sign for the Tourist Information kiosk. It was on a traffic island, with the belongings of youth on the move in heaps outside. At the kiosk we were sold a map and handed a list of places to stay, the cheaper ones ringed in biro. Most were very near, towards the city centre. Heading in that direction, beside a canal with hump-backed cobbled bridges, we found ourselves entering the sex-industry quarter.

'Hmm, pretty shabby,' she said.

We found the address of the first recommended hotel and stepped up into its entrance hall. A youngish-looking man wearing a lumberjack shirt was at work with a broom on the floor of a dining area. It was a cheerfully decorated place, making no allusions to the main commercial interests of the district.

'Beggars can't be choosers,' I muttered, turning to the man with the broom, hoping he understood English.

'Do you have a room for two?'

The man was glumly nodding his head.

'May we look at it?'

The room, in deep shadow, was on the third floor, at

a level with the upper part of a Dutch Calvinist church tower visible from its window; it seemed a glimpse of the street before the sex trade took over. The double bed was low. Alice sat down on a corner, testing its firmness, not liking to sleep on something too soft. She pronounced the bed comfortable enough. The room's one light bulb had no shade. It hung from the high cracked ceiling, pendulous on its twisted cord. A sink was set into the wall behind the door. But it would do till we found something better.

'Oh, by the way,' she said, after we'd both washed and gone down, 'what did you mean by "beggars can't be choosers".'

We were crossing the wide street called Rokin, a main thoroughfare lined with elaborately dressed windows of department stores.

'I didn't realize how expensive it was here. It's not that I'm short of money or anything. Just have to be careful ...'

'Puts a bit of a dampener on things,' is all she said.

After that Saturday spent going round the Rijksmuseum, the Van Gogh and Stedelijk Museums, then Rembrandt's House, we were making our way back from a Chinese meal, walking under trees alongside a narrow canal that led up towards the station. With nightfall, the streets round our hotel took on their especially business weekend character. And there it was, a thing I'd never seen before: as if the shops were all staying open very late, as if the women clad in scanty baby-doll nightwear were modeling unusually frilly bedroom suites in a furniture store window. Only it was they themselves, those girls sitting with strange patience on display, set faces bathed in a pinkish red light, who were the emporias' merchandise.

The dark pavements under the ground floor windows of those brothels, sex shops, strip and peep shows were crammed with jostling people: single boys, couples, gaggles of international executives. Here were men accompanied by girls who might have just encountered them. Outside the clip joints were the set frowns of bouncers and fixed grins of living invitations to step inside and see what was at that moment being revealed and up for grabs.

'Dope, coke, acid, horse, speed?' said a voice from a doorway. She shook her head definitively.

'No, man?' the voice called.

Flexing her knees up ahead, an Asian girl was making her play for passing trade. Perhaps she'd been selling too hard, for a man close by, instead of walking on, turned and started to abuse her. The girl herself hurled an insult at the man and spun contemptuously away.

'I missed a day last week,' Alice said. 'Do you think, to be on the safe side, we could use a contraceptive?'

There was a shop up ahead on the left. Racks of magazines in cellophane wrappings promised to reveal all you could conceivably do with a body of either sex, or both, so long as you paid, pulled off the wrappers, and cracked the spine. There were varieties of aids in red and black, leather, rubber, and nylon, electrical devices for satisfying desires, and pink inflatable models. The shop had a vast range of condoms. Some were bright-coloured, crinkly and crenellated. The cool summer night air and a faint scent of canal water greeted me as she took my arm outside the door.

What had the young man in a tie-dyed T-shirt said to the other in a black and chrome wheelchair? Provoked somehow, the man with no more than stumps of legs suddenly launched himself from his mobile seat. He was yelling and throwing punches at the groin of the one in the T-shirt. Astonished by this violent assault against such odds, the young man backed quickly away. He was fending off the other, who came up to his waist, and trying to appease, or at least to stop him. Yet at great speed, on hands and stumps, the infuriated disabled pursued the able, taunting and attacking him with murderous intent.

'Christ,' she said, 'do you think he's got a knife?'

We crossed the street and quickened our pace to pass by on the other side. There in that zone of splayed or interlocking legs, some failed deal, betrayal, or affront must have infuriated the still young, but badly disabled man.

Relieved to be back in our bare room, she drew the curtains for us. Even so, there was quite enough illumination from the street to make the light bulb on its twisted cord unnecessary. Over by the basin, preparing herself for bed, she took off her clothes, folding them neatly in the wardrobe to the left of the sink. As she did so, I was scanning across her suntanned back, the vertebrae at the nape of her neck, and pale stripe where her bikini strap went. I was sitting at the side of the bed, naked too, leaning over to place one condom in its shiny blue packet under a pillow. The quiet of the room was perpetually invaded by voices of traffickers and punters from the street below.

The Dutch headmaster and his wife, in bathing costumes, had scampered off towards the waves—running in a vigorous diagonal, glancing to each other as they approached the sea. They were a well-matched pair, both about six feet tall, equally athletic, fair hair ruffled by a stiff offshore breeze. We were standing in a defile between sword-blades of sand dune grass, fully clothed. I was stooping to untie my laces as Alice took off her sandals. We were both some inches shorter than the Dutch couple, and differently built—a skeletal long distance runner courting his bonny Scottish lassie. Nor did our hosts hesitate as the breakers whitened round their waists, but struck out energetically into deeper water.

Maarten Verhagen and his wife Nina would drive up to Bergen-aan-Zee most Sundays from May down through September. They were only too happy to enjoy their regular swimming party with the two young English people that Maarten had found hitching on the road outside Amsterdam. We had been standing on the grass verge of a dual carriageway leading inland to the north. Almost the first car to come up was Maarten's.

It was one of the headmaster's ways of honouring his father's memory. His dad had been a policeman in the Dutch capital all his working life. It was his practice to be a Good Samaritan for holidaymakers without funds or a place to sleep. Fortunately, Nina was as equally well disposed to strangers.

No sooner had he swung his light blue 2CV back onto the road than Maarten asked where we were heading.

'Forests and hills,' said Alice from the back. 'We thought it would be good to find a different Holland.'

At breakfast that same morning, the ordinary actions of pouring her a coffee or passing a slice of bread began to restore a familiarity. After making love neither of us so much as spoke a word, but fondly kissed and then fell asleep in each other's arms. Sitting down to eat at that table covered with a green polka-dot cloth, I was somehow not quite able to look her in the eye—noticing, instead, a small hole in the short sleeve of her white lace-trimmed blouse.

'Jesus, let's get out of here,' she'd said.

'Why? What's the matter?'

'Oh, don't be so coy. You know as well as I do it feels all wrong. Let's go out into the countryside somewhere, where things will be cheaper anyway.'

'What about Ann Frank's House and the Flea Market?'

'Another time.'

'Only place I know is Arnhem …'

'Fine,' she said, 'that's fine.'

'Perhaps we'll try to get to Arnhem,' she called from the back seat of Maarten's brand new 2CV.

'It is a good idea,' Maarten confirmed.

He looked about thirty, with straight hair parted in the centre and swept behind the ears; he spoke with a faint American accent.

'Please will you come to have lunch at our place?'

Alice leaned forward and prodded me in the side.

'Thank you, we'd love to,' I said.

When we arrived, Nina and two of their friends were drinking coffee in the tiny back garden of their maisonette. Whispering in English might have seemed rude, so we sat silently sipping from the cups offered us. Despite the luck of being taken up into the local society, I couldn't help feeling a pang at being separated from our intimate solitude. There were so few days in which things could go right. It was just after eleven o'clock when Jan and Lieke rose from their deckchairs and said goodbye in perfect English. Maarten then offered to show us the sights while his wife prepared a simple lunch. Nina—whose other language turned out to be French—was making a suggestion to her husband.

'Yes, good,' said Maarten. 'Our friend Jan is driving towards Arnhem tomorrow morning. We would like you to stay for dinner and spend the night here. This afternoon we will go swimming. If you will stay, I shall telephone Jan and ask him to come here tomorrow.'

'You're both so very kind,' Alice replied.

Maarten led us back through the open-plan living room, neat and sparse, with its Turkish rug and modernistic furniture. The 2CV stood parked in its bay beside a small grass patch with a few flowers growing outside.

'I will show you Volendam—and Edam where our famous cheese is made,' he said.

Maarten drove through the outskirts of Purmerend, the Verhagen's dormitory town. We were motoring along a straight, tree-lined road, tall narrow trunks rising high into the air. It was just like that famous Hobbema landscape. An enormous grassy bank rose up to the left.

'You would like to see the Ijselmeer?'

Maarten pulled onto the roadside and stopped the car. We all struggled up the steep green slope. At the summit, brilliant blue water stretched as far as you could see. The strong sunlight of that Sunday in early September glittered across tiny wavelets to the water's edge a few feet beneath us. There were thick-wool sheep sheltering in the shade of trees and enjoying the wind of that choppy expanse of lake, down by the waterline. In every direction, white sails fluttered and billowed. Spinnakers filled like maternity dresses. Cleats and halyards tinkled. Booms swung with the tillers' motions. Pennants of every colour flapped at mastheads. Yellow and orange lifejackets leaned over sides, or ducked and bobbed as the yachts changed direction, stretching onward and onward as if to infinity.

Maarten beamed with pride. The water and sails were completely hidden from the road—as if this man-made lake created to express self-esteem and love had been fearfully concealed from the everyday world of windmills, tilled land, grazing cows, and polder wrested from the sea ...

A cold wind was blowing at Volendam. We stepped out to look around, but contented ourselves with staring briefly across the turbulent waters. Maarten proposed trying some rollmops, so we divided one between us, then scurried back to his buffeted blue car.

Maarten was explaining how the land had been wrested from the sea, earth drained and made fertile. He described how the new republic used to protect itself against invasion in the seventeenth century by breaking the dykes, and restoring the ground once each threat passed. We were gazing out across the carefully tended, irrigated fields, the natural and the human seeming to collaborate so intimately, white sails gliding through the landscape—for the water they sailed on was concealed behind earthworks.

'What subjects do you teach?' Alice asked.

'In my school there are only five teachers and we all teach every subject.'

'That must be difficult.'

'No,' Maarten replied, 'the children are very young and

we are telling them the simplest things.'

'How old are the pupils?'

'They are from four to seven years,' he said. 'Would you like to see my school?'

'Yes, please, if it's possible,' she was saying.

'Of course it is possible, I am the headmaster.'

He drove quickly back between the flat fields of black and white cows and white sails. Maarten, being a headmaster, must be older than he looked, I thought. His car was once more approaching Purmerend.

'Our town is a new development,' he continued. 'It has been built because it is so difficult to find a place to live in Amsterdam. There are many young couples like ourselves and you see there are many children in our town, and they come, all of them, to my school.'

The car turned in through open gates and came to a halt on a small tarmac apron before the single storey brick building. Maarten unlocked the door and stepped inside. It was an infant school like any other, yet being his guests we couldn't but see it differently, presented through the calm, enthusiastic narration of our host.

'Do you have problems with discipline?'

'Oh no,' Maarten replied, 'and if there are some problems of behaviour we always ask the parents of our pupil to come and speak with us at the school.'

'Do you ever use corporal punishment?'

'No, never, in Holland, is it permitted. We have a rule never to touch the pupils. It is also best not to be alone with the pupil if you criticize them. I always leave the class door open.'

We followed the headmaster into one of his schoolrooms, its walls decorated with the children's paintings of simplified houses and trees, one with a big black sun in the sky. And this would be the mummy and daddy with tube-like bodies, thin stick arms and legs, the hands and feet like bunches of bananas, enormous heads and large, expressively misshapen features—one with each tooth careful picked out in a smile. Here again were the images of love and fear, as if from a COBRA exhibition; so the land flourished and the sea was kept at bay behind walls; these children were themselves the blossom of such needs.

But why did the Verhagens have no kids? Perhaps they were waiting till they could afford it, or maybe they just couldn't. Yet there seemed no such sadness between them. They were still young. There was plenty of time for them still too. It was not, of course, a thing to ask, so I let the thought slip from my mind.

In the dunes at Bergen-aan-Zee, we remained a moment still, watching Maarten and Nina's heads bobbing up and down in the sea. The shoreline stretched away in a flat arc before us. To the right of the defile where we stood, sand crested into hillocks topped with coarse pale grass. These sloped down shallowly almost to the distant sea's edge. A ramshackle booth was selling ice creams.

'Want one?' she asked, fishing in her purse for some coins.

Choices in one hand, footwear in the other, we set off into the streams and pools of the tide run and wide curving beach ahead. The waves came foaming over wrinkles in the harder sand, then the water would halt and pause, before, as though reluctantly, being drawn back into the undertow, leaving tiny burdens of sand, pebbles, or bladder wrack behind. Gentle sucking noises rose from our left and right feet in turn. Alice's white cotton trousers, rolled up below the knees, flapped against the goose pimples of her calves as she strolled along.

Perhaps it was the relaxation and calm of that moment's wind-refreshed peace. We had found such contentment and generosity by chance, and now life seemed to slope easefully away like the shoreline itself. While she walked, Alice's feet dug up tiny granules of the sand that stuck between her toes and on her bright red varnished nails. White frills of foam slid forward up the beach in intersecting flounces. Then don't ask me how but I let the baseball boots slip from my fingers. They dropped directly into the tide and began to fill with water. I bent down to snatch them from the sea before the socks stuffed inside were completely wet through and, as I did so, the remains of the ice cream toppled off the end of its cone, hitting the beach, and making what looked like the last traces of a sand castle washed away by waves.

'Oh you silly thing,' she said, as I blushed and bit into the cone.

The Rijksmuseum Kröller-Müller was separated from heath-land and pine forest by rows of specially planted trees. The Dutch bikes we had hired didn't have brakes on the handlebars. To stop or slow down you had to press backwards on the pedals. It wasn't easy to get used to the idea. Trying to squeeze the nonexistent brakes on the handlebars, there had been one or two unnerving moments in traffic through the suburbs of Arnhem as we rode out the afternoon before. Dropped off at a crossroads by Maarten and Nina's friend Jan, we got ourselves stranded with hardly any traffic somewhere near Nijmegen, and after a while decided to give up and take the bus for Arnhem. At the tourist office in the terminus, there was a poster advertising a modern art exhibition, so we decided on the spot to hire bikes as recommended and ride out to see for ourselves. First of all, though, we headed for the banks of the Rhine to take a look at the town's famous bridge-too-far.

As a plaque informed us, we had reached the site of the battle thirty-one years minus a few weeks after Montgomery's notorious error of judgment. In the shadow of the bridge that had replaced its fought-over span, bombed soon after the failed attack, we ate a picnic lunch of bread and sliced sausage meats from a nearby delicatessen, and studied the free tourist map.

There, on the riverbank, was the last time that Alice and I ever spoke of you. I know I was trying to keep you out of my mind, trying to concentrate upon the present so as not to risk spoiling it with the ghost of a comparison, a stab of guilt or remorse. But as she reiterated, and with again what appeared my best interests in mind, she really didn't believe you were the right person for me: too much the would-be manager, sentimental, materialistic ... as she more or less spelled out. Yet although I could see bits of your character and behaviour in lights such as these, her portrait didn't exactly coincide with that of the girl graduate caught up inside me forever.

'Oh, I don't know ...' I said.

'No, I think you do,' she replied.

The broad Rhine was flowing on past us, sunlight glinting across its waves, a laden barge coming up under the bridge. Moments such as these were what I had worked all those months at the National to experience.

'You're right,' I said. 'I'm sure you're right.'

She gave me an unconvinced, quizzical look, and I tried to smile it away. Doubtless, she'd meant it for my own good. As I say, she had woken up in New York; now she wanted me to wake up too. And of course it's what I was trying to do, but there beside the water's glitter, I must have dozed off for a moment. Next thing I knew, she was giving my arm a gentle shake, suggesting, as I opened my eyes, that time was getting on and, if we were going to go and see that art gallery, we ought to set off and find ourselves a place to stay.

So, back on our brakeless bikes through Arnhem's scarifying traffic, we headed towards the forests. Reaching the tiny village of Otterlo as darkness was falling, we found there were only a couple of private guesthouses recommended in the brochure, and freewheeled around its few streets to take a look. In the vestibule of what seemed the most homely, she suggested we stay for a couple of nights.

It was on a bright Tuesday morning, after the usual breakfast, when we set off into the Hoge Veluwe national park to find that art gallery. Gliding along avenues through forests of firs, she was following the signs along a road called the Houtkampweg. I was pursuing her flurried hair and broad back in the wind-ruffled pale yellow vest far lighter than her tan.

Suddenly we were approaching a deep glade within the trees. Expanses of plate-glass shone with reflections of the sky. White clouds were breezing across each segment formed by the grid of concrete beams. Inside, the rooms gave one onto another in a procession of plain white walls.

There were few other visitors moving round those spaces, figurative sculptures moving on armatures fixed to a rail above each invaluable item, before which they steadily paused.

The first piece we stopped at was called *Bride* (1893). I leaned forward and read that it was by Jan Thorn Prikker.

'Not exactly a household name,' I said.

'One to conjure with,' she came back.

Next to its art nouveau swirls there hung a greenish-yellow painting by Odilon Redon, *The Cyclops* (1898-1900), showing the head and shoulders of Polyphemus gazing lovingly and one wide-eyed into a glade where a naked Galatea lay sleeping.

'Creepy,' she muttered, and moved quickly on.

Beyond the numerous works by Belgian pointillists, whom in those days I didn't have time for, were three canvases by Juan Gris hanging in a row: *Glass and Bottles* of 1912 was clumsy in its handling, the paint a thickly applied impasto, its transitions stiff or blurred, the faint traces of lime green and pink failing to transform a dull bluish-grey tonality. Next to it was *Playing Cards and Siphon*, painted on panel in 1916. Landscape-format, the composition was formed as an oval with the area beyond that shape painted black, a black also appearing in the oval forming what looked like a set of intersecting shadows. There you could read most of *Le Journal* and pick out a cup, a glass, paper, the playing cards, a siphon and the table on which they rested. The intersecting parts of its grey oval, abutting crisply delineated representations and abstract shapes on the black rectangular support were no longer inventories of objects but a single whole composed of passages, outlines, and aspects. The third, *Siphon and Fruit Dish*, completed four years later, had a mellower and more wavering design, its moss green and turquoise patches contrasted with the overlapping areas of black and white.

'Lovely textures,' she said, in response to an appreciative humming sound, before moving on to admire the polished flanks of a torso by Brancusi.

'Isn't it sensuous?' she exclaimed.

Now she was moving on to the gallery's classic Mondrians—the paint of their matt white, red, blue, or yellow rectangles cracked in places and brushed with a dusty patina. She found them rather disappointing. We both preferred the earlier *Composition 10: Ocean and Pier* (1915) where the horizontal and vertical lines in black on a white ground appeared to shimmer like the waves at Bergen-aan-Zee.

'Practically Op art already,' she said.

Then there was a *Still Life with Cow's Skull* (1929) by another Dutch artist called Charley Toorop—the dark shadows and sharply delineated objects reminiscent of a Georgia O'Keefe. Turning to mention something about her Girl Friday job with Will, the photographer chap, I found her nowhere to be seen.

'What do you think of this?' asked her voice, disembodied and echoing in the silent spaces beyond a further white wall. Across the room and round a corner in shadow, a larger picture was displayed.

'*Nudes in the Forest* (1909-1910): by Léger ... never have guessed it was one of his.'

'Early work,' she whispered.

There were some whitish-grey tubes on the left, representing the trunks of trees, looking like lampposts after a car's ploughed into them. The red-brown striped spatulas would have to be hands. Various lumps and blocks appeared in the foreground, and one figure had arms raised high above his head, the hands together as if chopping wood. Other sections of body, looking like rusty spare parts for the Tin Man, were interspersed with muted green domes that must be forest foliage.

'Isn't it meant to be a study of volumes?' she said. 'I think he said the picture was "a battlefield of volumes"?'

'Didn't know you were a Léger fan.'

'Lots of things you don't know about me,' she said, murmuring out of reverence for the surroundings. 'Anyway, I'm not exactly what you'd call a fan.'

'Certainly a bit of a tussle … he's obviously been wrestling with it here.'

'Curiouser and curiouser,' she said, stepping up closer to study the pentimenti.

Next to it was *The Typographer* (1919) by Léger too, his name signed in printed capitals—bluish-grey ovoids, red shapes like containers, some bits of lettering, and a fragment of the typographer's hand.

'Have to say I prefer that oval Gris back there …'

'*Le jour de Léger est arrivée peut'être!*' she announced with an air of mysterious knowledge.

Out in the sculpture garden, mobiles were being propelled by trickling water. Maternal forms interlocked on humps of lawn. Couples were strolling among them, us leading and following each other into the sunshine. Blemishes of green light tinted wall surfaces; a fuller green of the trees outside impinged through glass. Here were flat squares of nature like a triptych whose panels coincide across the frame. Nearing the garden's entrance, we paused by the architect's drawings of the gallery itself. Only a few token trees appeared in his impression.

'To see it like that you would have to cut down all these trees,' she said.

'No, it's not at all faithful.'

After finishing off our picnic of rolls and salami this time, semi-reclined there among the Smiths and Caros, we had both settled down to some writing: Alice on a fan of postcards from the museum shop, me in a notebook, bought specially for that far-off September. After scribbling a few memoranda about the art works I had chanced to see, thanks to this bit of good fortune, I sat watching the motions of her hand and forearm, fingers delicately pushing and pulling the pen nib, then absently reading what was written. She was describing the coincidence of meeting a couple from Brooklyn Heights on the steps outside the Van Gogh Museum. They were leaving for the States the following day, so she'd barely enough time to catch up on their news. Then she put in a bit about how Rembrandt's house was rather empty of paintings to admire. Her handwriting was tiny, quite the opposite of yours, and she'd practically filled up the space left below the address. Soon she would have to turn it and write up the side. The card was to Isabel.

A crackle of automatic rifle fire reached the sculpture garden. The forest of Arnhem was a military training area, and the modern art museum had been built within a mock-battleground, encircled by gunnery ranges and tank terrain. We were relaxing in the heavily defended art area, surrounded by places in which it would be dangerous to stray. Soldiers with twigs in their hats and donned gas masks would be lumbering somewhere near with their heavy machine guns. Puffy white clouds were in convoy above them, taking their own route towards where, speckled with sunlight and peaceful, we were lying. Arm in arm, between the mobiles a few yards away, a teenage couple came strolling by.

'Couldn't possibly be English,' she said.

But her words seemed to echo far too loudly in the silence of that sculpture garden's calm. For their part, the young Dutch couple glanced over at the pair of us, but, evidently not that interested in hyperrealism, they immediately decided we weren't worth the trouble.

The grass around was speckled with coins of light printed out by the colander of foliage above. We too were covered in the spots of light, as if like Danae in her shower of gold. Through the leaves, across the brilliant sky, solitary clouds in strung-out procession were moving almost imperceptibly. Resting in the grass beside her, absentmindedly watching them, I imagined those clouds as thought balloons.

Not far away, behind coverts and bluffs on the shallow horizon, the far noises of battle simulation continued, excursions and alarums being played out in the distance: the white square defended against the red.

Alice let out a sigh, then closed her eyes and allowed her head to rest on the bank of grass, enjoying the sunlight on her neck and face.

'So what are we doing here?' she asked, pushing the short sleeves of her white blouse up to the shoulders.

Falling in love—is what I didn't say.

We spent that Wednesday hitchhiking and by evening had arrived at a place called 's-Hertogenbosch in North

Brabant, a long way from the tourist routes. It stood at a crossroads: one led back towards Amsterdam, the other in the direction of Brussels. We had talked through our plans in a roadside hotel lobby late that same morning. The barmaid was skimming layer after layer of watery foam from an overflowing beer glass. With each repeated gesture, she seemed to be bringing our promise-filled excursion to what felt like an unpredictably premature end.

The recommended hotel in the town was a place used by lorry drivers and commercial travellers. We ate a meal in the nominated café, where a discount could be obtained on the bill. Alice spent most of the time watching sparse traffic interrupt the blankness of the street outside.

'What will you do?' I asked.

'Have a few more days in Amsterdam,' she said. 'There's plenty of art still to see.'

We went to bed while it was still early, and attempted to make love slowly, as if piling on the agony of the separation to come; then, curling up together, I tried to go to sleep. Though our caresses on the night before parting might have seemed a vain attempt to re-join two people almost rehearsing their goodbyes, there was nothing to do but try. All that day she had said nothing about my imminent journey into Italy, the journey she would not be making, however much I might have wanted her with me in that other life. Lying awake with the scent of freshly washed hair and the faint note of her breathing, deciding, in so far as it would be up to me, that she would have to be my future, I found myself reliving the night before.

In the dark of the spacious double bedroom at Oterloo, behind drawn curtains, in each other's arms, we had formed two other areas of dark. Making love with the light off increased the sensation of touching, and though sensing still some intimately known dimensions, still I couldn't be sure about where each of us ended and began. Glimpses of her features, a shoulder blade or breast, an ear, or a stretch of neck would promise continuity. It was so hard to make out her facial expressions. Kissing with eyes open could seem such bad manners. But how would I meet her gaze and smile? Energetic, passionate, and yet a little too rushed: that's what our nights together had felt like to me. Overwhelming desire rearranged the features, our faces were so close to each other that her eyes moved into the bridge of the nose, they became so enlarged that the forehead shrank to the hairline. With our expressively misshapen features, confused images of love and fear, we were turning into those paintings by the pupils at Marten's school. Hanging upon each other's silence, moving as best we knew how: it made an undulating landscape with sudden and piercing surprises of perspective, vulnerable areas and delicate spots our hands could stray dangerously over. On her back the sunburnt skin still diaphanously peeled.

'Be careful,' she whispered. 'It's really tender.'

Then there was no wind at all. The fir-trees around that small guesthouse were absolutely still. We were those nudes in the forest.

Now she was moving away from me, stepping out of bed and walking quite naked into the bathroom. She turned on the taps. Her right leg arched slightly and foot on tiptoe, she was soaping herself with a flannel. Then she skipped back into bed, pulled up the covers, and that lovely young woman kissed me once again.

While I drifted off to sleep, my thoughts had gone

wandering back along the gallery walls. A one-eyed head was staring at a bride; bottles and siphons and playing cards were shattered in a broken heap on the floor; a pier was being demolished by high seas; tubular trees and naked foresters were shrinking in memory, dislocated nudes withdrawing into distance. Yet now the pictures were staring peacefully across the spaces of their corridors and recessed spaces, wholly unaware of each other. A full moon above the gallery cast its fair cool light onto the trees and clearings of Arnhem's silent, pitch-black forest and the sleeping village.

But now it was morning in our small hotel. We were sitting alone at a table with a thin white laundered cloth. On the wall above our heads was a carved crucifix. It would be a cloudy start to the day. The sun was fitfully filtering through lace curtains, enough to brighten the tablecloth with its patchy neutrality. On it were the now familiar objects of a Dutch breakfast: fresh crusty white bread, butter, a choice of jams, a small bowl of *haajeslag* as they're called, a sort of chocolate sprinkle, coffee pot, milk and sugar.

'When they write the biography,' she whispered, leaning over confidentially towards me, 'this will be called: *A Brief Affair.*'

I took another mouthful of bread and jam, hoping to let her painful words die their death between us.

'But it was nice while it lasted,' she added, winningly.

'Yes. No, I'll be in touch soon as I'm back. It's not that far from London.'

'You've got my Bristol address,' she said. 'Come over and

see me in the autumn.'

There was still some early mist outside, no more than the day would soon clear, and a faintly acrid smell from the nearby factories. We paid the bill and walked out across tramlines, up towards the corner where the roads diverged.

A brief affair: her joking phrase had seemed to seal off those days together. Approaching the point of separation, it was as if our few nights together in Amsterdam, Purmerend, Otterlo, and 's-Hertogenbosch had been framed and put behind glass, to be variously viewed by distant spectators passing before us in the gallery of lost-preserved time.

We soon reached the signposts. She glanced up towards the words. It was like a subtitled film when, only knowing a little of the language, your eyes flit between the moving lips and the white printed words which shimmer below them. But they weren't quite synced, and the lips didn't fit the phrases. The speakers' bodies were continually leaving them, even though appearing to be going on ahead. So the two of us gazed at each other, kissed once more, and—catching one another's eyes—began to turn away. I looked around and, with the sad relief of a tricky parting over, said yet again, 'Goodbye … goodbye.'

CHAPTER 9

When you emerged from the crowd at Brussels international railway station, with a red paisley handkerchief fitted behind your ears and tied under the fall of hair at your neck, my relief was strained with fear and anxiety. The scarf had been adjusted like a cowl around your face—a face in shadow. You were wearing your blue jeans with frayed white ends and the pale green flowery smock you'd made yourself; you were carrying a grey frame rucksack through the crowd that funnelled towards the barrier, and fanned out across the station foyer. Coming clear from among them, not noticing anyone standing beside the black wood kiosk, you took a few steps further, were beginning to turn around, when a sign of recognition flashed across your face.

'Let me help you with that bag,' I offered.

'No need—I've carried it this far,' you said. 'Have you found a hotel?'

Directed out into the nine o'clock dark of that September night, you turned and blankly gazed into my face. Then you strode towards the exit, leaving my hand behind.

'I've booked a place over on the far side of the square. No distance at all.'

Outside Brussels station, as we headed towards the hotel, traffic came pounding over the cobbles, cars veering past at the junctions. Beyond the railway lines, backs of dilapidated housing blocks loomed up out of the night, a rare lit window against the surrounding darkness.

'How was the ferry?' I asked.

'Rough. People being sick everywhere,' you said. 'I had the snack bar all to myself. We were late docking. There was just time to run for the last train to Brussels. It was actually moving when I got on. Count yourself lucky I'm here.'

'Have you eaten dinner?'

'In the restaurant car.'

The picture of a thick, white table cloth, a few scattered crumbs of fresh bread, an empty wine glass with a pale red stain, a wiped-clean plate and a railway waiter hovering to refill a coffee cup came over me like a pang of more than hunger.

'I haven't had a thing to eat since breakfast.'

But there was only further silence as we crossed the nighttime square. Raised railway lines were overarched by a mast-work of signals and gantries. Beneath that confusion ran tunnels with approaching car headlights that were picking us out, silhouetted in the glare interrupting urban darkness.

'Because I ran out of money … I'm glad you came. I wouldn't even have been able to pay the hotel bill.'

Leaving most of my holiday savings for you to change into traveller's cheques had seemed a convenient arrangement. Why risk carrying all that money around in Holland? Why not give you that assurance I would be here in Brussels?

'Alice not with you then?'

You must have been imagining your worst nightmare.

'No, most likely she's in Amsterdam …'

Dropped off by a travelling salesman near the centre of Brussels not long before midday, I had stumbled over temporary surfaces for pedestrians, along avenues congested by works in progress. They were building a new metro system. Past pleasant-smelling cafés, I headed by guesswork for the railway terminus in its enormous square. The room's window gave on to a vast empty space with the station, a large clock face on its tower, in one far corner.

So then, as we stood waiting in the dark, waiting for a gap in the traffic at another tunnel under its railway tracks, I was letting you know that the room had a shower, but, unfortunately, it didn't seem to work.

'Oh great,' you said, and it seemed better not to let you know why it didn't.

That morning, when I walked into its lobby with travel agents' posters for decoration, the hotel had seemed cheap enough. One of the images showed a man cheerfully chasing a blonde girl in a swimsuit through sand dunes, while the other was of a black waiter serving a cocktail to a richly dressed woman at a boulevard café.

Now the first thing to do was take a shower. The equipment stood in the same room as the bed. Water was carried from a fitting mounted on the wall, with flow and temperature controls, up a flexible tube and into the spray, attached by a bracket to the ceiling. I took off my clothes, stepped onto the plastic tray, and was trying to adjust the hot and cold tap, but couldn't seem to get it right. Suddenly, pressure forced the flexible tube off the shiny spray fitting above my head. A spout of lukewarm water gushed up from its free end. It splashed across the grimy white ceiling. It was raining all over my head and shoulders, drenching my hair in its downpour. It overflowed the shower tray, sluiced the plastic curtains, and sprayed onto the carpet that blossomed with a sodden, dark stain.

The double bed's soft-sprung mattress groaned. The hotel room had been emulsion-painted pale yellow many years before. Scales of pigment were flaking away at the angle of wall and ceiling, and there was a small heap of flakes on the worn brown linoleum in the corner near the door. After throwing a few clothes back on, I took a look at the shower attachment. Its plastic tube wouldn't stay fixed to the nozzle. The peeling emulsion told me to make something of that. The thin bit of damp grey carpet spoke wearily of all the other transients who had occupied the room. A frilly plastic lampshade, roses printed on its side, signally failed to cheer up the ceiling. With nightfall, it would try in vain to diffuse a weak, cold light. And it was too late now to look for another hotel.

By the railway station clock, the time was just twenty-three minutes past two. For some while now, across its intersections, the cars had seemed miraculously to be avoiding accidents, even though there appeared to be no markings on the roads. Vehicles continued nonetheless to wander around each other. The station's square was edged with small hotels with unlit neon adverts built on latticework above their roofs. The timetabled expresses would arrive and leave, and when a train roared outside the bedroom, the loose brass and enamel bed-head clattered against the radiator behind it. On the enormous clock face, large steel hands moved imperceptibly around.

All that afternoon I would raise my reading glasses as attention drifted from Gombrich's *Art and Illusion* to the long and short hands on the clock, then back to the closely argued text. Each detail in the day's altering light altered its aspects under my half-absorbed regard, and each was interfused with a spreading uncertainty as slowly but surely the horizon darkened and the clock became obscured.

Now it was nearly black outside. The drivers below had turned on their headlights. Through the gloom, I could no longer make out how long there was to wait. There seemed no need for me to wear a watch back then. Soon it would be time to go down and walk across the square once more to see what time it was. The shower nozzle leered from the wall. And what if you'd missed your connection?

But there was no need to worry. Here you were, and peering at the hotels round that Brussels' square, illuminated now with flickering neon. A sliver of moon shone a blur through the patches of drifting, darker-blue cloud. The frontage of our hotel grew more distinct, its name unlit, unreadable below the first floor windows. In silence, we entered the haven of the lobby's electric light, and presented ourselves at the varnished wood reception desk. A night porter gestured to the book where you were to sign your name. Behind the late-shift receptionist, a youngish woman was eating a mouth-watering cheese and lettuce sandwich.

'Passport,' he said, and reached out his hand.

You found the blue booklet in one of the small pockets of your rucksack and handed it over. He nodded us into the hotel. Then I led you up the two narrow flights of stairs to the room.

'Sorry it's no better. There's the shower. And every time a train goes by that brass bed-head rattles against the radiator.'

'Why don't we move it away from the wall then?'

You put down your backpack and examined the

offending object.

'Look, it's just resting against the bed,' you said. 'If you give me a hand we can shift it somewhere else.'

After the heavy brass object had been leant against the wall by the door, you pulled back the shower curtain and took a look at the broken attachment.

'No, this looks like it can't be fixed.'

Alone with you again, I felt your unfamiliarity like an accusation. Your sunburnt face, averted eyes, and the stillness of your lips were not as I had pictured them during those hours of waiting. It was as if we were tentatively reading each other, moving uneasily about the confines of that hotel room—as if it were the first night of an old-fashioned marriage, as if we'd never seen each other without clothes on, as if I didn't know how to kiss you. Oh but I needn't have fretted.

'All I want to do is sleep,' you murmured as you turned away.

PART TWO

CHAPTER 10

Where was I? Not curled up on a ferry's bunk bed, the hum and pitch of the ship a mechanical lullaby for the exhausted traveller, no, I was waking into sunshine. And not an Italian sun; the light was more diffused, from a much lower angle, it came streaming through a yellow-curtained window. No dream, this was me lying awake in broad daylight. The pleasant warm air of another clear morning in September, a late September day.

I must have slept like a stone, because it seemed no trace of any nightmares remained, no persecuting faces, no sleepless spells with thoughts going in circles. There'd been nothing but hours and hours of darkness. Hard to tell what time it was. Then slowly the room came into focus, the unfamiliar room with its oak chest of drawers, a rarely played guitar, and a decapitated teddy whose fur was cuddled threadbare. Placed on the shelf by the washbasin lay a human skull, a candle, and a Bible. So the room belonged to Kate. Then this was her bed with its summer quilt half slid off onto the floor. The alcove dormer in the roof-slope faced seaward. Your room was the one beside this one, but last night you had been put in a spare room on the floor below, next to your parents'. Now here I was, feeling wide awake in that attic back bedroom at the top of their house.

I could see the Isle of Wight from its window. A small desk had been pushed beneath the sill. Late morning, it must be, for the sun came flooding in through fully closed curtains. Placed behind the chair on the alcove's other side

145

there was a small bookcase containing faded and well-thumbed editions of Beatrix Potter, *Alice in Wonderland*, *Through the Looking Glass*, and *Complete Nonsense* by Edward Lear, J. M. Barrie's *Peter Pan* ... each prompting a stab of recollection. On the brightly lit desktop lay an empty inkbottle, a black crust of dried residue staining its label, and a girl's pencil case. Scratched in its wooden lid were love pledges of the lower sixth.

Better not get up just yet; they won't know what to say. I would need to make sure that you were already down. Your parents were light sleepers and would have breakfasted already. Kate was still away on holiday at that evangelical retreat she would annually visit in France.

Suddenly, like a rainstorm on the brickwork and gutters and windows of that detached house, water was gushing from a cistern. Then came the echo of somebody's footsteps on the landing. I pulled the sheets around me and closed my eyes: there was the taxidermist's fish in its box above the toilet at Isabel's flat, the broken attachment in a Brussels' hotel, and a magnolia wall from the guesthouse where we stayed on the outskirts of Otterlo; there she was walking from its bathroom with the sink taps left running, soaping her groin with a red flannel mitten, one leg arched slightly and foot on tiptoe.

Bottles and tubes crowded Kate's dressing table. In the bathroom mirror downstairs, you might be brushing the straight dark hair you were able to wash the night before, cut to the shoulders, parted above the left eye, your plucked eyebrows growing back and your cheeks without their colour, hair limp and tangled at its ends. You would decide to get it cut that day, and might be worrying about your looks, leaning close up to the glass and pinching the skin of your cheeks between two fingernails. Even then, her wide suntanned back kept returning, skin peeling in a curve between the shoulder blades. Perhaps she had already moved to Bristol. She wouldn't be expecting to hear from me for at least a week or two.

Out of bed, I drew the curtains, and sat down at Kate's desk in the alcove. Strong daylight broke over my head with the clear-cut chiaroscuro of sunshine falling across a sculpture. It made a well of light in the bedroom, a large bright square on the carpet. Through Kate's window I could see backyards of large red brick houses. They faced the fenced-off putting green, the tennis courts and a cricket field, and beyond them ran South Parade, the seafront promenade marked out by ornamental wrought-iron lampposts with flounces of lights suspended between them.

Across the road a concrete seawall gave on to a pebble beach subject to powerful long-shore drift. From time to time, a frigate or a passenger liner could be seen in the stretch of water visible from Kate's window. Now regattas of white sails fluttered and billowed as yachtsmen tacked or gybed, swinging their booms on the glistening water with the dazzling stripe of light. A spinnaker suddenly filled out like a pregnant woman's maternity dress. And there it was, the Ijselmeer: a gleaming silence locked in me forever.

Black against the channel's shining waters were posts in a row with waves lapping round them. They marked the remains of a submarine boom. There, too, the rotten wood stakes and planks protruded from a pebble beach, set there to prevent the long-shore drift that had destroyed them. The rose garden where people walked their dogs had clearly been constructed from what was once an emplacement; the rusted iron discs were gun traverses that could still be walked around as you strolled enjoying the garden's flowers.

Half way between the seashore and the Isle of Wight, one of the Spithead Forts lay silhouetted in the sunlight. 'Palmerston's Follies' was what the townspeople called them. He was the seaport's MP back then, and ordered the building of various fortifications during invasion scares around 1860. Perhaps the building of all those fortifications had dissuaded the French from attempting an invasion, or Napoleon III never in fact intended to launch his attack. Nevertheless, the local name your mother used for them did suggest a tradition of irony at the then Foreign Secretary's expense.

There were tourist trips organized to look around Palmerston's Follies. Though we once passed close on an Isle of Wight ferry, your family would never have dreamed of visiting them. Still those abandoned forts pretended to command the entrance to Solent Water and the Royal Dockyard. They were painted like a chequered flag in 1912 when the *Titanic* sailed past them to its doom, but were black now, stripped of their obsolete armoury. At night they would be glinting on the darkness, beaconed so as not to be hazardous, with the lights of Ryde in the distance. Running swell foamed against encrusted green slimed stonework, a lurid glow on the tireless spume.

CHAPTER 11

We had been treated with consideration on the ferry from Calais. Presenting passports on board, you were naturally obliged to explain why yours was a temporary document: without needing to go into any of the details beyond the bag-snatching in Rome, berths were provided, and a purser conducted us off the ship ahead of the queues and the crush at the dockside.

Back in London, we walked across the dusty dead ground beneath the Westway's fly-over at Royal Oak. Going up the stairs to your flat, you were relieved to find the children's quarters silent, the entrance to their living room closed. You had opened the door to that large, still under-furnished flat; two tower blocks, a cream and brown speckled church spire, and, further, a great gas cylinder appeared in the broad picture windows. The room had that silent inertness of a place just returned to, as if its few things were rebuking our presence, our having been absent. Your large black and white television stood in the angle by the window, a stereo rested on a low wooden table, its two vast speakers at the room's far corners, cushions and rugs neatly arranged on the floor. And there were my winter clothes, my books, paint boxes, sketchpads, art history notes—scattered about like the relics of an altogether different life.

The first thing you did was to telephone the doctor. He arrived soon after, and saw you in your bedroom. After just a few moments he reappeared clutching his bag; he glanced at me by the sink and stove, then hurried out of the door. I went to your bedroom: you were sitting on the eiderdown, a look of blank amazement on your face.

'So what happened?'

'I told him about the chill on my kidneys, and he was going to examine me. Then I mentioned Italy, in case of complications, and he just recoiled in horror.' You made the theatrical gesture with raised palms, wide eyes, and a twisted mouth. 'He said he couldn't touch me. As if I'd get him struck off or something.'

It was then you decided we should go to your parents' house in Portsmouth.

Your father met us off the London train. Once arrived, we were put into the different rooms and went straight to bed.

Feeling a little better now, despite the chill on your kidneys, you had started to report a conversation that morning with your mother.

'Mum's been in touch with Mr. Draper. We're going round to see him at his offices this afternoon. There may well be some things he can do,' you were explaining. 'Do you want to call your mother?'

'No. No, I don't think so—as far as she's concerned, I'm still on holiday with you. No need to upset her unnecessarily. No need to upset her at all.'

'So that's it, is it?' you came back. 'Whatever you do, don't mention any of this to your mother!'

'I don't think she'd be able to cope. Better keep it between us.'

'Right then,' you said. 'Get that jacket. We've got a bit of shopping to do.'

Your mother had also arranged an appointment with

a local doctor friend of hers. The fact that she didn't consider saving her daughter the public embarrassment by examining her herself only seemed to show how uneasy were your relations with your mother, or how what happened had only further troubled them; or perhaps it merely meant your mother wasn't qualified to ascertain whether any physical damage had been done.

When we reached the surgery, I stayed in the waiting area while you went through to a consulting room. Beside me sat a pregnant woman smiling with a mixture of awe and pity at a mum opposite her. The mother had a baby with a scalp rash, cradle cap, and there were two moaning twins at her ankles. Next to her was a grey-haired man with grey complexion, sunken eyes, and bony fingers intertwined upon his lap.

There were the usual heaps of women's magazines, day-old newspapers, and some brightly coloured plastic toys that the twins were ignoring. Public advice posters lined the walls: one suggested I have a full check-up if over thirty-five; another recommended that I try to avoid over-eating and to maintain a balanced diet; was I recently bereaved? Here there were some phone numbers I could ring. Wasn't it time I gave up smoking? As I strained to read a notice about cancer research without my glasses, a prolonged piercing shriek came through the thin partition between the waiting and consulting rooms. It was you. The others there looked up, startled. All of them sat as if bracing themselves for the next cry of pain. But only the sniffles of the twins disturbed the waiting room's silence.

Seven minutes later, you emerged with a nurse who smiled a kindly farewell and, glancing round the waiting room, said 'Mrs. Weekly'. The pregnant woman struggled to her feet and followed the nurse out of the holding area.

'What did he do? Why the scream?'

'You won't want to hear,' you said, now that we were safely outside. 'He was looking for damage …'

'Did he find any?'

'You want to know?' you asked me, then relented. 'We have to wait for the results … He had to insert a speculum. "This won't hurt," he said. They always do. "We're just going to take a little look inside and have a scrape around." It's cold when they first put the thing in. That's when I yelled. He said, "Now don't be silly." I really hate that.'

A stylist on Elgin Road gave your hair a trim without an appointment. Now a slight breeze ruffled the hair, cut to fall from its centre parting in two layers, thick and curving inward to the neck, then in a fringe down to the shoulders. We were walking between rows of redbrick terraces, narrower streets where the house-values declined. Identical door and window frames, foreshortened by perspective, succeeded each other, the one design repeated ad infinitum: but here with turquoise snowcem, there with Cotswold-stone faced walls; and now one had some coach lamps screwed into a featureless door surround. Here the old red brick was distempered pink. A sailing ship had been picked out in the front door's frosted glass. The house fronts were like thick make-up on anxiously aging faces.

We had got as far as the cemetery's few acres of white-veined marble, overhung by weeping branches of diverse species. Here was the gardener's house, outside it a standpipe and the buckets to help tend graves. Now we were glancing into windows of house-clearance businesses down the Albert Road: fender irons, sewing machines, electrical goods, unwanted presents, musical instruments, fog lamps for cars …

'She's offered to pay for a few days at a hotel in Dorchester if we'll go.'

'Who has? Your mother?'

'Who else? I've still got some holiday and mum thinks it would do me good to have time to recuperate. But that's not the reason. Actually, she's finding it difficult to have us both in the house. She wants rid of us. Over there we'll be safely out of harm's way.'

I was gazing abstractedly into one of the junk shop windows. It had an enormous heap of sand and wheelbarrow on display. So now they're reduced to selling the beach. About to make the remark out loud, I thought better of it, and turned instead to say:

'Maybe I should go.'

'Wouldn't make any difference. It's me that's the problem.'

Which sounded like an invitation not to keep my distance.

'How much does your mother know?'

'I wrote to mum when you'd gone on holiday with her,' you said, 'and I told her we were planning to meet up, then travel to Italy, but, you see, I didn't think we'd be staying together. When you left Paddington for the Harwich ferry, everything was over, I thought, and so that's what I told her. Then this morning when she asked me to tell her what had happened, I did, but she'd no idea what to do or say. She didn't even seem shocked, just numb. I'd hoped she might say something, anything, but she just couldn't. It's understandable, I suppose. But she's my mother, for God's sake. She probably thinks I'm tainted—more tainted than before. And I told her it was all right because I got

153

my period almost immediately. No need to worry on that score.'

'Did you tell her about the gun?'

'I did, yes, because of course she asked where were you all the time, and I told her you were there.'

'What about your father?'

'They've probably talked about it by now.'

'Do you think they'll say anything about it?'

'I don't know. Shouldn't think so. He never believes a thing she says, anyway. "Invention is the necessity of mother" and all that.'

On we went past the second-hand bike shops, antique businesses of the poorer sort, the junk dealers, sellers of soiled paperbacks, nearly-new clothes stores, a closed-down launderette, two off-licenses, a done-up stripped pine furniture business, a gun shop, three or four dingy cafés. Behind lay the crumbling commercial façade of a once prosperous seaside resort where Sherlock Holmes's author had set up in practice, a place still home to the exiled Sultan of Zanzibar and his wives.

'Town gets worse all the time,' you said, in a voice that didn't quite exclude a fondness for those streets that had certainly seen better days. 'Anyway, I said we would take the coach to Dorchester tomorrow, so we'd better go and book some tickets.'

Then you went into a chemist's for something to relieve your kidneys and upset stomach.

Mr. Draper had agreed to see us a little after two thirty. A late lunch finished, your mother drove us out to the appointment. At that time she was approaching sixty, but seemed much older to me, for she walked with a slight stoop, and her face was tightly wrinkled, especially round the lips; yet her eyes had a watery gleam when she smiled—and good bone structure meant that she'd retained the ghost of her youthful beauty.

You were sitting beside your mother, your small-featured face reflected in the driving mirror. We were being taken through the rings of urban growth, brick terraces with primary colours painted on gutters, doors and windows; the clear sky taut with vapour trails, brown leaves on the clearway's tree-lined flanks beginning to tumble; high-cambered, even curves led from the trunk road into an inland district of the city. Your mother's pale blue, slightly rusting Wolseley Hornet with its soft suspension rolled into corners as she swung the wheel.

The offices of Erwin, Sons & Draper were composed of two houses in a crescent of Edwardian terraces with rooms branching off from a central hallway, reached through an outer office. The entrance had an open door, a polished brass nameplate on the brickwork; an inner door, being opened by your mother, with a frosted glass window and the names of the solicitors again in gold lettering, let into the outer office with a desk and a bright-faced receptionist.

'Mr. Draper is expecting us,' your mother announced.

The receptionist stood up, left the room, returned and gave a fresh formal smile.

'This way, please.'

She was showing us into a spacious office with, for the solicitor, a leather-topped desk and chair behind it, for his clients, a number of lower, more comfortable armchairs in which to sink. As we followed her, your mother called to you from the door.

'I've some shopping to do, but will be back to drive you home, as soon as Mr. Draper's ready. I won't be long.'

Then she smiled at the solicitor and hovered at the doorway.

'Hello, Mr. Draper,' she added. 'I'm sure you'll do everything you possibly can.'

'Of course,' said the man. 'It must be a great relief to have your daughter back with you.'

'It is,' she said. 'You're both well, I hope? How are the children? Then I won't disturb you any longer.'

Your mother closed the door.

'Please do sit down. Please,' said Mr. Draper, gesturing with his hand towards the armchairs.

The solicitor was in his middle fifties, partner in a provincial firm with offices in many of the towns in Hampshire. His light hair was brushed firmly back from his temples, greying with distinction at the sides. Mr. Draper's face was large and round, with a small nose, clear smiling eyes, a mouth that when set between speaking suggested some discomfort, present or conditional. He sat slightly forward at his desk, which was tidily arranged, with a file ready beneath Mr. Draper's eyes. The desk included space for two photographs: one of his wife, a fashionable woman with something of a pout, exaggerated perhaps by age; the other of his son and daughter, Sarah smiling more than James in their double frame. Mr. Draper opened the top drawer of his desk, took out a sheet of paper and unscrewed the cap of his black fountain pen.

'So, how are you?' the family solicitor graciously began, addressing you directly.

You thanked him for his concern and assured him that you were feeling much better than you had some forty-eight hours before. Then you asked the solicitor how Sarah was doing with her Tort exams. Mr. Draper was confident that your school friend would pass this time.

'Based on what I understand from your mother,' Mr. Draper continued, getting down to business, 'I'd say you're both lucky to be alive.'

You gave a slight nod in recognition of this, which the solicitor took as his cue to continue.

'There are one or two inquiries and approaches I can make on your behalf,' he began, still addressing you alone. 'I shall be writing to Roy Jenkins at the Home Office today. He will be able to make inquiries at the Italian Embassy. You understand, I'm sure, that to do this I will need a clear picture of everything that occurred. I appreciate that this may be difficult and painful for you, and we can stop immediately should you feel at all distraught or in any way unable to continue.'

You were studying the pattern on your blouse, rolling and unrolling between your fingers the loose hem, worn outside an olive green cord skirt. You looked up and nodded at Mr. Draper with a serious expression.

'How did you come to be travelling like that, and in the middle of the night?' Mr. Draper began.

'We were camping in Rome: there's a campsite in the suburbs. It was early afternoon and we were somewhere near the Tiber, looking for a restaurant, somewhere not too expensive or crowded. We'd gone down a narrow, quiet street with high blank walls on either side ...'

'And a bar at the far end.'

Mr. Draper glanced up at me, and gave a faint smile; then, shifting his eyes back towards his family friend's daughter, invited you to continue.

157

'I was on the outside of the pavement and I remember hearing a scooter rev up, then looking back over my shoulder and seeing the Vespa with two boys on it moving very slowly at the far end of the street. I thought nothing of it. The next thing I knew, it had come up fast behind us and one of the boys was grabbing hold of my bag, which was held on a strap round my wrist. The strap snapped off when the scooter accelerated away.'

Mr. Draper was making notes.

'Could you tell me what there was of value in the purse?'

'I was taking care of almost all the money,' you explained, 'and carrying my passport too. We needed to change some cheques. All our traveller's cheques were in my name. I was carrying them with me. Richard's passport was in his pocket, and we also had a small amount of change in the tent.'

The high blank-walled street came back to my mind's eye, and again the commotion in the bar on the corner. We were chasing helplessly after the scooter.

'Come back!' you shouted. 'Come back!'

Then you dashed into the bar with its lime green tiled walls, calling out that you'd been robbed—in English. Neither of us knew the Italian word, but somebody understood and phoned the police.

A rifle lay between the seats of the car in which we were taken to the central police station. There, to our dismay, we discovered a long queue of tourists who had all been robbed that morning. After some time spent waiting in glum silence, you were able to give details of the stolen things to a police official. He completed the form, and gave us clearly to understand that there was, in fact, little likelihood of the property being discovered and returned. Sitting there waiting, I kept living over the moments leading up to the theft, as if trying to restore our earlier, fraught, though relatively secure condition. It had been too suddenly snatched away and couldn't be connected with the precarious and powerless state into which we had now been hurled.

Mr. Draper's office was illuminated by sunlight coming through a high window let into the wall opposite the door. The sash had been lifted a few inches to allow fresh air to circulate. Above the sound of your voice there came the songs of birds. Up over the roofline, a mass of swallows was gathering to migrate. Warm brown colours of the Roman buildings in the heat haze from one of its seven hills came back, and the tiredness on that long day's wander round the English Cemetery looking for the Pyramid of Cestius, then through Saint Peter's and under the Sistine Ceiling. While eating yet another ice cream, we came upon the Trevi Fountains. We sat on a stone beside the Colisseum, and smelt the dry grey dust of its excavated walls. Descending the Spanish Stairs from the twin towers of the Trinità dei Monti church, past the palm trees and Egyptian obelisk, we went on into that famous café just beyond the Keats-Shelley house at the corner of the Piazza d'Espagna. Later, after visiting the Villa Borgese and seeing a modern art gallery of Italian Impressionists, we stopped under a pergola to nurse sore feet and drink a coffee. That was the day before everything went so horribly wrong.

Now your account had reached the Villa Wolkonsky.

Mr. Draper, minutely attentive, continued to take down notes. You were saying that, of course, we barely slept the night after your bag had been snatched. The police had advised visiting the British Consulate in that elegant villa on Via XX Settembre, just by the Porta Pia. We arrived early that Friday morning, carrying all our belongings through the gate. Towards the curving stairs of an entrance we climbed—one that would become only too familiar as the day wore on. Despite all our efforts to be early, we nevertheless found ourselves at the back of a queue waiting for its doors to open in the gathering heat. Pushing inside at last, we entered the small public reception area crowded with people requesting permission to enter the British Isles.

'You were getting all hot and bothered, weren't you, because nobody seemed at all concerned about what had happened,' you said, glancing at me. 'Doubtless, for them, it was just another case of robbery. I imagine there's at least one every day. But you kept seething at the bureaucracy and officialdom. Which obviously didn't help at all. Yes, it was very trying. So, when, finally, it was our turn, the woman at the counter explained that I could have a document called a temporary passport—which would be valid for one journey only, direct to the United Kingdom, which had to be completed within three days. But her difficulty was, the official said, that the Consul couldn't issue any documents unless we could show we had means enough to make the journey home. Your first grant cheque will only arrive in October, and there were none of your savings left in England. So I was going to have to arrange for some money to be transferred from my bank in Paddington ...'

The Consular official suggested we go to a branch of Thomas Cook in the Via Veneto, no less, and showed us where to find it on a map. So then there was another tiring walk through a hot and dry late morning. But at last we arrived, two scruffy young people, in one of the city's most fashionable quarters. At the embarrassingly luxurious Thomas Cook's, the company would gladly arrange to have your money telexed, but needed your passport to do it. Without documentation they couldn't complete the papers to authorize the transfer. You explained that you couldn't have a passport until you received the money, but it made no difference. We would have to return to the Consulate and ask again to be issued with the temporary passport.

Back through the stifling heat we went. By now it was already after twelve-thirty and shops were closing for the long Italian lunch. At the Consulate, the same official repeated her statement that the document could not be issued to anyone without means to make the journey back to British soil.

'This was when you got really fractious and lost your temper with the consular people,' you were saying, to my embarrassment, 'but it wasn't their fault, and I had to quiet you down, didn't I, before asking the assistant again what more we could possibly do …'

The imagined sounds of moral disapproval and accusations of cowardice had been echoing around my head all day, but now there was this revelation reverberating in a stranger's ears. Yet everything you said was true. I had lost my temper with the wrong person. Whether because of that misdirected outburst or the nasty fix we were in, there at the Consulate you couldn't stop yourself from collapsing into tears. At this the desk clerk said that perhaps, in the circumstances, were she to speak to someone, it might be possible to make an exception. We were asked to wait while she had a word with her superior. The official's demeanour was entirely altered when she returned and beckoned, for the Consul himself had intervened on our behalf.

'So that's why we were hitchhiking,' I put in when you paused a moment, hoping to move the story along. This time you too glanced round before continuing.

The Consul had phoned Thomas Cook's, you continued, and been told that the company could not possibly consider bending its rules. Most unsatisfactory of them, but the young official explained that she could see their point. So the British Consul authorized, this once, release of the document without final signature, on the understanding that you returned immediately to the travel agents and arranged the telex. Then you would have to come straight back to the Consulate and have the passport validated.

At the Via Veneto once again: Thomas Cook's was closed for lunch. To kill the time, we took a look at the Carmelite Chapel made of bones, then sat on the rim of a fountain and pondered. Finally the cashier at Thomas Cook's told you that your bank in Paddington would not accept the temporary passport as proof of your identity. How did they know it was Miss M. J. Young there, and not someone using the document to defraud them? Signatures could not be matched, and they had no photograph of the client on file in London, nor would they accept answers to obscure personal questions that can sometimes be used when the banking arrangements are of considerable longstanding. You had moved what money you possessed only a few weeks before, when starting work at Belle Vue House.

'Soon as we get back I'm closing my account with that bank!' you hissed through gritted teeth.

Nothing remained but to go back to the Consulate. It was mid-afternoon, and still painfully hot. We had eaten nothing all day and were once more walking past the restaurants, pizzerias, and cafés with their various aromas. So what could the Consul suggest we do now? We were quite willing—as you said—to hitchhike back home. It was how we had reached Rome in the first place. But you were exhausted, dehydrated. You were anxious, and hungry. All you wanted was to be sent your money, and be allowed to take the first train for Paris. At the Consulate a third time, the officials were beginning to identify their professional status with our predicament. The Consul himself took up the matter by noting down details and telephoning your bank manager in England.

'And he told us, didn't he, that they'd not believed it was the British Consulate in Rome either, so he'd said, "Look me up in the telephone book, call me back, and if I answer perhaps you will believe it is the British Consul here." And they did too, didn't they ...'

'Please,' said Mr. Draper decisively, 'would you mind allowing Mary to tell me herself in her own words exactly what happened?'

My eyes lowered, half out of focus, to the mustard-brown carpet of Mr. Draper's floor.

'So the bank finally agreed to telex thirty pounds,' you recounted. Then, in Thomas Cook's, waiting for the telex to arrive, we talked it over and you decided you'd had enough of Rome. With only three days to get home anyway, we would go straight to the railway station and book ourselves onto the first express heading north. When your money had arrived we returned to the Consulate and finally had the temporary passport validated.

But a strike of railway men and stationmasters had been called on the whole network for forty-eight hours. There were notices everywhere saying as much. Neither of us could bear the thought of another night at the campsite. There was barely enough money to get back home, a hotel would be far too expensive, and, besides, we had no way of knowing whether the strike would be over in two days anyway. We'd had good luck hitchhiking in Italy, and decided we could make it in a night as far as the Swiss border. Then there would be trains for Paris.

A bus set us down near the autostrada and we walked into the gloom of a gathering dusk. It took almost an hour to be offered a first lift. An unending procession of headlights scrutinized us indifferently as we perched on the curved metal rim of a dusty crash barrier in near total darkness. Then it seemed our luck was holding. A red Alfa Sud stopped, its driver wound down his window, and when you shouted over the traffic roar, 'A Svizzera?' the man replied, 'Milano, ma sì ...' As was customary, we made a few attempts to talk. But the driver didn't understand. Through the night in total silence he drove us northward at top speed.

While you dozed off in the back, beside the driver I stared out at the road. The lightning started beyond signs for turnings to Siena. So finally, that September night, after uninterrupted months of sun, the rain returned. Bolts and flashes of lightning illuminated the entire deep blue sky, picking out pylons and power lines strung above surrounding mountain slopes. Rear lights of vehicles blurred across the screen as we passed. It was as if all the strains and stresses of our days in Italy had come to a head. Now they expressed themselves with all the power and force of that electric storm, its sheet and forked lightning, and the pelting rain that beat on the Alfa's windscreen as the car sped north.

The rain had been sheeting down for hours by the time the sports car pulled into a small service station, its asphalt forecourt badly pitted and now deeply puddled, glistening in the dark. After having his tank refilled, the driver went into the station's office and asked the mechanics playing cards in the back if there was anyone going further who might be willing to give his two passengers a lift. No one appeared to volunteer, but the Alfa drove off, leaving us there in the petrol station's office.

A short, dark-haired man with a moustache and a maroon tie came in some moments later. He spoke with the mechanics, and then made us understand, mainly by gestures, that he had to go away but would return. The man intended to come back shortly, yes, and take us on to Como. He asked did we have any money. Glancing at each other, we said we didn't—for safety.

'We felt so relieved,' you were saying. 'We thought we'd made it. Only there was something unnerving about the fact that he didn't pay at the toll. That was when we should have got out, at the toll. The man had already put his hand on my knee. I don't know why we didn't get out. And the attendant in the cabin seemed to know the driver too.'

Mr. Draper made a note of that.

'The driver couldn't speak any English,' you were adding. 'I'd been trying to talk to him in Spanish as he put our rucksacks into the boot of his white Ford Escort. So, coming round by the side of the car, I got into the front seat beside him, because it was my turn to talk, while you got in the back.'

'You were sitting in the back seat when the crime took place?' Mr. Draper had looked up from his desk and asked me directly.

'He was pointing a gun at my head.'

'Lucky to be alive,' the solicitor murmured, and jotted down another note on his sheet of paper.

CHAPTER 12

Visiting the family home was one exam your boyfriends had all been obliged to take. Both parents were themselves the children of *Aged Ps*, and consequently brought up under a code of conduct and behaviour a couple of decades more antiquated than that which the majority of their generation was required to learn. They had inflicted a similar fate upon their daughters.

A child of empire, your mother had spent her infancy in East Africa where her father was employed constructing a railway. She might occasionally regale a dinner table with her story of the restaurant where her parents had eaten, later closed by the authorities for cannibalism; she would sometimes refer to the other children she played with there as 'picaninnies'. For her education, however, she'd been sent to boarding school in England and was obliged to spend the holidays at a great aunt's home in Worcester, a house full of cats. Her toys were sent to Worcester too: when the wooden trunk reached her, the great aunt said she should have grown out of them, and they could be given to the poor children.

Your mother had lost her entire wardrobe of beautiful dresses in the Blitz, which, along with the story of the toys, was the explanation you always gave for why she was an obsessive collector of bric-a-brac, pottery, dated fashions, and indeed bargains of practically any kind. During the V1 and V2 raids she had worked as a nanny to the family of Joe Loss, the bandleader, and after the war had trained as a GP in London, where she met the de-mobbed man she would marry—who in those days bore a striking resemblance to the poet Eliot in early youth. Now a community doctor who worked part-time, she would spend her mornings doing post-natal clinics, adoptions, fostering and school health visits: weighing babies, checking scalps for infections, diagnosing ringworm and progressive deafness.

That evening, a meal of minced meat and potatoes and carrots passed without too many tricky silences. While we ate our platefuls, your parents exchanged what seemed like mysteriously barbed pleasantries about their respective days. Your dad was compiling an English Practice textbook for schools and had attended an editorial board meeting. Then he managed a satisfactory par round in the afternoon. Your mum had spent her regular morning with mothers and babies at the health clinic, then, while we were with Mr. Draper, fitted in a useful shopping expedition.

You mentioned between mouthfuls that we'd bought two tickets for Dorchester. The coach would be leaving at nine-fifteen the next morning.

'Let me take you to the station,' your father immediately offered. 'It will mean an early start, and we don't want you missing that coach.'

Your father then washed up while I dried. We began by agreeing about the linguistic corruption in saying 'pacifically' instead of 'specifically'.

'But you can hear it on the BBC,' he complained.

He seemed a little younger than your mother. He had grey hair, centre-parted, drawn back from a high, dignified forehead. There was some firmness to his slightly pursed mouth. His pale, deep-set blue eyes bulged a little, with an abstracted gaze. He had begun his career as a teacher of English in public schools. Later, he transferred to sixth-form literature and pedagogic method. Now he was a senior lecturer at the local teacher training college.

He possessed a fine eye for linguistic detail. An excellent reader of proof, he would annotate the books he studied with editorial queries and correct solecisms. He wrote to the publishers of dictionaries pointing out words they had unaccountably overlooked, improperly excluded, or wrongly defined. Raised as a Seventh Day Adventist, he retained a sense of the world's manifold corruption; it had come to express itself in points of usage and abusage. By this means he could hold himself aloof, maintain a sense of self-control and order, and try to keep the world he criticized at bay. Perhaps he could repay it thus for his mother's early insanity, the Arctic Convoy war he never mentioned, a pupil's suicide, the attrition of his marriage, or some barely perceptible and irremediable hurt done him long before.

Despite my family name, grammar and spelling have never been my forte. Still, those few years of practice had made me familiar with your father's preferred lines of conversation, and I joined in with the case of a teacher who considered the split infinitive a matter for eternal perdition, the examiner at university who deducted marks if students used contractions in their essays, and the trailing clauses that had got me into such hot water with tutors. Then he took up the crusade by deploring those who say 'disinterested' when they mean 'uninterested'. Here was a crucial distinction to preserve.

'Yet it's being eroded,' your father warned, and asked could I distinguish metonymy from synecdoche.

'I'm afraid I can't,' I had to admit.

So he explained that 'England' for a cricket team was a case of the former, while 'a bit of skirt' for a girl exemplified the latter. Then I volunteered the misuse of 'hopefully' to maintain the camaraderie of interests your father seemed almost to relish. He added that it was properly an adverb of manner and not an alternative form of 'I hope'. Was there any difference between 'judgement' with 'e' and 'judgment' without? Your father averred that the legal profession reserved the former for the pronouncements of judges, the latter for anyone's act of considered distinction making.

With only the cutlery and pans to do we shifted ground slightly and exemplified to his satisfaction a litotes and an understatement, the one being a negative of the contrary and the other any expression which states a case with restraint and for greater effect.

'El Greco was not a bad painter,' I proposed.

'God works in a mysterious way,' said Mr. Young, and added:

'How about an oxymoron?'

'Poor Rich', Alice seemed to whisper in a tone not quite of mockery.

'Can you have one made of two adjectives?'

'They're usually formed with an adjective and a noun,' your father explained, 'like Milton's notorious "darkness visible".'

My mistake, I reflected, as it dawned on me that 'Rich' in her witticism was primarily a proper name and only then the shadow of an adjective. Did we have our favourite zeugmas?

'She left in a hat and a hurry,' the washer-up offered.

'Making love and art,' replied the dryer.

Coffee was served beside the living room coal-effect gas fire. Your mother passed round a postcard that Kate had sent from somewhere in central France. A cousin had recently married, a baby expected late next spring. Then silence but for the sound of sips descended on the four of us.

'I'm feeling quite tired,' you said after a moment. 'I think I'll have a bath if the water's hot. It is? Oh good, and then it's off to bed for me.'

It would have certainly appeared discourteous to say much the same, to finesse an escape with you and leave the room together. Which is why I remained seated in that upright chair, wishing you 'Goodnight' and 'Sleep well' in a mistimed chorus with your parents. Your dad then rose to clear away the cups and saucers.

'As you may know,' your mother began almost as soon as he had left the room, 'Mary has told me about you and Alice Mac ... pherson? Is that her name? And I am glad we can have this little opportunity to exchange a few words, because I would like to be clear in my own mind at least what you expect is to happen between my daughter and yourself.'

The wall-clock's tick steadily interrupted a continuous low hissing from the soporific gas fire. Then there was a squeak from Mrs. Young's rocking chair.

'Alice McLeod is a friend of ours from when we were students. We both read the same subjects and had a holiday in Holland together looking at paintings ...'

Taken unawares by the directness of your mother's approach, it hadn't so much as crossed my mind that this might be an area of her concern. Evidently, it was not how she perceived the situation.

'That isn't quite what I understand from my daughter,'

she went on, as if inviting second thoughts. 'She wrote to me before you left for Italy, as I am sure you are aware.'

The hissing of the gas fire, and ticking of the clock, the squeaking of your mother's rocking chair continued. No reply came from me for so long that she finally felt obliged to begin again.

'My daughter gave me to understand that you had left her for this other girl, and that as far as you were concerned your "relationship" with Mary is now at an end. Is this the case?'

Once more no words came into my mind, and none came from my mouth.

'You see I need to know how I am to behave towards you both,' she was explaining. 'I would not like to have to act upon an assumed understanding between you that does not in fact exist. You do see that, don't you?'

I did. And I saw that breakfast table in the hotel at 's-Hertogenbosch. I heard myself promising to get in touch, intending to phone as soon as we were back from Italy; light falling across the white table cloth, over the butter, chocolate vermicelli, bread and jams, I heard her voice whispering the words: 'a brief affair'. And how could I never speak to her again just because of events that were none of her doing? She didn't even know what had happened. Write to her, I had to write to her. Suddenly there came a great longing to be with her again, to talk it through somehow, be understood and able to explain.

I was sitting quite motionless before your mother, her stilled facial expression now awaiting an answer. I was hearing the faint hisses, clicks and squeaks, trying to fend off her questions politely, unable to decide matters not yet understood, and trying to stop myself telling her straight out that it was none of her business; then standing up and escaping from the room. I was hoping for some inspiration, but no words came that would paper the cracks. It was as if my life had been sliced in two then roughly pasted back together. Only those who knew could unite the two parts across that jagged divide. There was only one person who could do that. What had happened had happened to you.

'No, it was only a holiday. Mary and I are still together, and you can assume we will be, I think, after term begins at the Institute in London.'

Her face lightened with an inward smile.

'Thank you, I really am so glad you have told me this. And my husband will be too, I'm sure. You know I have been very brave asking you, don't you? It certainly is a relief to hear.' Then, after a further moment's silence: 'Perhaps now you might let me run you a hot bath too?'

CHAPTER 13

Of those few days spent together in Dorchester, I can hardly remember a thing. Though we must have wandered out of town to look at Max Gate, must have peered into the reconstruction of Thomas Hardy's study in the County Museum, nothing of either trip remains. Like an ordinary break in a picturesque part of England, those days and nights out of harm's way have blurred into all the other such excursions and visits we were to make down through our years together. No, not quite nothing: perhaps unintentionally, it turned out your mother had booked us into a room for two with a little double bed. Waking in the small hours, it seems I'm lying there unable to get back to sleep, you not stirring, the sounds of wind and rain in the trees outside. If so, that will have been the first of many such nights. For years I suffered from the sound of rain falling in the dark. Starting awake, I would find there was nothing else for it but to lie in sleepless anguish, as if for no other reason at all, but suddenly remembering.

Your father drove us up the A3 to London at the end of that week and back to the flat in the Belle View House Settlement. The idea was that I would be allowed to stay there and sleep in the spare room until somewhere else could be found. Even this provoked a difficulty, because you had already agreed the spare room would be available for Roger—Captain Psycho's agent—while he was on his forty-eight hour shifts. So when you were off duty, you would let me sleep beside you in the double bed. That was how things continued through a chilly October, during which I disappeared for a couple of nights to Bristol. You knew about that, of course, and didn't outwardly object. After this, slowly but surely, there seemed less and less point in traipsing off each evening to Roger's spare room, and the idea that I was looking for somewhere, or planning to move out, gradually got forgotten.

All through the autumn, the days dwindling down from September, while the lectures of Michael Kitson and Anita Bruckner started at the Courtauld, I was keeping my proximity, you, Mary, living and working at the Home, your children no less alarmingly wayward. During those months in Warwick Crescent, where it turned out Robert Browning lived after his wife's death and his return with their son from Italy, I got to know Danny, the senior social worker and his series of girlfriends. Your co-worker Roger would tell us about his string of part-time clients. And we were soon only too familiar with the antics of Sylvester, Justin, Tessa, Althea—and Edwin forever combing back his Elvis quiff. Mr. Draper no doubt sent his letter to Roy Jenkins, probably during our staying in Dorchester, and, although we never heard from him about that again, behind the scenes the processes were coming to a head.

On a New Year visit to Port Isaac Bay, we rented one of the whitewashed cottages at Trelights. You had found the advert for a holiday let in *The Lady*. From the upstairs back windows I could see St Endellion church on its hill. When the wind was in the right direction we could hear its bell ringers practising. It was a freezing winter, and the dark evenings were spent playing game after game of bezique in front of a chimneybreast clad in stone with a brass fireguard. After a few days of exploring the environs, you seemed to soften and relent.

'You know, I never really intended to finish with you,' I made myself say into one of your thought-filled silences, your hand held high with the card you were threatening to play.

'You don't expect me to believe that, do you?'

Now you had slapped it onto the little table between us, and were holding the cards firmly against your pink cardigan.

'Well, I do, because it was me who kept saying we should stay together, wasn't it?'

Then you looked up from your well-concealed hand.

'Ah yes,' you said, 'I can see things haven't quite turned out the way you planned them.'

'You know I don't think I ever had a plan exactly—just making it up as I went along. I was sort of experimenting.'

At that, you played another card.

'Doubtless,' you said. 'So what do you imagine we should do?'

'Good question,' I agreed, and played one of mine.

We would take up the same topic the next day over lunch at the Heartland Head Hotel, its draughty dining room deserted, the walls lined with enormous framed jigsaws, difficult ones of facial features, dunes, or stretches of sea and sky.

Walking back along the winding road up towards St Endellion, we paused and leaned on an old field-gate. The dark winter trees were whipped back by fierce sea wind, wild grasses driven flat; it was exactly then that we found a way ahead. You were making up your mind to leave Belle Vue House at the end of the year's contract. You were planning to train as a hospital manager.

'We could try and find somewhere to live together … and a change of place might make a difference.'

'Are you telling me you want to mend your ways?' you asked with a faint smile at the appropriate, slightly antique-sounding phrase.

Yet by then my ways had been mended for me. So we strode on down to Port Quinn's hidden shore, found a smugglers' cove where the waves came pounding, a pebble beach with shards and wrack, soapstone and razor shells. There were a few shallow caves in the cliff face. Wandering in and out of them, picking our way among the tide pools, two young people yoked by violence together, it was here that the one future we could live found its course in us again.

Your summons to appear at the Court of Milan was waiting for you when we got back to Little Venice.

CHAPTER 14

It hadn't been easy to sleep on the overnight train from Paris. Bleary-eyed and stiff, with luggage for a few nights only, we stepped down to the platform and set off towards the ticket barrier. Then you stopped and looked up into an enormous, curved roof of smutted glass and steel. Ahead gleamed the vast advert for the *Corriere della sera*. On the fat iron pillars of Milan's railway station, I could make out its date of construction given according to the Fascist calendar: Anno IX. So what would that be? Counting from 1922 … but I hadn't had time to work it out before we pushed through the grey metal swing barrier, and crossed between the busy kiosks and timetable boards. Descending by way of a steep escalator, we were engulfed in the portentous marble of the central station's vast booking hall … built in 1931.

Roger, your co-worker, knew the name of a hotel, one which he happened to remember was within walking distance of the courts where your case was to be tried. It was on the Corso Lodi. Nevertheless, despite everything, the Belle Vue House director was reluctant to let you have the time off to go. We had spent a week of your annual leave together in Cornwall and there was no more due for months. Finally, after you flourished the documents from the Italian Embassy under his nose, the director relented and allowed you a few days' grace.

Nobody was forcing you to attend the trial. So why did you want to return?

'It's the proper thing to do,' you told me.

'But it'll be a torture,' I said. 'How can you do that to yourself?'

'I just have to.'

Coming from that vast edifice into a winter morning light, we bought a street map from one of the newsstands in the enormous square. There was a line of taxi drivers touting for custom under the shadows of various skyscrapers with huge neon adverts on their façades. Corso Lodi was somewhere down on our left-hand side, and quite a distance away along the Viale Umbria. Fearing the appeals of the taxi drivers and not understanding the tram or bus systems, I supposed there was nothing else for it.

'Wouldn't it be safer just to walk?'

'Safer than taking a tram in the wrong direction, like we did in Rome,' you said.

'We might find a restaurant and get some lunch on our way.'

So we set off briskly down the Viale Andrea Doria in chilly late January air. Walking close to the frontages, you were all but grazing the walls with your shoulder. The street was not crowded, but at intervals groups of men in business suits and leather overcoats or formally dressed women in thick brown furs would come striding towards us. Here were city people with marks of determination, masks slackened in a picture of settled dissatisfaction, or resignation, masks aggressively animated in unintelligible talk, or laughing out loud, their large teeth on show. A few yards further on, up above the people's heads, an enormous pair of spectacles, an optician's signboard, was suspended over a shop doorway. Underneath, a man stood still by the wall. Closer, it was clear that his eyes were wide open, but the pale blue irises didn't move at all, and a watery lightness transfigured the whites.

Around his neck he wore a neatly painted label on a chain. It said CIECO in red lettering on a gold enamel ground.

At Piazzale Loreto we had to turn right. Each time anyone came anywhere near us on the street you would convulsively tense. You couldn't but sense a threat in these people's very appearance, which was perhaps only the everyday suspiciousness of urban populations; and yet Piazzale Loreto seemed grimly reminiscent of the violent mood in films about the Spanish Civil War. A car pulled up some distance ahead and as its window was wound down, passersby stepped away and hurried on regardless. But, no, not all of them—for now one old lady had ventured towards it and was pointing out landmarks or directions.

On the far side of the Viale Abruzzi, plate-glass windows of what looked like a restaurant opened around one spacious corner. It had *Tavola Calda* in an elegant cursive script across the curtained panes.

'Let's try that one. It means "hot food", I think, not "cold buffet".'

'If you like.'

Seated amongst the tables of lunching businessmen, we had just started guessing what the menu had to offer when the door swung open and an old man came in. He was dressed in the style of the 40s or thereabouts with an outsized black corduroy jacket, white shirt and a soft, loosely knotted bow tie. Extremely thin hair was swept back from his forehead to make separate stripes across an otherwise shiny pate. He had a large waxed moustache—a modest parody of Nietzsche's. From behind the bar, where he was evidently welcome, the old man produced a jazz guitar with a raised bridge and f-holes in the sound box. Putting the short strap over his head, he supported the instrument high on his broad chest and paunch, a bit like Django Reinhardt, the guitar neck lifted above his left shoulder.

As he sauntered between the tables, this antique musician beautifully picked out and improvised tunes with casually struck combinations of arpeggios and strums. This was surely *Santa Lucia*. Pursing his lips and wrinkling his forehead expressively as he concentrated on the hands' techniques, he was playing variations on popular songs. Some of the diners clearly recognized snatches as he moved between them. '*Dimmi quando, quando, quando ...*' A couple were humming and crooning the phrases. They offered the guitarist a small paper note. '*Nel blu, dipinto di blu, felice di stare lassù ...*' Others there had pressed on the old man a handful of coins, which he deftly pocketed with barely a break in the recital.

Our soup arrived. It was made of pasta and beans, and piping hot. Tunes the musician played were inviting the diners to remember moments of the fleeting loves they shared. It must have been their gesturing hands and unintelligible Italian that set us at a distance from the workaday restaurant trade of shoppers and businessmen. You had your head down over the soup bowl, tipping the plate slightly towards yourself as you spooned up the liquid.

At a table not far away a scrawny fellow with bloodshot eyes was receiving a large white envelope from a sweating, overweight man. As the thin man muttered a phrase, the fatter one grew flushed and subservient. The thin man, his mouth set in an expression of aggressive intent, contemptuously snatched the package. He calculated its contents, flicking through the loose ends of notes, then turned it over to check none were folded.

'Did you see that?'

The Mafioso-like character was standing up and leaving the other to push his plate away and slump back in the chair. The waiter came and started saying something that sounded like '*carne*', but we almost seemed to disgust him by ordering a cappuccino and asking for the bill.

Paying and leaving the restaurant, we continued along the windy Viale Ascoli Piceno towards Piazzale Lodi. But what could have left such a restless feeling in the heart? What was it that seemed so uninviting in the city? It might have been the bare trees rising, their branches intertwined, along the wide paved-over central reservations. They divided the two carriageways of the avenue, its heavy traffic jostling for space between lines of parked cars on which the dust and grime had settled. More cars were parked around the narrow tree trunks at every angle, and in every piece of possible space. They looked completely abandoned there.

Here were the balconies with parapets, high-sided grey façades of apartments caked in smut to above head height. Traces of a foggy morning remained still on the air. The thick light made it seem like early evening, though it couldn't have been much later than two in the afternoon. Deep shadows gathered between cars under the trees; others edged out from the angles of pavement and apartment block frontages. Policemen armed with short-barreled automatic machine pistols were standing guard outside the banks. Bits of packaging and newspaper leaves came gusting over the crumbling road surfaces.

Posters for films currently showing were pasted up on fences and patches of wall. Most of them seemed to be for porno cinemas. Next to a bit of graffiti that read 'Titti ti amo' was an advert for *Ferita d'amore*. The blown-up stilled frame showed a half-dressed girl cut off above the knee. You saw that one and instantly turned your head away. Small black squares were sticking across the places where the girl's nipples would be, and these served to enhance the sense of something tormenting and forbidden: a fully clothed man with slicked-back hair was penetrating her, pushing her against a glass executive boardroom table. The girl was arching her back away from him, her neck curved even further, with a look on the uplifted profile that might have been agony or ecstasy. I glanced at it again, half-ashamed, as we went by, trying vainly to decipher the actress's inscrutable face.

Not far down on the right from the Piazzale we found the Hotel Lodi, its entrance set into a grimy apartment block façade. The lobby had the air of a shabby, poky-looking place, but Roger the part-time theatrical agent had assured you that its prices were affordable.

'*Una camera per due?*'

The woman on the desk, after taking the passports and having the register signed, led us upstairs to a dully painted but unexpectedly spacious and dust-free room. As soon as we were left alone, you said you'd better try and catch up on some of that lost sleep. Later we might try to find a pizza. While you were showering off the twenty-four hours of travelling and preparing yourself for a nap, I opened the yellow canvas gas-mask bag pressed into service for carrying books. It was French Army surplus—a native-speaker assistant at a local grammar school whom Alice was occasionally seeing at university left it in her room one evening, and never returned to retrieve it. Since she didn't want the poor-looking thing, she passed it on to me. It would serve as a book bag all through my Courtauld years.

Inside the satchel was an envelope containing a few sheets of typed, headed paper. The first of the documents was in Italian. It consisted of the official summons from *il Presidente del Tribunale di Milano*, with a black official stamp on it dated 28 Nov 1975. A second document explained what it said.

(translation)

WRIT OF SUMMONS

The Chief Judge of the Court of Milan, Italy -- 2nd sect. hereby orders all competent writ-servers to summon, charging all expenses on the Public Treasury, the person mentioned below to appear before the said Court at the hearing of the 28th day of January, 1976, at 9 a.m., to be examined in the criminal proceedings instituted against:

Cesare Moretti, under custody charged with assault (Art. 519, Penal Code) and private violence (Art. 610, Penal Code) Milan, 27/11/75

The Chief Judge: sgd.
The Court Clerk: sgd.
A true abstract. Milan 28/11/75

sgd. -- Court Clerk

Person to be summoned:

1) YOUNG, Mary Jane, born Lyme Regis on 8/1/54, residing at Belle Vue House, Paddington, London;

2) ENGLISH, Richard, born on 14/2/52, residing (illegible)

_____

A true translation. Rome, 18/12/75
The Translator
(Renzo Arzeni)

This was how we had found out your assailant was in custody. The *squadra volante* at Como must have arrested him after noting down wrongly the dates of birth, and, as the translator's parenthesis indicated, mangling my home address. And what exactly did 'Private violence' mean? It was a literal translation of the Italian document's *'violenza privata'*. The word in the dictionary was *'stupro'*: we were going to attend *'un processo per stupro'*. So would we have to be asked about our private lives?

Beyond the window, dusk was already falling on Corso Lodi. The sky was invisible, cut out by apartment blocks beyond the avenue's tree-lined central reserve. The leaf-less branches were heaving up and down in a strong wind. A woman, her head turned, leaned into the gusts, and then disappeared beyond the frame. A man stood waiting to cross the road. A car was pulling up, its window wound down, words exchanged; the doorways of shops seemed made for such encounters. Across the street those niches were deserted, but, further, a shop-girl had come out of the small electrical suppliers and, with the aid of a long pole, was lowering its grille for the night. A city was like this: glimpses of streets and bars, people getting off a tram, cars abandoned and vandalized. Some kids were playing five-a-side football beneath the trees, indifferent to the cold and wind; their pitch was dead earth, kicked to bone-hardness by innumerable passersby.

Attached to the translation sheet, a covering note had been stapled:

URGENT
Italian Embassy 14 Three Kings Yard,
London N.1.
London, 2nd January 1976.

218

Dear Madam,
    The Italian Ministry of Justice has asked this Embassy
to forward to you the enclosed Writ of Summons to appear
before the Court of Milan on the 28th January 1976
at 9 a.m. to be examined in the criminal proceedings
instituted against Cesare Moretti, who is at present under
custody charged with assault and violence.
    Should you decide to appear as witness in the penal
proceedings (appearance is not compulsory) you will
be paid: a) cost 2nd class return rail ticket; b) lire 1.400
(about one pound) for each day of the journey; c) lire 2.500
(about Lst. 1.70) for each day you are required to stay
there.
    Please acknowledge receipt informing if you intend to
appear before said Court.

Yours faithfully,

    (G.Titone)
    Assist. to Labour and Social Affairs Councillor

Mrs. Young, Mary Jane
Belle Vue House, Paddington,
London W2.

All along the walls of the Corso Lodi were innumerable
election posters, pasted across one another like papier
mâché, some with the hammer and sickle on them, many

in shreds, the promises of yesterday already waste paper. At this distance, overlapping and interrupting each other's messages, they looked like a street-art collage. Over the top of them, and at eye level everywhere else, many more informal slogans had been daubed and sprayed. There was a mash up of what must be political parties: PCI, PSI, PR, DC, MSI, CGIL, CISL and UIL. The word 'LOTTA' was used all over the place. *'Boia chi molla'* said one. Round about it somebody had painted a row of those little backward-facing swastikas. There were other slogans, both printed and painted, that seemed to be attacking the terrorist groups, the Brigate rosse—the ones who were to kidnap and murder Aldo Moro just a couple of years later.

But now Corso Lodi was dark and still. You were lying fast asleep. Perhaps we would venture out towards the centre when you woke. I glanced down at the papers on my lap to check again the expenses that we could claim after the trial. 'Mrs. Young, Mary Jane' … and it suddenly struck me that the girl who lay not far away, evenly breathing now in the low double bed had been addressed by the Italian Government as if she were, in fact, a married woman.

The *Tribunale di Milano*, unlike the central railway station, was built in the style of 1930s futurist modernism: a blank pale grey stone frontage cut into with tall, narrow slots of windows. We walked the few hundreds of yards back along Corso Lodi past the Porta Romana to where it intersected with the Viale Piave and there it was, on the opposite side of the square, the *Palazzo della Giustizia* with the *Tribunale* inside. It was approached by a high and steep flight of steps. Our eyes were obliged to lift skywards as we climbed towards its bleakly imposing façade.

Inside the entrance was a small, green-painted wooden cubicle. After glancing at the summons documents pushed under its glass screen, the custodian explained indifferently, waving his hands, where we were to go. His words emerged too rapidly to catch, and nor did I know how to ask him to say them again—but this time more slowly, please. The custodian's casual manner didn't appear at all encouraging. We were meant to be somewhere to the left and on a higher floor; that was what his hands had seemed to say. Stairs led to a balcony around the entrance atrium with a thick marble parapet. The vast interior height of the room was emphasized by occasional appearances of men at a distance in dark suits.

An official-looking person emerged from an office.

'*Dov'è questo … processo, per favore?*'

The man shook his head firmly, meaning either that he couldn't make out the words in my accent, wouldn't help us anyway, or that he didn't know. A number of people shrugged similarly before someone raised a finger towards the ceiling.

'*Terzo piano!*'

After emerging from the lift, we had only stood there a moment, exchanging guesses, looking confusedly around as if for inspiration, when a man in a black uniform came up and spoke.

'You English?' he asked. 'What you want?'

The man took one glance at the documents and led us down a corridor, past closed doors and towards a blank yellow marble wall. Here the passageway branched off to left and right, widening into an anteroom. It was merely a larger corridor. A small crowd of men and women were gathering there. The man, who must have been an usher, disappeared into an inner room through a polished wooden door.

'Hope he's telling them we've arrived.'

Placing ourselves by the door, against the wall, we vainly tried to become inconspicuous. There was a commotion beginning at the corner where the corridor widened. Two carabinieri in parade uniforms were escorting a prisoner to trial.

You needed just one look to recognize the man from four months before. He was not wearing handcuffs, but heavy chains with links that hung down from his wrists. He'd grown taller and larger in memory. Coming from his prison cell, between the two guards, badly shaven, Cesare Moretti appeared shrunken, pale, deprived of any dignity.

From the little crowd outside the court, there came a small, poorly dressed woman, walking with a limp towards the defendant being led into the courtroom. She was shouting something at him; the man was interrupting her in that same brittle voice. One of the guards detached himself from the advancing group and attempted to hold her at bay.

Then this must be his wife.

The accused had a wife who was lame. You glanced around at me in a rapid acknowledgement of the fact. Then I remembered the World Cup football. This person might even be some boy's father, you could picture him kicking the ball to a child on waste ground between apartment blocks by railway lines—like those down which our train had rolled through the outskirts of Milan. The man's imaginary son was wearing an Inter shirt and trying to kick the ball, but it slithered off his toe at a crazy angle.

All through that autumn, the days shortening from September, while I was starting at the Courtauld, you were working at the Home, Alice throwing herself into teaching practice, all through that autumn, Cesare Moretti had been waiting in custody for this trial.

No sooner had he caught sight of the crowd around the door to the court, than the accused man stopped in his tracks. He had certainly recognized us. There was no doubt about it; there was clear surprise on his face. He suddenly swung round and spoke to someone else standing by him—his lawyer perhaps. They hadn't expected to have to deal with prosecution witnesses. The advocate was murmuring something to one of the guards, the carabinieri with their silver bomb cap badges. Now all four of them were turning round and disappearing in the direction from which they had come. His wife had been trying to speak with her husband—whose presence plainly upset her. She continued to cry and yell at him. He was telling her to shut up, and had asked the guards to remove him. Then the accused man's relative found herself alone in that milling crowd once more.

'Do you think he told her he was innocent?' you whispered.

'And his lawyer, for that matter.'

'Because he didn't expect to see us?'

'Maybe it's so we don't see him,' you wondered, and then, to yourself—

'It was though. It *is*.'

The accused man's wife had limped back to where the journalists and advocates stood talking. The sight of

her husband had badly unsettled her. She was accosting
anyone who'd stay and listen. It must have been her view
of the case she was stating, moving from one to another
as they listened or rebuffed her. She needed to wear non-
matching shoes with different thickness of sole. One of
them retained the caliper. She was dressed in an outfit of
blue, grey and black, like mourning, clothes that made her
seem older than perhaps she was. Her hair was a mousy
colour, plenty of salt and pepper in it, and perm'd, perhaps
for the occasion, into stiff close waves. The woman might
even have been Cesare Moretti's mother. For a moment she
reminded me of Gran back at the National.

Her dark eyes were fixed upon us, and now, to your
evident alarm, she was crossing the marble corridor. We
were standing a little apart, against the yellow wall, beside
the courtroom door. The woman stepped up extremely
close to you, cornering you against the doorframe's edge.
A sequence of rapid-flowing words poured from her
mouth, directed at your presence there. Though we didn't
understand what she was saying, it wasn't at all hard to
catch her drift.

'Stop it!' I tried to shout. 'Stop it! Get away!'

But the woman would not be stopped. You were shaking
with tears, your head lowered to withstand the shrill tirade.
There was swearing and insults—*Dio*, *puttana*, *marito*,
and, as I pushed myself between you and the woman, the
words *schifosa*, *dolore*, and *perché*? *perché*? There was some
incomprehensible wailing, a lament against fortune in the
form of two unwanted foreign witnesses. Would she never
stop?

Jostled, and receiving no answer to her impassioned
questions, the accused man's wife suddenly turned and

hobbled away. Someone behind her must have shouted that she should leave those two alone. Had the presence of these witnesses borne in upon her the possibility that her husband might not have been telling the truth? Who was guilty? Had that girl trapped her man, that girl, the whore, trapped him into whatever really happened?

Now, still staring towards you, she was haranguing her listeners, begging patience of the men and women by the courtroom entrance. You were still wiping your eyes, trying to recompose yourself, when the usher appeared from the courtroom and guided you towards its heavy wooden door. I began to follow, but the official's hand-gesture plainly indicated that I was to stay outside.

You had been in the courtroom now for really quite some time. The accused man's wife was still a mere yard or two away, restlessly talking to whoever would pay her any attention—a strained, distraught voice piteously rising and falling. The answers the men were giving seemed to betray a perceptible irritation. Were they finding it burdensome to support the woman in her view of the case, not given time to express an independent opinion? Were they contradicting what she was saying? Studying the movements of their faces and hands, I found it impossible to tell. Who were they discussing now? The men had raised their eyes from the woman's upturned face and were looking across towards me standing still by the door. At the mere thought of what they might or might not be saying, I found myself starting to redden. Then one of the men walked casually over.

'*Lei è il marito della ragazza qui dentro?*'

Not understanding a word he said, I shrugged my

shoulders and showed him the palms of my hands.

'*Io non comprendo.*'

'You are the—married with the—girl there inside?'

The man hadn't asked it aggressively at all. No, rather he was asking me an all-too-pertinent question about what relation there might be between us. But I would hardly have known how to explain in English, so shook my head in a vain attempt to deflect the man's curiosity.

'*Un amico.*'

The man appeared surprised.

'*Ah, il fidanzato?*'

I made no reply.

'Fiancé?' he asked, pronouncing the word accurately in French.

I hesitated, racking my brains for what else I could say, then nodded.

'*Ah sì, il fidanzato della ragazza,*' the man said, and seemed satisfied.

Had you ever dreamed of such a thing? Five years before, not long after we started sleeping together, you had missed a cycle.

'What if I'm pregnant?' you asked me below the blue Alhambra.

'Of course if you are, we can always get married.'

And we had continued on into the Italia café, for a plate of their homemade minestrone, you explaining how soon you could be sure.

Not that it made me your fiancé, of course, but what else could be said that wouldn't require fluent Italian and far more perspective, far more perspective altogether? Now the journalist or advocate had turned and was heading towards the small conclave of his colleagues, attended by the wife of the accused.

'*Il fidanzato della ragazza,*' he repeated.

There were nods and smiles of comprehension, even a few sympathetic glances in my direction, now the man sounded as though he were arguing with the distraught woman. Perhaps he was telling her that she should think what it must be like for him, that young English boy over there, to have a wife-to-be violated by a stranger. The woman grew mournfully agitated at what the man appeared to have said. It must have been some contrary viewpoint he was putting to the woman. My convenient lie had clearly contributed to her distress. A helpless anger suddenly overwhelmed me—still standing there, eyes half-focused on a patch of the yellow marble wall. Then the courtroom door opened and there you reappeared with the usher following closely behind you.

Hardly had I managed to exchange glances with my '*fidanzata*' than the court official was gesturing towards the room out of which you had emerged: '*Di qua.*'

I entered a large high-ceilinged room, panelled in reddish-brown wood. To the left was a group of judges seated in a row behind a raised dais and bench. Before this judicial panel, a lower stage stretched into the floor. On it, two wooden chairs were placed. There were rows of benches for the public, down on the lower level. The accused man sat forward on his seat in the front row, a guard on one side and his lawyer on the other. I was invited towards one of the isolated chairs before the bench.

Above the tribunal of judges, at present in conversation with a woman leaning forward at the bench, a large mural dominated the room. It must have been one of those commissions the fascist authorities went in for to give the impression they were creating a new renaissance in Italian culture. They were to make Mussolini into the semblance of a *condottiero* art patron—borrowing some of the caché that had accrued to the Mexican muralists and the Depression's WPA projects into the bargain. It was painted mainly in reddish browns, far too like that reddish clay earth, and managing to appear both shrill and muddy. The subject of the painting was Cain and Abel, its composition clearly indebted to Goya's picture of the two men fighting with cudgels; here the semi-nude figures with exaggerated muscles were struggling in a murky sunset. The mural had been painted in an extremely free hand. The outlines of the combatants, though drawn with mannerist distortions, were blurring into each other and into the background, an indistinct rocky landscape where the two dusty bodies grappled on forever.

The woman descended from the bench and occupied the vacant chair. She couldn't have been much older than twenty-five, but seemed so, in professional woman's jacket and skirt with a white silk blouse. Her freshly washed hair was drawn tightly back behind her head, and held in place with a discreet navy blue ribbon tied into a bow. She had a thin transparent plastic envelope on her lap. The judge in the middle uttered something to the woman. So she must be the court's English interpreter.

'Are you English, Richard?'

'Yes.'

'Were you born on 13 March 1952?'

'No,' I said, not thinking that it mattered much. 'It was the 18th of February, 1953.'

The woman seemed slightly flustered by these trivial differences. She was relaying them without question to the panel of judges.

'Were you with Miss Young, Mary Jane, on Friday the 19th of September 1975?'

'Yes, I was.'

'And did you witness what happened early on the morning of the day following?'

'Yes, I did.'

'Where did the … what happened this night … occur?'

'In a car.'

Again the woman appeared uncomfortable, with a slight flush about her features. She was lowering her eyes to the documents placed neatly on her lap.

'Will you please tell this tribunal what car it was?'

'Ford Escort—dirty beige.'

Then some more unintelligible words passed between the translator and the panel of judges.

'Where were you in the car while this happens?'

Now the translator was blushing as she asked the question.

'Lying on the back seat.'

'Please tells us all you saw.'

'It was raining, and he had a small gun, a black automatic pistol, and he was holding it in his right hand, pointing the muzzle over the driving seat towards me. He'd climbed across onto the passenger seat, and that's where he did it—while I was lying in the back—and when I moved he waved the gun and shouted at me not to …'

The translator was taking notes, she didn't look up while I spoke, or so much as glance at me when turning towards the judicial bench and reproducing in Italian, I supposed, exactly what had been said. The young woman was having difficulties, and kept stopping as if in search of a word, or ruffled for some other reason, then would glance down at her papers, cough and start again. When she finished, the president requested her to ask another question.

'Can you see the man who menaced you and committed that crime here in this room?'

He was sitting there: his roughly-shaven oblong face, hair in thick strands swept back from the hairline, his small mouth turned up at the edges, the dimple in his chin, a fixed, mask-like smile on his narrow lips, a smile without a history.

'Yes. Yes, I can.'

The accused man's lawyer stood up and spoke to the president of the court. The president, in turn, said a phrase to the young translator.

'Did you … from this man … receive at all any payment?'

We're standing in a doorway. It's the mechanics' office on that petrol station's puddle-covered forecourt. The man wants to know if we have any money to pay for the lift to Como. Perhaps he means to rob us. For safety, *for safety* one of us has said that we don't. It'll be needed for the train tickets to Paris and the Channel ferry anyway. Then come the words exchanged at gunpoint in a car parked on the hard shoulder, pitch dark outside, windscreen wiper blades beating back and forth, sluicing the rain off its flooded glass.

'*Amore, Amore!*'

'*A Como, per favore!*' you urge.

'*Amore prima, amore!*' He is waving his gun. '*Como dopo …*'

'He's going to kill us,' I hear you whisper. Then to the man you insist—

'*Como prima, per favore, prima Como.*'

'*Amore, amore,*' he repeats.

'Shall I try to get the gun?'

'*Tu: zitto!* … *Silenzio!*'

He's snatching at your blouse. It has started to tear at the buttons. There's a brooch pinned above your breasts. I begin to edge towards the nearside door.

'*Sta giù! Giù!*' he yells. '*Sta giù!*'

The man is shaking his automatic pistol in the dark, jabbing downwards with it, meaning lie down on the back seat floor and shut up.

'*Apri! Subito!*'

He is having trouble with the brooch's fiddly fastening.

'Don't do a thing,' you whisper to me. 'I think it's our best chance.'

The man named Cesare Moretti is unzipping your jeans, lowering himself on to you now.

'He could kill us after … Just be ready to run for it.'

The man's grunting now as again I try to slide as silently as possible towards the car door handle, but once again he shouts: '*Non muovere! Tu, silenzio!*'

Tensed and passive, you let the car roof float above you, concentrating on his tie. You're wondering could you use it to strangle him with.

I'm thinking: this is how we die. We aren't going to grow old. Suddenly it seems such a pity. I hadn't expected life to be this short. Yes, it's a shame. In the back, lying down, I'm praying to the God that half an hour before I would have argued wasn't there. Oh Jesus, just to do the best thing. Help us to get out of this alive. Now the man is straining to finish. Will there be a momentary chance to get away? He's panting, panting, and he comes.

Can he really be intending to drive us into Como?

'No,' you say, you don't want to now. Cesare Moretti's hand with the pistol in it has dropped back down to his side as he clambers off you. I open the door and step out into the downpour, keeping as low as possible; but the man simply gets out too, leaving his pistol on the dashboard, and lifts up the car boot lid. I grab the rucksacks and step away into darkness, onto the reddish muddy earth of the road's verge. There are deep cracks in it from the long summer heat. They're beginning to soften, to melt at the edges. Pulling your clothes around yourself, you climb out as quickly from the car, and now this man, to our astonishment, our relief, has gone back round to the left hand side, ducked in, and is driving away. It's then we see the number-plate.

'Remember that,' you call out, standing in the soaking uncut verge, watching as his taillights blur into the stormy distance. But now the car's turned, its headlight arcing, and driven back down the wrong side of the carriageway. You throw yourself into the soaking wet grass of the shallow embankment falling away from this side of the road.

'He's coming back to kill us!' you're shouting, droplets glistening on your face. Saying nothing as we lay there, the smell of long dry foliage and moisture in my nostrils, my eyes turn towards you lying prone beside me, feeling so close to death, sensing us alive there in the rain.

When the headlights disappear and there's no more engine noise, we begin to run down the hard shoulder into the dark. The rain pummelling our faces has cooled the

September air. At the first car to appear, we step out into the beams waving our arms to make the driver stop. But it continues through the downpour as if we aren't even there. This is obviously far too dangerous. We should try to find an emergency phone. And I'm sure I pressed the button for police, but there it is, pulling up beside us, a breakdown truck with a crane.

So now I'm here—it dawned on me as I sat there before the young woman interpreter—to corroborate your innocence? Moretti's defence is that we made some kind of financial arrangement? That what had happened amounted to a payment in kind?

'No, we didn't,' I said.

'You paid no money to this man?' the translator was asking.

'No. We did not.' More conversation ensued between the judges on the bench. At last, the English translator, evidently relieved, turned back to me and said,

'Are there any other details you remember and want to tell this court?'

'No,' I said, my mind a blank, 'I don't think so.'

The interpreter conveyed this response to the judges and reported their reply.

'Thank you,' she said. 'You are finished.'

But I didn't appear to understand.

'You are finished,' she repeated.

Beckoned to by the interpreter, the usher stepped forward and made to lead me back towards the courtroom door.

'Thank you,' I said, in the direction of the judges,

stepping outside with barely a glance at the curious smile of the man sitting there in his chains.

Outside, the usher explained we were welcome to stay until the trial was over.

'You wait the verdict?'

'No,' you were saying, 'we have to get back to England.'

Here once more were the lawyers, the advocates or journalists, and staring hard was the accused man's wife, but dejected-looking now, as if her anger and frustration had spent itself in those tirades. She stood silent in her helplessness as we were escorted away. And then there came over me the sensation of a vast burden lifting while we were being led from that corridor outside the courtroom, out of the lives of Moretti and his wife; it seemed that the woman with the orthopedic shoe might even have envied us. There we were, free to go, relieved from the consequences of whatever it was her husband did or didn't do on the night he came home in the small hours of that distant September night.

'You have expenses?' the court usher asked.

'Yes,' you said, 'we need them for the train back.'

The usher took a look at the summons documents, then led us along another series of corridors and down in a lift to the *Tribunale di Milano*'s accounting section. At the grille we received the various travel expenses and daily allowances in Lira. As you handed me the money for safekeeping, an unwanted thought struck home: the judges had asked if we received any payment, and no, we hadn't … or at least not until now. You were doubtless thinking no such thing, and, of course, that thought, and all the others, remained entirely unexpressed.

The usher was guiding us back up to the main atrium and the entrance doors.

'Buon viaggio!' he said, and vanished back into the *Palazzo della Giustizia*, as we descended its precipitous steps down into the chilly air.

Not far from Piazza Duomo and Milan's famous porcupine cathedral, we re-circulated a part of the expenses on a lunch of something or other.

'Did they ask you if we were given any payment?'

'Presumably he couldn't claim he didn't do it once we appeared,' you said, 'so he changed his defence to a payment in kind—or something like that.'

'Perhaps he went away to change his plea ... or his line of defence.'

'Maybe,' you said. 'But I don't really want to talk about it anymore.'

You didn't want to talk about it. There and then, in the hope that time would do its work, we enveloped ourselves in the silence of what was meant to be forgetting—like the flash of white sails on the Ijselmeer, that stripe of light on Solent Water, our September in the rain and trial at the Court of Milan were locked inside as if forever. I couldn't take responsibility for the damage caused, for there was no one there to acknowledge the gesture; I couldn't distinguish that gesture from being actually responsible for the hurt, when all the time trying to act as if nothing had happened. The flashes of memory and inexplicable blanks tangled up inside me, like the thin brown tape snagging out of a snarled cassette. They formed a knot of shame and guilt for something that, I now begin to see, had been done to me too. They left me, as it seemed back then, with nothing more to say.

Even now, trying to look back, to recall what happened after we went down the steps from the court building, it's still almost impossible to conjure up anything else of our brief visit to Milan. We must have returned to the hotel and collected our luggage, and definitely walked back to the Central Station taking exactly the same avenues down which we had come. Perhaps it was approaching the station this first time that I noticed the oddly Italianized name Giorgio Stephenson carved around the roofline of its over-decorated façade.

Again under the enormous vault of the booking hall, we agreed that there was money enough from the expenses to book couchettes for our night's journey back across Europe. With an hour and a half to spare, we ate a hasty dinner in a restaurant by Via Scarlatti. Then there will have been just time enough to make it back to the right platform and into our seats before the express pulled out across the maze of lines and points beyond that fascist station's high glass arch. Under gantries past its signal box we trundled, off towards Domodossola, the Swiss border, Paris, a stormy crossing, and an English winter.

CHAPTER 15

'Come on, let's go and look round the old places …'

You were dressed for a walk in September, stepping from the college flat's living room where a ruffled sofa bed had been made up under the window.

'Jean's still asleep, by the sound of it,' you said, proffering me my jacket. 'We can be back before lunch.'

Never able to get a good night's rest on an unfamiliar sofa, I had given up pretending to sleep before dawn and was sitting over one of Jean's books in her kitchen when you finally appeared. Jean Walsh, you remember, the playwright; we got to know her during that year she spent as a writer in residence at the Art College. Jean had been offered the post after her series of fringe successes culminating in the West End run of her first hit satire, *Money for Jam*, about the deregulation of the City. She was coming to the end of a two-year stint as a community theatre fellow in our old university town. It was almost fifteen years since you and I had left. The council was starting to sandblast the house-fronts and lower the housing density towards the end of our three years in the place. Now the transformation appeared all but complete.

Still dominating its skyline of sloping slate roofs was the Mill tower: a slender imitation of an early renaissance campanile. It had been saved by preservationists, and was part of the town's industrial museum. Trying to keep up the idea of a future in exhibition organizing, Alice had volunteered to work there when she came back from New York. The historical displays in the museum were just beginning to be put together. She typed up labels, cut out large squares of hessian sack to use as the ground for object displays, all in the hope that a vacancy would come up, but it quickly transpired there'd be no salaried positions for years—and, besides, she had no museum curator qualifications.

One Saturday afternoon those years before, we three had climbed to the eighth floor of the main university building. Up there, in a large empty space used as a practice room by student bands, a not-quite-in-tune piano stood open in the corner. Immediately after catching your breath, you wandered over and started to pick out the Labour Party Anthem with one finger; Alice managed to conjure some of its words from the air. Below us, smokeless and still, lay the panorama of that threatened Victorian townscape. It must have been only a few days before she left for London. Suddenly the prospect seemed emptied of purpose, the painted flats and props of a flopped kitchen-sink drama.

'All this can be yours!'

It was just such a view of the place that had prompted your professor to make that remark. She meant, of course, the rashes of social problems breaking out all over those streets of terrace houses. But that day, up there with you and her, our university town had felt like the stage set of the Mill which Jean's agit-prop students were building out of cardboard.

The evening before she'd showed us around the theatre's deserted auditorium.

'What's the play about?' you asked, walking up to centre stage with a faint squeak from the floorboards at every step you took.

'The Chartist lock-out,' Jean replied from the middle of

the front stalls. 'It's a documentary dramatization.'

'When was that? What happened?'

'In early 1849: Bester, the mill owner, brought in blackleg Irish labour, shut out the work force, and broke the strike.'

'Not exactly a happy political message,' you said.

'No,' Jean agreed, 'but though the Chartists were defeated, their lessons weren't forgotten, and it was then that the Trade Union movement in this industry really began to gather momentum.'

'Reminds me of all the school plays I was in,' you said, near the wings now, in a stage whisper.

'Oh your paws and whispers!' I could still remember Alice saying.

The student stage designer had attempted to represent the imposing mill tower and factory in a squat and corrugated form.

'Doesn't look much like the real thing,' my voice came from down left, a smear of black powder paint on one index finger.

'That's not the point,' said Jean. 'We couldn't possibly make the flats look like a realistic factory even if we tried. So I'm getting the kids to work on alienation effects, symbolic tableau, direct addresses to the audience by narrators, using historical documents, rapid shifts from scene to scene on stage at the same time and picked out with lighting changes ... You know the sort of thing.'

But looking out from Jean's kitchen window that morning, I had gazed a good while at the real campanile. There it remained, with the aura that an artwork could attract. Stripped of its function, that complex of buildings represented nothing but a value, the meaning to something that no longer existed. And it was just such a magical aura that Jean's student play seemed designed to dispel—as if the only thing which prevented life turning into virtual art was the unending effort of historical memory, as if the only way to forgive and forget was exactly to remember.

CHAPTER 16

That autumn evening, the best part of fifteen years' back now, Alice had been standing in the park by Cabot's Tower. Suddenly, as dusk descended, the household lights of Bristol suspended themselves in necklaces of crescents and terraces, glinting through the darker branches of autumn trees round the navigator's monument.

Not quite with your permission, but certainly your acquiescence, I arranged to meet her at the end of October. Whatever Mrs. Young had expected or wanted, it was impossible simply to pretend that the days spent with her in Holland never happened. I wrote a letter with the barest outline of how things had gone after our parting at 's-Hertogenbosch. In it I told her how you had met me in Brussels. I mentioned how the next day we managed to get to the German border with a series of short lifts, and were then found by an Austrian heading for Graz. Dropped in a bad spot outside Munich, we'd been rescued by Peter Bastian, a Frankfurt doctor visiting his grandmother in the Trentino.

He had taken us to stay the night in the village of Brunik St George. Then, the next day, we were driven to Florence by a pair of Austrian couples coming from Sweden to spend their summer car-factory earnings. I barely so much as hinted that you had been robbed in Rome, and then said how things had gone horribly wrong on the way back home. But then I just didn't know how to put it. The words were so flat and brutal. I was sorry I hadn't her telephone number … 'but please write and I'll call you. It's too difficult to explain in a letter. I need to talk. Perhaps we can meet somewhere soon. Please do write—with much love.'

When she replied, I did call and took the bus from Victoria Coach station one Friday afternoon to spend a few days together the very weekend Pasolini stopped his car in Ostia and picked up Death himself.

Alice had been standing there waiting at the city centre depot. It wasn't much of a walk from the hollow of Bristol's city centre to her flat in Cayninge Gardens. She showed me the way up the main street, past the university, through elegant squares of Georgian terraces, across the green and into a dignified street of cream-coloured stone buildings. Once merchant's houses, they were now mostly divided into rented accommodation for the student community or better-off young married couples.

When we reached the house, she offered a coffee and we sat sipping from her Liberty mugs in dark wood chairs by the windows of a second floor bed-sitting room. Above the desk hung a print of Cranach's *Adam and Eve*, the couple's sorry story in their coolly rendered flesh. Her print of Joan Eardley's Glasgow sweetshop had been taped-up over a blocked-in fireplace. She was wearing a fawn mohair cardigan and a blue velvet skirt.

'So how was Amsterdam?'

'You already know,' she smiled. 'Only stayed one night. Being a girl there on her own, men kept coming up and accosting me. It was all very unpleasant. I did have a look round the Flea Market, though; but then took the first boat train back home.'

I could picture her alone on the deck of a ferry: the sea breeze blowing out her reddish hair as she leaned on a rail gazing into the turmoil of the small ship's widening wake. Gulls swooping and rising around its stern seemed to twist like question marks in a still summery sky. Sipping at the rim of her mug, she described how she had spent a quiet week with her parents in Edinburgh, then packed up her things at Sydenham and moved into the flat found by some fellow-students back in late August.

Leaning against the work surfaces in its kitchen, pretending to a little composure, I asked her what she might have in mind for the weekend.

'The film club's showing Chabrol's *Juste avant la nuit*,' she said. 'We could go to that if you think you can cope with the subtitles.'

'Pushing against an open door: isn't there something a bit more cheerful?'

'Oh—how about something I'm learning to cope with: *Zero de conduit* by Jean Vigo?'

'You've seen it then. Me too.'

Alice looked puzzled, or I thought she did, and not for the last time that weekend. Sniffing the air ostentatiously, I complimented her on the aroma of the risotto. She was adding some white wine and stirring the rice in a large frying pan. Dropping the cinema idea, and whatever other plans she might have thought to mention, she started to give an account of her flat-mates. It was a houseful of girls all training to be teachers.

'Cayninge Gardens!' she said, with another of her smiles.

After eating the risotto, we went back down into the town centre and decided on the spot to see *Two for the Seesaw*, which turned out to be showing at the film club. After the black-and-white love story of Robert Mitchum, a divorcing lawyer from Nebraska, and the young Shirley

MacLaine, a Greenwich Village dancer, we walked back towards Clifton, the dark of our autumn evening all but banishing memories of that summer's heat.

'You look tired,' she said, curling up on the wall side of her bed after kissing goodnight.

'Coraggio! Coraggio!' a policeman kept repeating as I tried to get to sleep.

The next morning, she gave me a guided tour of her training college, its library, lecture rooms, and cafeteria. Alice was doing her teaching practice at a large comprehensive on the outskirts of Redland, and talked about discrepancies between the theories presented in lectures and the day-to-day realities of timetables, classroom discipline, about the sheer exhaustion from work loads teachers had to learn to bear. Waiting in the library while she dropped off an essay, I drifted along the shelves pulling out volume after volume at random, flicking over a few pages, and then pushing them back where they came from.

'*Book*worm!' your voice kept repeating. '*Book*worm!'

It would be a weekend of desultory wanderings. She needed a new lampshade for her bedroom, and that afternoon we shopped for one in the craft section of a store on Whiteladies Road. Then she took me out along Bristol's deserted and decaying docklands to the Arnolfini Gallery, a museum space on the waterfront, where a Patrick Caulfield exhibition happened to be on.

Alone in a large high-ceilinged room, we gazed at the peculiar interiors and still-lives, their blank sweeps of strong colour broken by thick, child-like lines of drawing. The most provoking ones for me contained segments of neatly painted, postcard-style views inserted into their spaces—a photographic realism located in the schematic frames of their period modern interiors. They seemed copied from travel brochures or the pictures fastened to the walls above the passengers' heads in continental railway compartments.

What did I think of them? Nothing positive came to mind, so I shrugged my shoulders and put on an uncomfortable face.

'Not like you to be lost for words in a gallery,' she said.

Then, with an almost imperceptible shake of her head and slight wave of the hand, she made it clear we might as well leave. Perhaps she had already realized that we would no longer be able to share those sorts of experiences—at least with the meanings they had briefly implied. My clumsy reserve made it all too obvious. There are things you can't come back from, however much you may wish you could, or even pretend you have. Yet as we walked over the cobbles of the wharf and headed for a department store coffee shop she liked to frequent, it wasn't at all clear which of us was bringing our involvement to an end.

'So how's the course going?' she asked.

'Difficult to get excited about the provenance for "school of" works destroyed in the bombing of Dresden,' I said. 'But there was a good lecture last week about a lost masterpiece mentioned in the literature which turned out to have been painted over by the artist himself. The slides of the x-rays clearly revealed it.'

'All sounds rather intangible.'

'Like in the galleries—where you're not supposed to touch the precious works of art ... It's always been a puzzle, that—the way painters can have their finger marks all over some reclining nude or odalisque until it's finished, and then it becomes something we're only allowed to stalk about in front of, gaze at a moment, then move on.'

'Well now, darling, are you absolutely sure you're in the right field?' she asked me in her teasing vein.

'It's much more technical than I thought it would be: stuff about the chemical formulas for the pigment they used, theories of restoration, enlargements of the paint strata as evidence for the artists' procedures. Don't seem to be able to concentrate on one thing at a time. Actually finding it a bit hard to concentrate at all. But it's only the beginning. It'll start to make sense before too long, I'm sure. How about yours?'

'Even stepping into the classroom's a bit scary,' she said, 'but of course you've got to be brave.'

That evening she introduced some of her trainee-teacher acquaintances in the crowded back room of the Coronation Tap. Stood there sipping a half of bitter, it was difficult to hear yourself think. The cheerful noises of people who didn't seem to know each other all that well only made my silence seem even more cold and aloof. We left after a couple of drinks.

It was Saturday night. So, as if for old time's sake, I tried my best to make love to her. She kindly put up no resistance; that was never her way. Rather her generous person had come to feel like an emblem of complicity. Why dwell on it? My one summer of half-innocent youthful confidence had gone forever. Displaying the foresight of the truly realistic, she had been right after all: a brief affair, yet with how long-drawn-out an aftermath, at least, that is, for me.

'Don't worry,' she said. 'It doesn't matter. It's alright.'

During those three days she never so much as mentioned what had happened in Italy. Perhaps she was just being tactful. Whatever expectations she may have had for that weekend and later, she must have quickly seen they would come to nothing. I might have wanted to live as if nothing had changed; I might have wanted to keep open that possible future. Still, the fact of what had taken place kept returning in the words of a song, a laugh animating her features, or bits of my no longer tanned face glimpsed in the mirrored pillars of some department store interior. We looked almost exactly as we had just six weeks before, but nothing now could feel the same. The only future to be lived had changed its aspect in the two of us too. We would walk the afternoon away, and end up by Cabot's tower as dusk was closing in.

'What are you reading?' she asked, noticing the top of a Penguin paperback pushed into my jacket pocket.

'Novel by Wyndham Lewis ... *Revenge for Love*. It's about art forgery, among other things.'

'Interesting title,' she said, with yet one more of her wry smiles.

CHAPTER 17

Over the next three years, we continued to meet now and then. Alice moved back to London after qualifying and took up a post at a high school in Brockley Rise. Now, the rabbits securely back in place, she and I were 'just good friends' once more. Meeting outside the ICA, we seem still to be climbing broad steps towards the clubs and Piccadilly, off to catch a show in Cork Street, perhaps, or at the Royal Academy, disappearing into the crowds of another all but forgotten afternoon.

How did we stop meeting altogether? The last time we set eyes on each other had been a pure accident. There she was standing in the queue for tickets to a concert at the Albert Hall. As I gazed towards her, not quite believing it, because there were thousands of people crowding around, she turned—and her start of recognition was one to which I couldn't but respond. Was she pleased? She didn't introduce me to her friends, momentarily glancing down the queue towards mine. Maybe she wondered were you coming to the concert too. But, no need to worry, you weren't. She mentioned, as if her words were suggested by the chance meeting, how she had recently heard from some other old boyfriend of hers at university. The name meant nothing to me. All the same, it produced the unflattering sensation of being a closed chapter in her past, located beside other episodes, other brief affairs.

'Good to see you,' she said. 'Let's talk more when we're inside.'

Once past the box office, I went searching around so we

could continue the conversation, but I wasn't able to see her anywhere in the crowded concert hall. Perhaps she had even tried to look for me too.

Then, four years later, a Christmas card arrived by a roundabout route. It contained a telephone number. She was still living in the capital.

'It's the year for mending contacts,' she said.

'Let me phone you again when I get back from Italy. I'm just going over for a few days research.'

'Glad you're still gadding about,' I heard her say.

One week later the card had mysteriously disappeared, the phone number with it. When I asked, you vehemently denied throwing it away. More years of silence followed, till again by chance news of her married life and motherhood arrived via that dinner with my sister, who had met her, you remember, at Isabel's wedding. For some time after that I would imagine her ferrying her children to a playgroup, or smartening up her daughter for Brownies, wondering what she should do with the letter—the one sent after my sister found an address through Belle. Perhaps it never reached her. Whatever, it resulted in silence.

Then, a few years back, I was trying to sort out the chaos of my office bookshelves after yet another hectic term. A thin brown pamphlet with nothing printed on its spine found its way into my hands. I was just wondering whether it was one more bit of college ephemera that could be tossed in the trash. But it turned out to be the catalogue from an exhibition of sculptures and bas-reliefs by Jean Arp at the Galleria Schwarz, Milano—a show that ran from the 8th of May to 4th of June 1965. Published along with the reproductions of exhibits were various examples of the artist's poems in French, including one called '*les pierres domestiques*' which still did something for me when I gave it a go. Underneath the English phrase 'For Arp, art is Arp', attributed to Marcel Duchamp, she had written 'For Richard, a token of my arpreciation (not in the best line of McLeod wit, but one tries). From Alice, Christmas 1974.' After standing there amongst the chaos, lost in memory a moment, I closed the catalogue and put it back into the bookshelves, but properly filed in the Dadaist section— making a mental note to see if the Gallery Schwarz was still there at Via Gesú 17 next time I was in Milan.

Alice. Yes, I hope she's content, her marriage happy and her family thriving. What attracted me to her, what created that particular fondness and desire, remained caught inside, as if it were a puzzle without a piece. Of course, the years would alter the feelings about how we might have been experimenting, trying to invent our lives— whether needing to change or become what we thought ourselves likely to be. Is it self-forgiveness that alters others' characters in memory, or the complacency of middle age? Alice McLeod: it stood for somebody gone for years, for a trace of what remains, what was once a living person, now these words.

CHAPTER 18

Lifting the reading glasses and staring out at our university town's altered skyline, its pale yellow frontages of once smut-grimed sandstone now delicately contrasting with the grey-blue roof-slates, the wide tree-planted spaces between thinned-out rows of terraces, I found another coincidence coming back to mind. Again at Victoria Coach Station, taking the bus for Cornwall with you that New Year, I'd looked out of the window at another one leaving for the West of England—and there inside it, making me blush with shame, was Alice's face. She was evidently absorbed in a book or magazine and didn't, thank goodness, look up or look round. It was by no means the last time we saw or spoke to each other, but, as her coach pulled out ahead of ours, it couldn't help but revive the confusion of our previous partings.

In London one early February night just after we came back from the trial in Milan, two Courtauld MA students who were to become friends for quite a few years invited us round to their flat for dinner. The kitchen was a low-roofed extension from the main rectangle of a terraced house in Hackney. Phil and Molly, another apparently inseparable couple, rented the downstairs flat. Beyond the dark window lay an indeterminate space of yard and garden, then the back wall of a similar arrangement in reverse. The heads of our two hosts, glancing and nodding, were two bright ovals in the un-curtained rectangle of the kitchen's rear window.

You had curled yourself up on the sofa in front of an

electric fire. Again you seemed to be worrying about your appearance, feeling at some slight roughness on your chin and cheeks. Your skin was always sensitive, and reacted visibly to anything upsetting. Your feet, in thick red socks, were tucked up underneath you, your legs curled in close fitting jeans, matching a thick winter shirt decorated with small pieces of bright-coloured material cut and sewn like a quilt onto the rough blue ground. You had just closed the curtains for Molly and settled back onto the sofa. The only sound was the regular, mechanical click and jump of the needle in the record's run-off groove.

'And what would anyone like to hear?'

'Anything,' you said, 'anything at all.'

Flicking through the vertical stacks of LPs at the bottom of their bookcase, I dug out a collection of Elvis Presley's Sun Sessions.

Now Molly was stirring the cheese sauce, made with chopped ham and peas that Phil was tipping into the pan. Stretching across her boyfriend, one hand on the salt, the other holding a spatula, Molly turned her neck slightly, pointing her face with its side-fall and natural wave of blonde hair, upwards into Phil's; his face, clean-shaven yesterday, with a stubbly emphasis of chin and smiling mouth, moved to meet Molly's. As they kissed tenderly, my envious eyes were deflected to the red clay tiling of the kitchen floor, where tiny flecks of onionskin lay preserved in its more remote corners.

The grey metal pan with darker heat marks around its sides exhaled a gust of steam and seasoning as Molly carried it over to the table. A bottle of wine from Frascati had been placed at its centre, the cork removed and then partially reinserted. There was a brief hesitation among us about where each should sit.

'No formalities,' said Phil. 'Put yourselves anywhere.'

After we'd complimented them on the food, the talk momentarily faltered.

'So what have you been doing with yourselves?' asked Molly, as if to save the situation. 'Wherever have you been, dropping out of sight like that?'

'Nowhere much,' you replied.

Neither of us had any desire to spoil the evening. But then Phil would have to say he didn't believe it, adding that my absence from the seminars had been noticed. I told them we'd been on a flying visit to Italy, to see the Bernardo Luini in the Brera.

'Only for that?' Molly asked. 'What are you, made of money or something?'

Which obviously wasn't the case. But finding it impossible to talk with friends about what happened had the unintended effect of making them seem so much the less friends. Just as in Bristol, everything beyond us took on a somehow weightless air: in Hackney on that first occasion when it happened, you smoothed over the silence by coming up with the more or less plausible tale that the Italian police had caught the man who snatched your bag in Rome. When Molly looked slightly puzzled and then exclaimed how it must have been exciting, you said it was simply a bureaucratic formality, identifying the man, boring really, and changed the subject.

'You're right. I'm left. She's gone,' Elvis sang.

In among the glasses, cutlery, Parmesan cheese, salt and pepper pots, and a half-empty bottle of wine, the sound of his yodeling voice came filling up the silence between us, matched the twang of Scotty Moore's guitar—

'You're right. I'm left. She's gone.'

'Come on, if you're coming,' you repeated, your hazel eyes bright, as you opened the flat's front door. You had obviously slept soundly and were eager for the exercise.

'Why not let's see what the old square looks like?'

We were walking beside the rough-hewn walls of the park. Inside were its couchant lions, their sandstone smutted and scratched, begrimed with bird-droppings and smoke. There was a lake as well, but back then it had been silted up and used for dumping rubbish. Pram chassis, bed springs and frames protruded from what remained of the water. As we approached its glistening, renovated surface, a flotilla of ducks came swimming in close formation, then they veered left to the bank and one by one waddled out onto the grass. The ducks were familiar enough with the habits of humans to expect a bag of crusts and crumbs. They were to be disappointed. Neither of us had any bread, but still we stood surrounded there in silence for a moment.

'I wonder if they pitied us,' you said, 'the neighbours who used to take us to feed the ducks on Southsea Common?'

'Pitied? Why?'

'Because we were brought up so strictly and strangely,' you went on. 'They must have known what my parents are like, and given us treats when we played with their children.'

'Don't you think everyone feels that way about their parents?'

'No, I don't—and, anyway, it's nonsense to think everyone feels the same, because they can't possibly have all had the same reasons for feeling what we felt.'

Fair enough, I thought, learning one more lesson as I did.

On the stone beside the park's other gates I could make out that daft bit of Sixties' graffiti: 'Tomorrow is the first day of the rest of your life'.

The wind was picking up as we walked along the moor side, crying through the high branches of trees. You were fastening the top button of your blouse as you walked.

'That September when we were packed off to Dorchester by my parents,' you said, 'you know it wasn't the first time it had happened to me.'

'Really, when else?'

'Remember that time we had a day out to Kingsdown, so I could show you my grandparents' house, Pine Cottage? Mum and dad sent me there when Katie was about to be born.'

The pinewood and orchard had mostly disappeared when we went there, its croquet lawn of fond memory divided into building plots. Where you used to play, bungalows, chalets and holiday-haciendas had been erected. Pine cottage itself stood separate behind a beech hedge in a surround of gravel that wasn't there in your grandparents' day. The two-storey house had been imported in kit-form from Scandinavia— the first of its kind anywhere in England, you said. It had a decorated frame, with deep eaves, and was clad in cedar-wood shingles. We had trespassed onto its more recent pebbly drive, beyond the name *Pine Cottage*—just as it had been, but repainted on a different plate. That had seemed an idyllic day, you happily revisiting a place so replete with memories; but as you looked from the drive and waved I had the sudden piercing sensation of being no more than a vague phantasmal presence in your life.

'I'll have been just four when it happened,' you were saying. 'Both my mother's pregnancies were difficult. You see she was very ill before my birth, and when Kate was due, granny came over to collect me. I was probably only in Pine Cottage for ten days or a couple of weeks, but it seemed much longer. Mum must have stayed in hospital quite a while after the delivery, because I also remember going with dad in a taxi to collect her and Katie from the hospital. I can still hear myself being told she was my sister.'

'Don't suppose it's that unusual … or maybe wasn't. It happened to my grandma on my mother's side.'

'You know, most people in my class had a holiday relaxing after their A-levels but not me, oh no, I was packed off for the whole summer to work at a religious community—thirteen miserable weeks of putting on weight.'

'And what was the brilliant thinking behind that?'

'It got me away from my boyfriend at the Poly, didn't it? I never saw Simon again.'

'Which is why you were "available", I suppose, when we bumped into each other at that student disco.'

'Perfectly true,' you said, with a mysterious conjuring gesture of the fingers after a moment's silence.

We had reached the bridge above a disused railway cutting. Gazing down at its trackless shale, wild grasses and willow herb indicating where the lines had been, I recalled that it was exactly the spot one blustery night Alice had said that if she stayed here it would ruin her complexion.

'Can't you see how it's finished off everyone else's?' she said.

But even if we were allowing ourselves this bit of

a nostalgic looking round, it was surely better not to let her name drop from my lips. Adapting Dorothy Parker's witticism, you would now and then comment on the gamut of emotions from A to M; but really you preferred not to hear more of her name than your own faintly sardonic allusions to its initial letter. It seemed clear enough I would never really be forgiven for that, but then why should I be? Did I deserve it? So in silence once more, and parallel with that disused railway, we continued along the moor-side road.

There had been so many moments like this one when it felt as if you would never really forgive me, let alone forget. You might be standing on the bathroom scales or looking into the washbasin mirror.

'Have I lost any weight?' you'd ask. 'Is my face improving?'

And your questions would sound curiously like the sessions of trial and judgment to which your parents used to subject their daughters' boyfriends. It was impossible to say the right thing. I would always be weighing my words, attempting to make amends for that ever more far off mistake.

Perhaps a return to our student flat would help put that sort of thing behind us once and for all. No such painful thoughts had naturally crossed my mind back then: the world was all before us. But now we were heading in the direction of the past, towards St Luke's Square in fitful September sun. First, though, we must walk in front of the church that gave its name to the place, and then cross over towards what was the old workhouse. Later the great stone edifice had been converted into a municipal hospital. As we cut through behind the back of the building, its rows of ward windows glinted in the sun. You could imagine patients wanting to move nearer to the stove in winter, nearer to the air in summer, hoping they could change to the beds nearer the door—the ones that meant you would soon be discharged. Those rows of apertures, gas-lit in a foggy Victorian dusk, looked like a glimpse into other people's nightmares, their fears of euthanasia.

To enter the Square we crossed the cobbles of Fairfax Terrace, closed at the higher end by a blank wall, alleys leading to left and right, at the lower, by a row of house-fronts on the far side of the road. One side of the street had been sandblasted too, and closed to traffic by laying some flagstones over the cobbles. Bollards prevented cars from crossing the pavement, and there were three enormous concrete bowls for flowers that either had never been planted, had long since failed to take, or had been unable to survive the younger inhabitants of the place.

'Remember when you threw out your old paintings? The kids from the houses around must have always been rummaging in our rubbish, only this time they found your masterpieces. Weeks after, coming home from the health centre placement, I used to find those old self-portraits of yours caught in the nettles and dock.'

The terrace house with our tiny flat on the first floor was in the furthest corner of the square. We walked round behind and down the alley with weeds pushing between its cobbles, a shrub turning yellow in the corner of one backyard. The past ten years hadn't improved it at all. Faded net curtains still hung behind the rotten frames of what had been our student flat. Some of the panes were broken, patched with pieces of cardboard and tape. A great swathe of wallpaper was hanging from the wall you once painted a warm ochre emulsion with cream gloss skirting boards.

Gazing up at what were kitchen windows, I could just about picture the bedroom where the best of those daubs, as Dr. Green had called them, were hung on the walls. How little we'd had to do with the place. In a brief parenthesis, as if before our lives, we two had grown and then moved on, leaving, or so it appeared, absolutely nothing behind.

'Difficult to imagine we ever lived here, don't you think?'

'Oh, I don't know,' you said.

During our time, just a few doors down, there'd been a brutal murder, a man stabbed to death in his bed. The police made house-to-house inquiries, but when they came to us, we were no help to the officers who called. It was the son, enraged by a family inheritance quarrel, who, it turned out, had committed the crime.

'They don't keep it as tidy as we did,' you said, hardly able to conceal a shiver. 'Could the place really have been this bad back then?'

In the years since I fluked, as you would put it, my lecturing job at the Art College, Winchester had become our home. It was there we spread sideways and put down roots. The decade spent in a comfortable Hampshire town had certainly mellowed and altered us. I had even got used to the idea of living in a place where the leaves came out in spring like wallets flourishing old one pound-notes, notes which would turn into ten shilling ones come September.

Two little Asian girls had stealthily tiptoed up behind us while we were staring through those windows at the musty nothing that was once our student home. When we turned round and looked at the little sisters, we found ourselves stared at in return. The children couldn't have been more than four and six, dressed in a combination of traditional sari and British kiddy clothes. Despite the mortgage, the overdrafts, the credit card bills, those girls made me feel too comfortably off, too uncomfortable, as we intruded into their different existences. What's more, those two girls had produced a twinge of sorrow, our story overlaid with other hopes and disappointments.

'Probably never seen anyone like us down their street before,' you were saying, as we stepped back across the uneven cobbles of Fairfax Terrace. Yes, over those ten years you had stayed with your sense of social injustice. Entirely able to keep your intimate anxieties and public concerns in different boxes, you had changed jobs at regular intervals through the decade. You'd remained in health care management, though, the latest move taking you to a senior post in the Regional Health Authority teaching hospital. Now you were working to have the government guidelines implemented in the traumatic stress and bereavement counseling services. A couple of years later, you would edit a collection of papers on the subject.

Hands in pockets and the last of a smile on your face, you were leading the way across Ireton Road, through towards Jean's college flat in the Halls of Residence. Now the streets were quite deserted. No one lived here any more. The area had been badly run down a decade earlier, but now there were just the shells of buildings, some without windows and roof, the floors caved-in, walls stripped or scorched from fires.

'It's as if a bomb had hit the place,' you said.

We were walking along Mount Pleasant, its large houses set back from the road, and in what had once been the front gardens of wealthy people's homes were only the burnt out shells of cars under trees scorched and blackened. Surely these buildings could not be saved.

'Was there a riot or something here?'

'One of the Yorkshire Ripper's victims was discovered in Mount Pleasant,' you said.

'So had they started before we left?'

'I'm sure they had. There were notices warning the students never to go out unaccompanied in the evenings.'

The paving-slabs were hollowed-out by weathering and footsteps. They were unevenly cracked and fissured. A puttying of moss had swollen out from between the flags.

'Why?' I asked, aware of the surface being broken. 'That's the question they never seem to answer.'

'Denial. It's denial. You know, the people at Belle Vue House didn't believe it had happened, even after we went back for the trial. They thought I was drawing attention to myself. At least that's the line the psychoanalyst at consultation took. You see it couldn't have been a rape, as if even a girl like me must have been asking for it. I was speechless; I couldn't believe a professional like him would have had such an archaic attitude. Sometimes it strikes me the responses I got were harder to cope with than the rape itself.'

Not that long before, you had mentioned, almost with equanimity, how for years after coming back, you half-wanted to have been killed. You would find yourself imagining that the night's events were running like a film projected on your face—so that people who glanced at you in passing could see exactly what had happened.

Flinching at your saying 'the rape itself', I also saw how my objectless affections had attached themselves haplessly and without hope of response to near-strangers. Reactions to small failures and criticisms would incapacitate me for months. They would make the outer world of sunlight, ruffled grass and shifting clouds almost an irrelevance, *like a dying ember*, a seeming affront or token of what was lost, now perhaps forever. The detail and sequence of events, occasional phrases, glimpses in darkness one September in the rain, and its residual feelings remained trapped inside me. And there was the decisive moment of our lives, formed like an unspeakable absence, a social embarrassment, an apparent affront to others' sensibilities. Even the concern for my poor mother's moods had prevented me confiding in her. Her entire ignorance of what happened that night was one she would take to her grave.

'You know, I've never been able to talk about it to anyone …'

You were waving your hand to suggest we take a left at the corner, round towards the university campus.

'Maybe it was easier for me,' you said. 'After all, I was the "victim", the innocent one. No, I'm not suggesting you were guilty. You weren't. But, anyway, you know what I mean. You have to let it go.'

A stiff wind was rustling the leaves surviving on the branches of the badly scorched trees. Your short-cut dark hair, a few traces of grey in its fringe, lifted slightly in the quickening breeze. The last of your smile seemed to come back more warmly. Mortar had crumbled away between stones of the wall we were walking beneath. It bulged unnervingly. The capstones, not sandblasted, leaned away above. A patch of dust had appeared on the toes of my shoes.

'Somehow it's like it could have been me. Even wanting to make amends, you feel like an aggressor.'

'No, no,' you said. 'No. The motives are different. It couldn't be the same. You know you shouldn't hang yourself up on that hook now.'

The campanile of the Mill reappeared on the skyline. But just which Italian town was that bell tower supposed to recall?

'More ruined lives, more wasted, ruined lives,' I said, thinking out loud.

The distant moors were variegated with large patches of shifting shadow, the sky overcast in that direction, the wind quicker, clouds moving rapidly towards us. Now a layer of slate grey cloud covered the whole township. The temperature suddenly dropped. Separate spots of a darker tone began to pattern the pavement all around. There was a faint whispering in the foliage. But, as we approached the university area that day, the rain was no more than a passing shower. We were quickening our pace as you reached out a cupped palm.

'Just spitting,' you said.

And already the clouds were breaking up, their edges tinged with sunlight, patches of blue about to re-appear. Relishing the cool spots hitting my cheek, I could almost touch just how much that September in the rain had made us what we were. Coming back to England that time all those years before: it hadn't been anything like melting away because you couldn't stop crying, or being transformed into birds as if a relief from unendurable suffering. Death had cuffed us across the cheek; it had let us both go with a warning.

The cloudburst was already over. Refreshed, the air

hung still again, the street silent and deserted.

'I don't think I've ever said this,' I started.

We were almost at the stairs to Jean's block.

'But, you know, I'm grateful.'

The shower over, grass around our friend's flat was a deeper, glistening green. You moved closer and curled your fingers around my arm.

'For what?' you asked.

'You saved my life. The worst thing that ever happened to me, well, it happened to you.'

'But,' you said, knocking on Jean's flat door, 'you know very well it happened to us both.'

The tramway was creaking and grinding up a sunlit moorside. It was a short chain of open carriages rattling on their rusty, uneven track. The frayed cable slid along rollers that guided its movement up the centre of the rails. Some of the rollers were rusted solid and the wire scraped stiffly across them. The cable would tauten, and then inflexibly go slack. The lines ahead were almost enveloped in grasses and rosebay willow herb. The cable disappeared into a bower of sunlight and undergrowth towards which the insecure transport was noisily moving.

'Relax,' said Jean, 'I'm sure it's quite safe.'

She was wearing her uniform of green dungarees and cowboy boots, her frizzy red hair alight in the wind and sun.

'Can't think why we never came here before.'

'Probably wasn't working,' the playwright suggested. 'I bet it's got a preservation society. They'll have come along after your time and got the thing running again.'

From the tracks up to the hilltop the tenuous line of the cable ran obscurely through patches of shade ahead. It beckoned, as if drawing us further on towards the young people we once were, people for years thought far better dead. The train slowed into its upper station. Between simple wooden souvenir booths, we followed the hilltop path through woods. Brief bursts of a heavily distorted music came echoing through the September leaves.

'By the way, what happened round Mount Pleasant?' you asked. 'I don't mean the Ripper. But wasn't there some kind of riot?'

'There could have been, things being that bad round here,' said Jean. 'Actually a garage pump exploded and set the whole area alight.'

Now we were approaching a tiny, run-down fairground. There was something attractive in the roundabouts' amateur paintwork: long since faded through the bitter northern winters, these bright swirls and curlicues were like a child's dream of immediate pleasure. And in fact there was one little boy, about three or four years old, playing among the attractions. He was kicking a soft yellow ball with black patches painted onto it, like a World Cup football. The child, with chuckling face, would get something into his head and toddle off in an inexplicable direction, then turn and run back. Toppling over on the cinders, he would pick himself up, his face on the point of tears, decide he wasn't hurt, and then zigzag back over towards his parent.

'Just kick the ball to your dad, son,' the half-attentive man called out.

I was sitting on a flaked wooden bench. Its green paint had been chipped away to show the rutted, weathered-grey wood underneath. You were studying the boy with a curious look. It was almost a smile, with wrinkles at the corners of your eyes, but your top teeth were biting slightly into your lower lip, as if you were trying to imagine a possibility but couldn't. Then you had glanced across at the father and practically scowled.

Jean came over and began to tell us about how Heathcliff, an orphan discovered in Liverpool, as she said, might well have been an Irish tinker's child. We had driven out late that morning and looked around the Brontë parsonage straight after lunch.

Not far off, a couple of lads were fiddling with a loudspeaker on one of the rides. Suddenly it started up, rumbling distortedly: '*The leaves of brown came tumbling down, remember ...*' But the sound cut out once more. There was a small wooden hut at the end of the fairground. It was a refreshment kiosk, where a woman sat knitting. On the counter stood a row of large glass domes. Inside were a few stale cakes and scones, hermetically sealed for eternal preservation as if in some bizarre experiment.

One of the amusements was a toy train on its circular track. And there was the same little boy seated inside the engine driver's cabin. His father was resting against a low wall on the far side of the rails. The man was making smoke rings for a minute's peace. The boy was absorbed in the circular motion of the train. It was how he was steering it caught my attention, for however much the little boy turned his wheel, the train just kept going on round and round.

Now he was restlessly glancing and twisting to where his dad stood smoking. But the father seemed caught in a dream of his own. The boy had quickly reached the point of boredom, and began to shout at his parent, calling to be released from the seemingly endless reiteration. At his shrill cries, his crescendo of anguish, I suddenly felt a terrible nausea like that lost desire, rising as if in sympathy with the little lad, to be anywhere else but here, to be hurrying home across the park and going in through the back door under the washing line.

'Why don't we go and look round Saltaire?'

'In a minute, we've only just arrived,' you were saying, both women evidently wondering whatever had got into me.

'They're planning a motorway link that will cut this place in two,' said Jean, stepping down from the lower station.

You had finally agreed to leave the fairground, and after descending by the Shipley Glen Tramway with postcards and souvenir pencils, we were crossing parkland behind council houses with their lines of washing fluttering in the direction of Saltaire itself.

'One of the proposed routes,' Jean went on, 'goes right through the middle of Salt's village. There's a preferable one that would circumvent it, passing not far from these fields right here.'

'And an ideal one would be not to build it at all,' you said. 'Has a decision been made?'

'No, I think they're still at the planning stage, or it may have got to the public inquiries, the petitions, re-applications, all that. You might have seen the Saltaire Defence Committee's posters: *Over Our Dead Bodies!*'

Gazing down towards the village, its mill and canal, a habitable space removed from careering cocoons of cars and lorries, I could imagine the carriageways with their steep scrub slopes, the rumble of continuous wheels, an isolated hurrying mobile world, its flickering mirages of glass and lights, the service stations with their cuddly toys in plastic bags, and lay-bys and emergency phones. A question began to form itself. It hung suspended in the air. You and Jean were pursuing the line of your conversation, getting onto environmental damage and air pollution, passing close by a family engaged in a game of French cricket.

Now we were entering the groves of rhododendron bushes that formed a part of Titus Salt's parkland. And here was the statue they had raised, some time after his death, to commemorate the work of this philanthropic industrialist. Surely there was much more graffiti bespattering it now than when we had visited the place all those years before? Yet there he was still, the frock-coated Victorian dignitary with his eyes uplifted towards the moors.

From whence cometh my help ... and the memory of that psalm brought back one more lost picture of mine. It was a large canvas, five feet by three, completed during the last summer at university. Titus Salt's stone eyes, which gazed up away from his mill and village, were painted as if yearning after a more anarchic life than the one that he had set apart from those Yorkshire moors through his organizational skills, the power of accumulated capital, and a commitment to civic virtue. Salt, in the lost canvas, was gazing towards a landscape of impossible fulfilment, the sodden mildewed cobbled streets of Howarth, just a short journey by car from here. There was a deep satisfaction in the rocks beneath over-furred with slippery moss, but in the painting Salt's civic order was played off against the allure of Bramwell Brontë's emotional chaos. Though we might feel an affinity with the graveyard atmosphere of the parsonage, it was to Titus Salt's world we would always be obliged to return. That was what the picture had meant to convey.

Those years before, the paternalism of Saltaire had seemed to suffocate its inhabitants: a life regimented around the little streets of worker's cottages, the enormous Nonconformist chapel, the mill, and, across the river, a playing field in which, at this very moment, a school cricket match was in progress—the warm afternoon had brought people out to picnic and relax. But why did my landscape have to dramatize such mutually exclusive and equally self-thwarting opposites? Saltaire seemed far less restricting now than it did those years before. Why had it turned out this way? True, things were going better now for me at the College. Soon our weekend up North would be over; the working week ahead was already beckoning. In less than an hour, we would have to drive back south to King Alfred Terrace as fast as we dared, making enough time to finish your various presentations for that Monday morning.

How many years was it now since I stopped carrying round an artist's sketchbook? Those untouched white cartridge pages were the last stage in the fading away of that youthful ambition. There was always going to be time to work up the studies, the bits and pieces cut from magazines, which might one day make a canvas or a collage. Artists made time. They stayed up all night retouching their *pentimenti*. But it hadn't happened for me. For so many years, after what had been witnessed, the minutely detailed appearance of things no longer seemed to matter. It was unbearable to look and look so hard, to gaze hour after hour at some marks on a flat, textured surface trying to fathom how they might be amended. Those days in the living room at Belle View House, trying to paint the Little Venice Basin and the flats beyond, I could feel the old impulse drain away. Besides, studies at the Courtauld required so much time and concentration. As the months went by, I got used to the habit of absorbing information about provenance, digesting theories of representation, mugging up the history of aesthetics, checking the sizes and materials in catalogue raisonnés, deciphering pre-war x-rays and the like.

You and Jean were continuing on while I hung back under Titus Salt's statue staring blankly at the well-supported cricket game. Still deep in conversation, you were heading around the far end of the pitch, passing behind a small group of players and parents who were avidly watching the innings. Slow left-arm round the wicket bowling was regularly foxing the young batsman, probably a tail-ender. Or perhaps not, for at that very moment the receiver made contact and with a loud crack the polished red ball flew off towards the boundary nearest the scoreboard.

'Nobody's going to reach that one,' a voice said from somewhere.

The scoreboard frame, on which the black plates with large white numerals were hung, was now being manually updated. There came some well-deserved applause. The boys had run a three. You and Jean were strolling on together by the river. As I was about to catch up at the bridge, two girls came walking past me from the opposite direction. They were dressed in what seemed ethnic peasant costume. One was pushing a light baby carriage, a child inside the transparent plastic canopy. The other was carrying a bat, ball, and other playthings. Each wore a straw hat fastened underneath the chin with thin white elastic, and each had on a maroon pinafore-style dress over an embroidered white blouse. From the snatch of conversation passing between them, it seemed they weren't British. But whatever were they doing here? Could the child be one of theirs?

Crossing the grey-painted wrought-iron bridge across the Aire, it felt as if something had suddenly made itself apparent. But was it only one more hankering, another restless yearning to be anywhere else but here? Or did it perhaps promise some miraculous change, as if there were still someone else inside me calling to be allowed into the light? Suddenly here again was the need to relive it all, to have the entire thing happen inside, the events unfold once more with a meaning and sense of their own.

We stepped down towards an old boathouse on the riverbank. It had recently been converted into a café and restaurant, its white-painted bargeboard gleaming there in the afternoon sun.

'Shall we have a pot of tea?' Jean asked.

'Why not a cream tea?' you suggested.

'Go on, be a dear, and order us one,' Jean said to me.

You were sitting at a table outside on the terrace when I returned, and had started on a different theme. Jean's drama residency would come to an end at Christmas— but, ever resourceful, she already had quite a few irons in the fire.

'Keep this to yourself,' she said, 'but last week I was interviewed by the Bolton Octagon for the post of writer-director.'

'How did it go?' you asked.

'Well, they certainly expressed an interest in all my ideas

for revitalizing the place: community workshops, travelling shows for clubs and schools, that sort of thing, and they seemed impressed by the need for fresh scripts with a more up-to-date flavour, picturing the multicultural realities. I'm thinking of doing something about the motorway proposals,' said Jean. 'And I can bring in the northern tourist industry.'

Everyone has a book inside, as they say; Jean, it seemed, had a library in her. She was just then complaining about the innumerable scripts she would have to turn down about happy miners off to the seaside in a charabanc.

'I can well imagine,' you said. 'And did they offer you the job?'

'Haven't heard yet. It would ease things if they did. How about you?'

You were as busy as ever. There were the complaint procedures you needed to reorganize. You were putting the finishing touches to a consultation document about the matter, and would have it done that evening. Back over the river, people were climbing in and out of boats. On the far side, in the distance, under Salt's statue protruding from the trees, the cricket match continued, and a sudden burst of clapping and cheering let on that an innings had come to an end. Nearer, circles of friends were settling themselves on the grass, playing games of catch with family and offspring, chatting together, eating picnic food. Further removed, there were couples lying intertwined.

The two girls dressed in what looked like their national costumes had also settled themselves in the grass and were throwing the ball for their toddler to chase. A larger group, gathered in a ring nearby, fell into talk with the two maroon girls. Perhaps these two were from the Trentino or Ticino, the areas south of the Alps that we travelled through to reach Italy, and then managed to get home across all those years before. Perhaps they would be speaking in faintly imperfect syntax about the boy's age, where it was they came from, the Alto Adige perhaps, how long they were planning to be in Yorkshire, when they expected to go back home.

The tea had arrived. Jean leaned forward, being mother. You were helping yourself to a piece of scone with jam and cream, taking a large bite and, rocking back on your chair in the sunlit afternoon, allowing your eyes for a moment to close. Yes, you were right. You were right enough again. It was time to let it go.

CHAPTER 19

Visiting Milan in recent years, riding on the airport bus from Linate, it's been getting more and more difficult to catch even a glimpse of the city that we came to for that trial. There might still be the odd policeman armed with a short-barrelled automatic standing guard outside a bank. The bus might still be shaking over uneven road surfaces or getting stuck in traffic beside a grimy apartment block's exterior. Yet, waiting for the bus to move, I would see mothers dropping in and out of shops with pushchairs, or men deep in animated conversations by the doors of bars. I would see the usual sights and sounds of a busy metropolis. There, once more, were the broad avenues with tramways running under trees down their centres, a few crisp leaves still gusting about months after autumn was over, the avenues and piazzas appearing no more threatening than an average London street—and rather less so, if anything, than some of those around about King's Cross.

True, you can still see the occasional hate-daubed parapet, or waste-ground littered with abandoned cars; but the porno cinemas have long since given way to video shops, and the spectrum of political slogans from the hammers and sickles to rashes of reverse swastikas breaking out everywhere have been multiply painted over, or covered up by spray-gun graffiti art like the stuff on railway coaches everywhere. Now the underground system, at least beyond the central station, is clean and efficient, with escalators that start to move as you approach them. Strolling around the surprisingly compact central streets, it's almost impossible to see what was so threatening back then in the appearance of this city's inhabitants. Milan's the centre of fashion, of course, and people do dress to make an impact. Yet now they appeared, for the most part, to be calmly going about their business—calling 'Buon lavoro' to each other as they set off in their different directions.

Climbing the steps of the Metropolitana a few weeks back now, I resurfaced once more into the middle of Piazza Duomo right opposite the main façade of its famous white stone Porcupine. It was a bright sunny day just before Easter, the sort of day that tells you not to take life too personally, and one that required the sunglasses slipped into an inside pocket on leaving my hotel. Polishing their lenses with a handkerchief, I headed straight towards the statues on the shining cathedral's bronze doors.

There I found the emblematic slumped gypsy with a sick-looking child-in-arms begging by the entrance. Familiarity with the scene across the square allowed plenty of time. I took a few coins from a pocket and stooped down to drop them into her basket. At that moment, a couple of German women in late middle age came out through the sprung cathedral door, revealing how dark it was inside. A glimpse of that darkness visible, the flickering patterns of sun and shade on the flagstones of the Piazza Duomo, accompanied by the musty smell of old incense mixing with their rather stronger perfume, all seemed to say how much better it would be to remain outside.

Yes, half an hour early, on a day like today, everything said there was really no need to go straining my eyes again to make out the works of art in the shadowy side chapels of its five different naves. This would be, after all, the last afternoon of a flying visit to put in one final bit of spadework on my (probably) forthcoming monograph, *Genre Painters of Nineteenth-Century Italy*. The book's practically written—and, so long as the last of the footnotes can be nailed and all the transparencies for illustrations tracked down, it might even be got out before the cut-off point for the next round of government research assessment. Our head of department has been dropping dark hints lately about the width of my bibliography, and that long-meditated, much revised book had anyway stayed a skeleton in the cupboard for far too long. What's more, I had an added reason now for the occasional research trip to Italy.

A year or so back, growing restive in the dog-eat-dog environment of London's advertising industry, my sister had suddenly found herself falling in love with an Italian entrepreneur and, on what seemed an impulse but proved a lucky break, emigrated to Lombardy. She soon mastered the language and on the back of her London experience was engineered a job by her fiancé as an accounts manager with a Milanese agency. So, given my interests, during vacations or on bits of study leave, I could easily be tempted to fly off and pay her a visit. And that's how I came to be waiting for my sister to escape from the office for a leisurely lunch one spring day almost a quarter of a century after first setting eyes on Milan.

At one of the piazza cafés a waiter immediately loomed over my chosen table. Not bothering with the menu's range of choices, I ordered a cappuccino and a small San Pellegrino. There were still twenty-five minutes to kill, or more should Christine be unable to get away. The coffee wouldn't last long; but the bottle of water ought to keep the waiter off my back a while. The order quickly arrived. Sipping at the warm coffee, with the sudden onset of a familiar sinking feeling, I realized I'd left the hotel without so much as a magazine to read. So, in the shadow of the sun umbrella, with nothing else for it but to sit and wait, I let my thoughts go drifting back over the years.

Not long after she first became involved with her businessman fiancé, I spent an evening with them out in the suburbs of Milan. That must have been the first time I'd passed any length of time in the city since our '*processo per stupro*', as I learned it hadn't been. No, it had been *violenza privata* all along. The flat my sister occupied while she and Giovanni waited to marry was comfortably furnished, with every amenity, and the meal her husband-to-be prepared was delicious, particularly the *osso bucco*, a Milanese speciality, but it wasn't difficult to imagine why they were eager for her to move.

Cinisello Balsamo was a raw development of high-rise blocks on the outskirts of the city. It had been constructed to house southern immigrant workers. The area was a Kingdom of the Two Sicilies at the end of an autobus line from the station, buried in the heart of Lombardy. As we walked along the street towards her flat, the old women's eyes tracked us eerily. Nor was it difficult to associate that place and those eyes with the people's looks at the Agip petrol station or at the trial, and, indeed, with Cesare Moretti himself. Out of her brief residence in that part of the city, I started to imagine a history for your violator's blank smile: a southerner, he might have migrated to the north in search of employment and was living with all his family in some such vast district of poor apartment blocks, no love lost between them, under the shadow of who knows what frustrations and resentments.

And I could certainly remember wondering out loud as we were walking down towards the River Itchen by way of the water meadows whether he might have been a family man. Speculating like that naturally led to the question of what had happened to him, whether he got a long sentence or not, how it had affected his life, the lives of his family. It must have been a Sunday in early autumn, because we were out on one of our habitual afternoon strolls to St Cross. We'll have taken the usual route through cathedral close, down College Street, past No. 8 where Jane Austen died, over the stream at the little footbridge, then out of town along the towpath and into still fresh-looking countryside.

Yet even so much as mentioning Cesare Moretti or his imagined children that day had, at first, seemed like another big mistake. Your face lost its animation. Yes, you'd insisted on going back to Milan for the trial, but hadn't wanted to remain for the verdict. That would have felt, you said, like taking judicial revenge; of course it was also your way of coping with the whole business. You would do precisely what you believed was right, not concern yourself at all with what its consequences might be, for better or worse. Still, though firmly established now in one of the caring professions, you weren't going to have me milking sympathy for the family of your aggressor with my bits of remembering and fictional reconstruction.

A light breeze was rustling the leaves on the branches of the oak and ash, the sycamore, and chestnut trees. Scales of ivy and moss patches clung to their trunks and boughs. Down in the river sallows with their small gnats and leafy reflections, the air stood thick with light, and still.

Your cheeks flushed to a rosy hue, you were lifting your eyes in the direction of Twyford Down, to that rolling curve hacked into a white chalk cutting through which a stream of trucks, buses, and cars rumbled on towards Southampton and the coast.

'The fault was mine. The fault was mine,' I would quote to myself, and for years it seemed as if I were to blame for everything. Yet if what once appeared a precipitous slide of events had never happened, if we'd found things to enjoy in Italy and come back to a different autumn in England, there would have been little that needed forgiveness, little with which to burden myself down the years. A brief affair, that's what she'd said.

How self-important long-nursed, guilt-like feelings can seem to become. Our trusting innocence, or innocently self-interested calculation, had provided that man with his opportunity. We could have told him that we had money to pay for the lift. He was obviously poor. It was also a stroke of his bad luck to have found us there that September in the rain.

If he did try to defend himself with his idea that the rape was a payment in kind for the lift, then the fact of the gun looks difficult to explain. We had always assumed that he went away from the service station saying he'd return because he had to go and get the pistol. It's more than possible, though, that living in Milan during those leaden years of the mid-Seventies, he had a gun in the glove compartment anyway. So why, if he went to get the gun on purpose or had one with him, didn't he use it? Maybe it wasn't even loaded and he just waved it to get what he wanted. Perhaps he thought we would go back home and he would get away with it anyway. Perhaps he'd even got away with it before. No, we never found out for sure that he didn't get away with his bit of 'private violence'.

Over the years, on those occasional research trips to Italy it would have been perfectly possible for me to make inquiries at the *Palazzo della Giustizia*. As my Italian got better, I could have asked to read a transcript of the trial, as if discovering what happened to Cesare Moretti would definitively close the case for us. There was equally the risk, of course, that finding out how he got away with it, or had been given a light jail term, might start a whole host of unwanted emotions. Frankly, it's likely that if he didn't get off scot-free then he received a short sentence. There was no medical evidence of rape having happened. It was just our word against his.

So why was there even a case to answer? Perhaps it was because Mr. Draper sent that letter to Roy Jenkins. If the British Government had made a formal enquiry, then the Italian authorities might have needed to show that justice was appearing to be done. Britain had joined the EEC only two years before. If that was the case, then he might just have been given a serious sentence—so that the British Consul could be officially informed of the outcome. Yet no one ever contacted us about what transpired, and everything else points away from such a conclusion. You were never interviewed by any women police officers. The only woman in the room when I was being cross-examined had been that embarrassed interpreter.

Recently I read in an Italian newspaper how some politician announced that a girl wearing jeans couldn't, strictly speaking, be raped. She had to have consented.

Which probably only went to show that he'd never been obliged to do anything by having a gun pointed at his, or his loved one's, head. So, despite the opportunities, I had never gone back to find out for sure how the trial had ended. And sitting at that café table in Piazza Duomo, still waiting for my sister to arrive, it didn't look likely that I ever would either. By the Itchen outside Winchester, all those years before, I'll have agreed with you that it somehow seemed better not to know, as if it weren't any of our business.

'It wasn't,' as you said. 'It was Italy's.'

Italy. And it wasn't as if you hadn't tried, but you simply couldn't get to like it, nor ever feel at home there. One year I booked a holiday on the Ligurian coast, but for whatever reason we seemed doomed always to relive that first journey through the country. Every day, around lunchtime, we would end up quarrelling about where to go or what to eat. Visiting Portovenere, we managed to get as far as the hillside cemetery, a resting-place above the sea for tourists to pause between the white-domed Christian temple and its mountain commanded by a cavernous fort.

The little seaport's graveyard was completely deserted. Relieved by its quiet, the walls of the dead lain out in terraces like olive groves, we stopped and caught our breath. Tended jam jars, used as flowerpots, nestled in the dust. Mounted over the names of the dead were tiny faded snapshots. It seemed as if the family albums had given up their ghosts. Posed in their Sunday best, those old people seemed faintly to smile with the assurance of an everlasting life. There, head framed in its entrance arch, a sepulchral niche railed off with rusted spears, you had paused to be photographed.

Unfortunately, back home in King Alfred Terrace, when we got them developed that one came out as nothing but a blur. The camera must have shaken at the crucial moment. I couldn't make out your sunburnt forearms, the bruised thighs you had that year from moving furniture around, or your features bitten by mosquitoes. No, you never got used to Italy—which, given my research interests, was to prove a problem. So, in the end, the only practical solution was for me to make brief visits to the galleries and archives on my own. I would stay in cheap hotels or be put up by the odd expatriate scholar I happened to meet through my work. It was while away on just such a trip, the one to see the Pisanellos in Verona, when Alice's Christmas card with the phone number mysteriously disappeared.

But why, today of all days, why torture myself with those memories? For years I thought that giving you most of the holiday savings to change into traveller's cheques made out in your name was the crucial mistake, the thing that causally linked my infidelity, if that's the right word for it, with the bag-snatching and our overnight hitchhike home. Now it seemed there was far too much casual happenstance interspersing the sequence of events: the forty-eight hour rail strike, the decision to hitchhike that we made together, and the good luck of that lift in the Alfa. The fault was nothing like mine alone. There was no clear blame for me to take, however bereaved I might feel by that fact. Yet what if I'd simply realized as much all those years ago, and acted upon it immediately? It was as if my exculpation from the lack of blame somehow required the long years it would take.

Then why go on torturing myself? Why did I have to be chained to a memory?

It was such a lovely spring morning in the Piazza Duomo, with a dazzle reflected off the cafés' sun umbrellas. The large paving slabs were variegated with patches of shifting shadow, a bright blue sky flecked with soft white clouds moving rapidly above the grand Vittorio Emanuele arcade and the Palazzo Reale that edged the square.

Though spring is here, I thought, and let the lyrics of the old song play across my thoughts yet one more time.

CHAPTER 20

Remember how we bumped into each other leaving one of those cattle-market discos from the first term at university? Out of our simultaneous apologies there came that flurry of shared views about what a waste of time those bad scenes were, what trashy music they played, and how everyone was only after what they could get. Which is why, understandably enough at that tipping point in our lives, we opted instead to head for the bar and get to know each other better.

By Christmas, others had caught on to the idea that we were an item, as people like to put it now. Your parents and my mum had both had us down to stay. We were already in the habit of escaping from halls for weekends of walks in the Dales or Moors. So when, for the second year, it came time to move out of college, of course the thing to do was find a bed-sit together.

Sharing that tiny flat for the next two years, we fell into the uninterrupted conversation of lovers who were also friends, friends who would talk over everything and everyone as if for richer or poorer, in sickness and in health, till death would tangle up the tapes inside us. That's how we went about forming our conspiracy of two. It would stand us in good stead through those years of university, what with the mind games people played, the mental cruelty of tutors, or the usual character assassination that competitive types would go in for.

And then there was the star system. Over cups of coffee in a college snack bar, friends of ours would privately grade the people they were paired with for tutorials and seminars. They were the first to accuse me of being a bookworm, of spending my life in the library. But how did they know if they weren't there too? We have our spies, they'd say.

Ah yes, their spies ... You remember the time Alice and I were walking beside the lake and, thinking out loud about how life imitates art, I happened to notice that the reed beds looked like a Japanese print.

'But wait a minute now, the reeds aren't the cliché,' she suddenly said. 'It's your idea of them that is.'

And so I will have carried that off-the-cuff cutting remark straight back to you in search of repairs to my wounded *amour propre*. Not that you gave what I wanted to hear—far from it. You too had a line in what I needed to be told; and, given the very different subjects we studied, you were ready on innumerable occasions with prompts for me to become less self-absorbed. You know how it was: I would be going on again about the 'bricks and mortar, grass over fields, the shadows of trees ... the little figures here and there' in a Dutch genre scene, when you would counter with one of the case histories you had to write up for your finals dissertation.

'You have a class problem?' is how the tutor I shared with Alice responded if any of us so much as dared to ask how our work was progressing. The first time it happened to me, I thought he was referring to my accent.

Then when it all got too much, you would find the address of some B & B and we'd escape for a day or two, explore the countryside around, take a tour of Skipton Castle, visit the remains at Bolton Abbey, walk across the stepping stones there, or climb up the Wharf to the Strid. It was on those excursions that you always seemed to be most yourself, doing the things you liked so much: looking round old country houses, picking through antique shops, staring into estate agents' windows, and, most of all, taking those long country walks.

You would gaze up at the crags, the dry stonewalls, the heaped clouds that cast great moving shadows across the moors. Your lips would be set in a determined grin as we battled against the stiff gusts blowing along ridges and backs of hills. And I suppose it was that limestone landscape of springy turf and curving river, narrow tracks and beck-side paths, which really got you under my skin. Your chestnut hair would be blowing across your face, your long slim fingers reaching out to unhook the cord that held a farm gate closed. You'd be vaulting a stile, or leaping from stone to stone across a shallow ford. We would be scampering down a dale- or moor-side in time for hot drinks and sandwiches in a Kettlewell pub ...

Yes, it was definitely those long walks and the endless talks we had that helped to establish our fondly self-preserving cabal, our conspiracy of two that went such a long way to binding us together.

CHAPTER 21

Only ten minutes later than expected, my sister had come striding across the square with a wince of stage embarrassment distorting her tanned face.

'Sorry—bad hair day,' she said all in a fluster, sitting down, crossing her legs, and immediately launching into a series of explanations for her being so on edge. The graphic designers had screwed up her portfolio of magazine and hoarding ads for *Intimissimo*, the women's underwear firm whose brand image she was revamping. The public relations team at the client company had been on the phone all morning about how her ideas were completely bloody hopeless and the sketches even worse. Her boss was breathing down her neck about when he could announce to the world another major advertising coup for his agency. Giovanni had left a message on the answer-phone to say he wouldn't be back that evening from his trip to Zurich. And if that weren't enough, Leopardi, their cat ... But as she kept on about her job, her life, her problems with 'abroad', and even their domestic pet, a strange bit of TV from the night before came flickering back across my mind.

It had been her idea for me to book a room in the little hotel by the Porta Ticinese. The spacious flat she and Giovanni now owned was way out by San Siro in the Via P. A. Paravia. That would have been far too inconvenient for the brief visit planned to Milan's gallery district, and a day trip to Emilia Romagna. So, after taking the air a while, strolling amongst the book stalls, antique markets, going past soloing saxophonists with accompaniment tapes around the Naviglio, I headed back, ate a tuna salad nearby, then returned to my hotel.

Single rooms in modest places like that one always find me at a loss, being no more than alive and left to my own devices. After no time at all in such confined spaces I'll start feeling flat as a faded news cutting pasted to the back of a personal box like one of Joseph Cornell's—or, come to think of it, the one with that prize fish in James's bathroom. Scholarly tomes that in any other circumstances would provide hours of absorption just dull over the minute my glasses go on. So there was nothing else for it last night around ten but to go to bed and hope against hope for a good eight hours' uninterrupted sleep. Then, just about to snuggle down under the covers, I noticed the remote on the bedside table and decided on impulse to see what Italian TV had to offer that evening.

I was channel hopping between food ads and game shows—their scantily clad, tall hostesses crowding around the breast-high presenter, his evidently dyed and transplanted hair groomed to within an inch of its life. No, thank you. Suddenly, looking like they'd stepped out of an old master painting, one with a gilt-moulded frame, two characters flickered on beside a broken Doric column. The first was another dumpy man, dressed as a waiter, his head bowed, standing and waiting silently with, in his arms, a high and toppling pile of the day's newspapers. The other was a suave commentator, his mouth talking nineteen to the dozen, face and hand gestures seeming to say that, no, he was merely expressing his opinion. The previous user had left the sound turned down. I couldn't hear a word he was saying. Still, it gave every impression of being an advertising company's idea for a party political broadcast, doubtless on behalf of Forza Italia, since the logo in the corner of the screen indicated that this was one of the channels owned by Silvio Berlusconi himself.

'Where do you want to eat?' I asked, interrupting the apology for her lateness that my sister was working up into a routine of complaints about the job that, actually, she loved.

'Sorry,' she said, 'no time for a meal. I'll just have a toasted sandwich and a cold milk right here, if that's OK with you.'

'Sure, same for me—but another San Pellegrino instead of the milk.'

My sister summoned the waiter and dispatched him with an order in grammatically fluent, but faintly accented Italian.

'So why don't you quit advertising?' I asked just to tease her. 'You don't need the money now, and do you really need the grief?'

'Might as well tell you, then, mightn't I?' she replied.

'Make a change,' I smiled, lifting my sunglasses to look her in the eye. 'After all, you never tell me anything.'

'Vanni wants to start a family.'

'What? You're not ... Congratulations!'

'Hang on a minute,' my sister laughed. 'It's just an idea. After all, my clock is ticking and, as you say, we can certainly afford it. And really I've got about as far as I can in this job. The next step up would be hiring and firing, juggling budgets, that kind of thing—whereas my thing's the contact with the clients. I've been talking to my boss about going part-time, but he's not very keen. So Vanni's going to put in a word, and if nothing comes of it, well, I'm thinking of taking up knitting!'

'Come on; let's order something stronger. We could drink a toast to that.'

'Did you get what you were looking for in Parma?' she asked.

'Well, yes and no,' I replied. 'I did get to see the picture, but finding a reproduction could well turn into another *Divine Comedy*.'

'Why so? As if I couldn't guess.'

The *Soprintendente della Galleria Nazionale* at Parma had sent a fax to the office at the Art School. In response to my courteous request, it ran, she hereby communicated to il Dott. English that he would be able to view the following below-listed work which was not at present placed on display: C. Preti, *La lattante*, inv. n. 89, by making an appointment with la signora Serra at the following telephone numbers.

So I arranged with Marta Serra, as her name turned out to be, to visit Parma for the day. She would arrange for a viewing of that particular work in their picture store. When told that, unfortunately, I didn't know the town, let alone the Galleria Nazionale, she kindly arranged to meet me in a bar opposite the Teatro Reggio, just off Piazza Garibaldi. A taxi from the station, she said, would of course drop me there—though it was, in fact, no distance along the via Garibaldi in the direction of the famous Battistero, quite visible from the Piazza della Stazione.

Marta Serra was already waiting outside the bar. Dressed in a high street reworking of the Stoke Newington drabby look, she was a studious professional who specialized in the works of Parmigianino and Correggio. Marta was left-handed and, as she raised the espresso cup to her peach-coloured lips, I noticed the wedding ring. Her husband, it turned out, was a manager at Parmalat. Their two boys were attending the Liceo Classico. When she reciprocated with a polite enquiry, I decided to tell her there was no Mrs. English—without going into the business of how you hadn't changed your name after we got married. Marta couldn't, unfortunately, miss the faintly hapless note in which I referred to you, and graciously she let the topic drop. Coffees downed, we set off past a more than life-size, socialist-realist sculpture of a partisan. He was standing above the body of a fallen comrade in a strong wind that ruffled his hair, holding a Sten gun that must have been air dropped by the Allies.

Across a vast square called the Piazza della Pace we headed towards La Pilotta—an enormous, ugly palazzo that looked as though half of it had been pulled down to create the desolate space across which we were strolling. When asked about its half-built look, Marta explained that it had been designed by an engineer, not an architect, and was bombed by American Liberators during the assault on the Linea Gotica in the final stages of the war. For the last fifty years the city council had been divided about what should be done with this vast bombed site right in the middle of their town, while the citizens had arranged for a covered market to be held there once a week. Divided, I thought, like most of Italian history—all the other Septembers of confusion and betrayal, when the country was yoked together by violence.

The offices for the *Soprintendenza per i Beni Artistici e Storici di Parma e Piacenza* were themselves in a bit of a state. The staircases and corridors were covered in heaps of building gear, rubble, and concrete dust, but through the middle of the old stairwell rose a futuristic glass and steel lift which seemed to be suspended by a hair from the ancient ceiling some six floors above. Up in the lift we went, and stopped on the top floor. Marta pointed out the rooftops, the domes, campanili, skyscrapers and cranes of Parma. Then she showed me the way along a corridor into the spotless new offices of the Superintendent herself.

Out came the explanation that not only did I want to see the picture by Preti, but also that I was writing a book called *Genre Painters of Nineteenth-Century Italy* and would need a transparency of the work to be used for the illustrations. Which is where things began to get difficult. The Superintendent was one of those people who likes to hold office and demonstrate she has power, but not exactly to use it, since this would involve the trouble of getting something done and something right. So she announced in no uncertain terms that though they did hold some negatives of a reproduction, I would not be able to purchase or take any of these away. Furthermore, should I wish to arrange for the painting to be photographed at my own expense, I would first have to provide full details of the publisher of the book, its size, its print run, purchase price, and so on and so forth. But by this point it had became only too clear what the obstacles were, and I managed to put in that perhaps before deciding whether to go to all that trouble it would be best to see the canvas itself.

Thankfully, the Superintendent left that task in the capable hands of Marta Serra, who positively burst out laughing when we were safely inside the futuristic lift and descending to the floor where her far more modest and not yet restored office space was located. The gallery's library housed its books in dark wooden shelves all along the walls with other cases jutting out to form alcoves in which the scholars and archivists worked. There were volumes in precarious piles all over the floor, and plaster flaking from the high vaulted ceiling. Marta explained that the place was due to be refurbished, but somehow the funding had got put on hold. She confided that her boss, the Superintendent, happened to be one of those political appointments, meaning she was somebody's relative and didn't actually know anything about the history of art in Italy—or anywhere else for that matter.

Perhaps Marta would be able to arrange for a reproduction of the picture to be sent to England? She couldn't promise anything, but would see what might be done. Then she led the way through a maze of public galleries, across the immense and spectacular wooden *Teatro Farnese*. As we went, she described how the court engineer had constructed the space so it could be filled to a certain height with water. That way small ships might be sailed below the audience for the purpose of staging masques with naval battles and such like. Once across the imposing structure, restored after its damage during the bombing, we ascended some further flights of stairs back up into the roof space of La Pilotta where the gallery's deposits were located.

Born in 1842, Cletofonte Preti lived around Reggio Emilia, the neighbouring town to Parma, for all of his thirty-eight years. He painted 'La Lattante' in about 1875, approximately half a decade before his death. Marta pulled inventory number 89 out from its storage rack on the rolling frame to which it was attached, and I was immediately struck by what a fine picture 'La Lattante' actually is, further convinced as I was that it would make a suitable subject for one of the later sections of my long-meditated book.

As the title suggests, it represents a young woman of poor origins breast-feeding a thriving child in the corner of a humble brick-floored bedroom. The youthful wet-nurse is standing in bare feet resting her weight against the end of the bed, its pillow visible behind her arm, and her dark green dress set off by the light blue and white check of the bedspread. The woman wears a loose cotton blouse, pulled down off her shoulders so that she can feed the baby with her right breast. The child's one visible arm is raised and divides the bosom, its tiny fingers reaching towards her clavicle. The baby's kicking legs, the woman's smile and lowered eyes all show reminiscences of Madonna and Jesus treatments by Preti's far more illustrious Renaissance predecessors. There were signs of *pentimenti* clearly visible around the young woman's breasts and the feeding baby's arm.

The wet nurse has a ruby-red earring dangling against one cheek, and a matching red headscarf which only half covers her thick russet hair. The skin of her head, torso, left arm, and bare feet are lit by a very strong warm light source—a putative window beyond the right edge of the picture. Against the left wall, jutting into the lower corner of the picture is a beaten-up wooden chair with a woven-reed seat, fraying at the front. Underneath the chair, on a bar connecting the two front legs, a white dove is perched. A small piece of the paint on the right side of the bedspread had chipped off, revealing a patch of bare canvas. A new transparency would reveal that damage, and I mentioned the possibility of restoration.

As if to excuse the poor condition of the work, Marta mentioned that Preti had been more or less an amateur painter and the technical quality of his pigments was far inferior to those of Scaramuzza. He had also painted a genre piece with a wet nurse, *Il baliatico*—which, since we were there, she was only too willing to show me. But a glance at inventory number 82, its grey skin tones and cool palate of dark reds and blues, made it clear that 'The wet-nurse' by Cletofonte Preti had everything that was needed.

'And how about the Gallery Schwarz?' my sister asked, as we were sipping the white wine and nibbling at the toasted sandwiches brought to our table.

'Didn't find it, I'm afraid. Don't think it's there any more.'

On the evening of my arrival from Linate, in an uncharacteristic fit of tidy-mindedness, I decided to see if the place where the Arp exhibition had been held in 1965 was still in business. A glance at the tattered old street-map bought all those years before, the city coming to pieces at each worn-through fold, showed that the via Gesú runs parallel to via Spiga and via Monte Napoleone. It was only about five or six minutes walk from the Duomo or San Babila and, approaching it, I quickly picked up the signs of a distinctly smart area—one lined with designer-label emporia.

The via Gesú itself turned out to be a narrow, elegant stroll of about two hundred and fifty metres, with no bars and no trees, past eighteenth-century buildings that had become five-star hotels and the like. Far less Japanese tourists crowded its pavements; but they were there nonetheless, burdened down with enormous artsy carrier bags, eyeing the windows of its Chiara Boni boutiques. Number 17 was on the left, converted into two shops, mirror images either side of the door: one for Chinese antiquities, the other selling Italian rarities like the Venetian vessels arranged about its window display. A 1920s-style picture of a musical instrument had been placed in the entrance. Gesú, it went without saying, would have overturned quite a few tables in the temples of mammon that lined his street.

'Come to think of it,' she said, 'I seem to remember reading somewhere that a guy called Arturo Schwarz left a whole load of weird art to the State … probably the same bloke who owned your gallery.'

'What? Sorry, what were you saying?'

My sister looked across the café table. My sunglasses where thankfully hiding the state of my eyes.

'On your metaphysical worthlessness trip again?' she asked rather sharply. 'Want to talk about it, you old spirit broker?'

'Water under the bridge …'

'Whatever it is,' she said, 'best let it go.'

It was just the phrase you had used those years before.

'Better still,' she continued, 'let your self go.'

'Taking a break from all that,' I said, as if the solitude of my present existence could be made to look like a conscious decision.

Of course I've sometimes wondered if the fact that I was left with nothing at all was, frankly, my own fault. But somehow that doesn't sound quite right. It's perfectly true that, like Italy during the Civil War, we were yoked together by violence. The links between us forged by that night's events had quickly made my involvement with Alice seem as if glimpsed in a department store mirror. And what was immediately true for her had come to seem the case for anyone else I might happen to meet. Nothing vicarious about it, you had been my life. Trying to do the right thing, I took the road that appeared at least to make sense for two of our lives. Yet, after all those years of making amends, all the attempts at an ordinary existence, all the second chances that you allowed, it was as if the only way either of us could truly get away from that violence was by getting away from each other; as if our relationship was to violence itself and not to the other person. There again, after ten years or so, perhaps we did get away from those haunting scenes. But the private violence was still what yoked us together. When it all appeared to be recovered from, when there was no longer the need, or apparent need, to work on it, to make amends and live up to them, then suddenly it seemed there was no longer any reason for us to stay together.

Our talking over everything and everyone began to go round and round in circles, and our conspiracy of two turned in upon itself. The petty irritations with each other's habits, the slurping noises and forgotten bath water, just seemed to crescendo into major issues. Then it began to seem as if I were perpetually elsewhere in my mind; and the thought of taking off on the next bit of research was always asking to be acted upon. Slowly but surely, there was nothing else for it. The past was past; the present a routine; the future stared back at us, empty of purpose. Whatever it might have held, that future had come to seem no more than the time it would take for us to grow more or less gracefully old.

'And how is Mary?' my sister asked.

'Getting on with her life,' I said, repeating the set phrase for dealing with the question of your continuing existence. 'The last time we spoke she was arranging to move the long-stay geriatric patients out of their hospital beds and into the private nursing care beds. The fees are still supposed to be paid from the National Health purse. You know what they're saying. It's to make more beds available for the urgent ops. They want to close the old wards with their stoves and chilly windows, just trying to fulfill the patients' charter, shorten waiting times, keep the whole Health Service out of the red.'

The moment we decided to separate, you moved to Cornwall. It's a part of the country you have always loved, and so you bought a cottage with the money from your half of the mortgage. Our house loan from your mother was made on the understanding that we would be getting married, which of course we duly did. After having lived together for so long there seemed no reason not to—but separating also meant having to buy you out of that part ownership, by re-mortgaging our marital home in King Alfred Terrace.

'Glad to hear you're still on speaking terms,' my sister said.

'The odd phone call, birthdays, Christmas … it's mostly me that does the calling, and always her new chap who answers.'

'So the break-up was amicable enough then?' she asked and, answering her own question, 'I mean, I've never heard of a painless divorce.'

The last time we parted had happened by the strangest of coincidences to be on the steep slope of Whiteladies Road in Bristol. We were pausing outside a bookshop door. With a vague sense of having done this once too often, I stood there waiting beside you, my life, and the person with whom I had shared the most decisive events in that life, for one more moment longer.

'Please try to appreciate,' I was foolishly saying apropos of one indebtedness or another, 'that I've other responsibilities to think about now.'

It was just a few months after you had moved down to Truro and taken up that management job at the local infirmary. We had decided to meet half way, in Bristol, to exchange a few possessions, some old books and records that had got confused together. Unfortunately, over an Indian meal, we ended up bickering about the details of the settlement. The burden of the newly enlarged mortgage payments had certainly contributed, when it suddenly dawned on me that Whiteladies Road was almost exactly the spot where Alice and I had said goodbye those twenty-odd years before.

'No, *you* try to appreciate', you were saying, 'that your "responsibilities" can be nothing to me any more.'

You turned away. You had a train to catch. On the point of calling out to you, I stood there rooted to the spot, the warring factions of sorrow and anger squaring up inside me. Then as you strode off down the slope of Whiteladies Road the sense of having done this once too often returned with no less force. The echo of your voice seemed to mingle with the absence of another's, like a rhyme or a form for those broken attachments, now quite beyond repair—unless the bare coincidence of a raised and a choked-off voice could make amends for all that doubled loss.

Her lunch break long over, my sister stood up and, opening her purse, made to offer money for her share of the bill.

'No, no, I'll stand you,' I insisted.

'My turn next time, then,' she said.

'Thanks for doing this,' I managed. 'Oh and give my regards to Gian.'

'My pleasure—I will,' she said. 'Have a good flight, and do get that book finished!'

Then she leaned across the table to offer her cheek, which received a fraternal peck, then proffered the other one too. So, in Italian style, that got kissed as well.

'*Ciao, ciao, baci, baci,*' my sister called out as she glanced back from halfway across the Piazza Duomo. 'See you the next time you're over! Oh and next time you really have to come and stay.'

Back under the sun umbrella, as my sister disappeared down the Metropolitana steps, I thought about ordering a second glass of wine and wondered how I might while away the rest of the afternoon. *Though spring is here, to me it's still September*, I thought.

No, I couldn't say *September in the Rain* has become my favourite song. But over the years happening across versions of Harry Warren and Al Dubin's classic, I would buy and play them until, patience exhausted, you called out again to take the glimmering touch song off. Eventually I burned a CD with all the different versions, and played it in my office so as not to upset you. After we separated I did try to give up listening to the thing, but quickly relapsed, I'm afraid to admit, into what must seem like a bad case of repetition compulsion. Needless to say, after all those hearings, I had the deceptively simple words off by heart and without ever having tried to learn them. It's such an inspired notion to make the bridge lyric rhyme on just its last word, and then only with the title phrase. So the *sweet refrain* leans backward and forward to touch that *September in the rain*.

One time a colleague at the art college, a print-maker who plays piano in a local jazz combo, tried to teach me how to vamp it in Eb. Not that I ever quite mastered the changes: the shift up from Ab6 to Cm7 in the middle-eight would always fox me, because in the verses you have to go from Ab6 to that fancy Db7. Still, those prolonged attempts and the pains in my fingers and forearms increased admiration for the subtlety with which the two composers had married words with music—and for the artistry on all the various versions I came to know and perhaps too obsessively savour.

Going back to classes at the end of each summer vacation, I'd be strolling down King Alfred Terrace and across the park by way of the children's playground towards the art school's lecture rooms murmuring its lyrics. *The leaves of brown came tumbling down, remember?* And the park's trees will seem to be shedding their foliage in harmony. *The sun went out just* like a dying ember and, just so, a cloudy autumn day might perform the lyrics, while glimpses of what happened, what was and wasn't said, and *Every word of love I heard you whisper* comes drifting indistinctly yet again across my mind. Naturally enough, there'd be days like this when the infants and mums on those swings or roundabouts are scattered by an afternoon shower and the *raindrops seemed to play a sweet refrain*. So as I'm humming its middle-eight, or imitating the ever-so-apt variant play-out lyric on Frank Sinatra's version, *that September … that brought the pain*, Alice and you, and all the others, our youthful selves among them, come hurrying back to life inside me once again.

Yes, *that September … that brought the pain.* Though I much prefer the timbre and backing on Dinah Washington's rendition, she doesn't sing that phrase. Old Blue-eyes doubtless improvised it to the sound of Nelson Riddle's strings in some long ago Hollywood studio. And, if you want my opinion, George Shearing's cool instrumental doesn't sound in the least bit hurt; but the way Sinatra sings that phrase, with his characteristically syncopated pause, has come to substitute perfectly for the knots of feelings I can't escape still caught in me from our own *September in the rain.* Doubtless you'll say the point of all that listening was simply to turn the tangles of bodily discomfort into a pleasing pain, a painful pleasure, or any of my other oxymoronic emotions, like that nostalgia for Queen Square, the Italian Hospital and the times of our youth.

And so it's there in Milan, while I look around at the Piazza Duomo in a mid-afternoon of a warm April day, look around at the pigeons and passersby, sipping at my extra glass of wine, immediately, as if the words of the song had been right all along, those glimpses start up again. There's her suntan peeling, the white sails on the sea, a damaged attachment, accelerating Vespa, sheet and forked lightning, you there among the soft toys for souvenirs, an orthopedic shoe, Cain and Abel wrestling, the yellow marble halls … And there, in present memory, like an eternal recurrence, are such places as the Arturo Schwarz

Gallery here in Milan, places to which I may never return, however strong the hankering to relive these things exactly once again. Then on this warm April day, in a city changed almost beyond recognition, it's as if we never were here in the leaden nineteen seventies, years to which, willy-nilly, no one ever can return.

Even wanting eternally to return places too much of a burden on you and her and the others who lived those years with me, and who have their own reasons for not wanting forever to go back, love's limits as present as ever they were: the suntan, white sails, a damaged attachment, accelerating Vespa, lightning, soft toys, and those yellow marble halls. Which is how at last I must have got round to telling myself there in Piazza Duomo, Milan, that the next time I happen to be up in London it's probably just as well if I make a point of not getting off the Tube at Holborn, not walking round by way of Boswell Street to stand for a moment in front of the Italian Hospital yet once more, its ornate black cupola still surmounted by a crucifix, *Ospedale Italiano* and *Supported by Voluntary Contributions* picked out in faded red lettering.